A Devil's Hope

Book Two of Hope-Marie
The Wolfe Legacy

J. R. Froemling

To Benjamin, the love of my life.
He is the Mick to my Hope-Marie,
the Harold to my Stella,
and all that is in between.
AWOO!

The Wolfe Legacy

Hope-Marie Wolfe
Mistress Giselle (1978-1983)
A Devil's Hope (1985- 1988)

Elijah Joseph Wolfe
The Naughty List (1986)

Table of Contents

Playing Hard To Get

December 2, 1985

Castian bounces on my knee making gurgling noises and sucks his fist like it's the best tasting thing in the universe. He loves the train. Helena sleeps in the carrier nestled between my legs on the floor. With Magellan at work, I don't have a car of my own. The doormen at our building happily get us a cab or help us out when we wander.

Today is special. We're heading to the Oyster to check on the progress of Le Salon, and to catch up with the Rittendorfs. Our last conversation was weeks ago and resulted in the need for a cash infusion. I never realized how much starting a new sex club would cost.

The train comes to a halt and I gather up the bag and children to quickly step onto the platform. The tick of my heels echoes faintly as I make my way across the platform to the stairs. Castian has discovered the puffball at the end of his adorable cap's ties and gums it with great gusto. Helena does not approve of the wintry weather and makes a squawking noise while I adjust the blanket over the carrier. Their grandmother in Spain sent him an assorted amount of winter gear because she's convinced we don't have enough for Castian, and that we live in the North Pole. Castian's waddling and snowman shape while in the gear makes me smile. She, thankfully, has sent nothing for Helena to wear yet.

A few quick steps and I hail a cab. I'm not going to carry these two that far. It's too cold to be walking to the Oyster from the station and I still have issues from my streaking incident. On cold days like this I think of Tony. It will be two years in February since his death. For all his faults, the man was there when I needed him. I'll never forget him and what he did for us, or what he did to me. I ignore the incredulous look the driver gives me about taking an infant and toddler to The Blue Oyster.

I get Helena's carrier secured with little fuss. My gaze turns out from the cab while I hold Castian in my lap. I wonder how Tony's son is doing. I kept in touch with Margaret Scapelli for a few months after Tony's death. I wouldn't want to be in touch with the one that got away, either.

Fifteen minutes later I stroll into Harold's office. Stella and he are already there. Their beautiful baby girl sleeps in the playpen in the corner. The juxtaposition of a playpen in a strip club makes me chuckle. I drop the bag and peel us out of the winter gear before I turn and hand Castian off to Stella, while I set Helena in one of the chairs in front of Harold's over-sized desk.

"He's getting so big!" She snuggles him into her lap.

"And heavy," I bemoan. "Mick says he's shaped like a footballer."

"You're lookin' great, kid!" Harold wraps me up into a tight hug and I reciprocate. He's a Wolfe by proxy. "Thanks for comin' in. I know it's cold out there."

"Of course, anything for you, Harold," I bat my eyelashes at him and grin.

"Cute. About Christmas. We're having a soft open for The Salon--."

"Le Salon." I correct him.

"Whatever, and I need you to work."

"No. Le Salon doesn't open until July. We agreed not to open it until then. I have finals next week. The club isn't ready. You said, yourself, we're being iced out on the liquor license. Magellan and I already made plans to run the gauntlet to see both sides this year. I know you would never deny Helena's grandparents seeing her for her first Christmas, would you Harold?" I jut my lip out, pouting at him while giving him the big doe eyes.

"Don't give me the puppy-dog look. You know it doesn't work on me." He brandishes a finger at me.

Stella snorts.

"Hear me out. We need to have a soft open. The Scapelli Christmas party is the perfect start for The Salon--."

"Le Salon. We don't even have the kitchen operational. Is the bar even put together yet? Last I heard, we were behind on the stage and there was a problem with electrical." His lack of respecting the brand name grates on my nerves.

"Not a problem. Got some guys on it. We're catering that night. License is dealt with and will be ready. Scapelli's covering the costs. I need *you*, kid. Mistress is great and all, but the boys get excited for *you*. I got you booked solid for the night. All sixteen mini sessions booked and paid for."

"One problem, Harold. The Scapelli contract."

"Hate to break it to you, Hope-Marie, but that contract means shit now. With Tony dead, there's no reason to keep it up. The rest of the Scapellis behave." Harold shrugs. "Besides, it's for The Salon--."

"Le Salon, Harold. Say it with me. Le. Salon." I pucker my lips and motion with my hand toward him as I enunciate the words.

"Lay Salon."

"Le."

"Lay." Harold rolls his eyes.

"Eu, no Ey. Like you're hocking a loogie."

"Whatever. I'm not French. That's your job. Back to the Italians." He waves his hands dismissively. He's trying to be funny.

I inhale slowly to prevent chucking the paperweight on Harold's desk at his head. I'm irritated that he thinks I'm going to forsake my entire family for the Scapelli Christmas party. "No."

"What do you mean, no?" He shakes his head and blinks in disbelief at me.

"No. Nein. Nyet. Nada. Non. Not happening. Exactly what I

said. I'm not telling any of my parents that I'm going to skip Christmas to dominate a bunch of horny drunks, and they'll maybe get to see their granddaughter in six months when I graduate."

"Oh, you're graduating from high school! That's great. We don't have to lie on your application anymore," Stella teases me while still bouncing Castian on her knee.

"You damn well know I'm graduating from Columbia. I'll be getting my bachelor's in psychology with a minor in sociology." I hrmph, "With honors."

"Wait, you're serious?" Harold blinks in surprise. I ignore the astonished looks between the two of them as Helena begins to fuss. With an easy motion, I scoop her out of the carrier and bring her up. I don't even hesitate as I shift my blouse around and unclasp the bra.

"Whoa! Hey!" Harold dramatically throws his hands up.

I roll my eyes. "Really, Harold? You tried to convince me to let some weird prick milk me when Castian was born." I toss a blanket over the exposed side and shift in pain as she gums the shit out of my nipple.

"Fine. Uh, when are you done with your school stuff again? I may have a compromise."

I raise a brow. "Last final is on the thirteenth." My eyes narrow as I see the gears turning in his scheming brain.

"And you're sure Mick can't take them?"

"I am." I try not to grin at him trying to weasel out of me traveling with them. "Helena's still feeding. I'm not sending him with formula."

Harold pouts at me. "Fine. My plan is we'll fly you out to Kansas-."

"Missouri."

"That's what I said, we'll fly you out to Kansas--."

"Kansas City. Missouri."

"Whatever. We'll fly out there in no man's land on the fourteenth." He pulls up his desk calendar. "You'll stay out there until the twenty-third--."

"And you'll fly Mick with the kids to Spain from KC on the twenty-fourth?"

"To Spain? You're killing me, Hope-Marie."

"No Spain, no deal. And I still get my quitting bonus."

"No. You're getting paid to work, plus holiday, plus the airfare, *plus* international."

"Then I'm not flying back until the twenty-fourth, and you'll pay for Mick to fly with the kids on the Concord."

Harold and I stare each other down as if we're going to duke it out like Rocky Balboa.

Stella chuckles from the couch, and she coos to Castian, "Your mommy drives a hard bargain."

I bite the inside of my cheek to keep from laughing at the comment. "Harold, I love you to death, but you aren't my boss anymore. We're partners, and you're asking me to give up my entire holiday, and family. You're the one that said family's more important than anything."

"Fuck," Harold groans as he throws himself back in all his dramatic glory. "Okay! Fine! I'll fly you to Kansas whatever, then Mick to Spain, and you'll be here to work Christmas for the party. No bonus."

"Deal," I reach out and offer my hand to shake. After getting Helena burped and settled back into her milk-induced slumber, Harold and I take a tour of Le Salon while Stella stays with the kids.

He wasn't kidding when he said he had been slave-driving the guys. There are workers everywhere. They pay us little mind and I'm beyond excited at the progress. All the details of the salons themselves are perfect. From the lighting to the feel of the furniture, everything sets the tone of a French salon. We won't bring in the bondage gear until after final inspections. Our public play salons are going to have a playground of sin in equipment.

The Lion & The Gazelle

With all the business in order, I gather up my kids, and we make the trek home. I dread the conversation with Magellan. When we enter the building I let Jimmy, the day doorman, spend a few minutes with Castian while I sign for the mail.

Our apartment is in decent order. The mess bothers Magellan. I get the kids nestled in their cribs to finish their naps, and I turn into a whirling dervish of cleaning. I pick up all the toys and toss them into the basket, wash the dishes, and start the laundry. I even dig out all the ingredients to make rock soup sans rocks, snails, or anything of that other gross seafood. By the time Magellan comes strolling in, the table's set and I'm setting up the highchair.

"Mhmm, smells good," he coos as he kisses me on the cheek. He's tense and he quickly parts from me to head into our bedroom. I barely have time to dwell on him as I'm summoned by an angry, hungry Castian, soon followed by the as demanding Helena.

I duck into their room to deal with diaper changes and defer screaming with pacifiers until Magellan swoops in to take Helena from me. We head back to the dining room, and I get our little lion into the highchair with his bib firmly attached.

Magellan coos down at Helena as I grab dinner from the oven

and set it on the table.

"You feed his highness, and I'll take care of our princess?" I say as I reach for Helena.

As I work myself free to feed our daughter, Magellan's eyes twinkle and drift from mine down to my breasts. He quirks a brow with the silent question of whether I'll remove my shirt.

My cheeks blush as I remember when I could be that obedient. He would command I go topless when I fed Castian this way. With Castian awake, and older, we don't feel comfortable playing our game that far.

He sulks when I shake my head no and turns to feed our son with great reluctance.

I make quick work of Helena's meal and deposit her back in the crib to come and enjoy dinner.

"With your right hand," he says without looking at me, as he zooms a spoonful of baby-food into Castian's mouth. "Then tell me what it you want since you cleaned, and cooked my favorite dinner."

"Yes, Sir." I serve our food using my off hand. I've gotten adept at performing this task. It's still awkward and requires me to focus. We eat quietly while Castian plays with the few Cheerios I left on his tray for dessert. "Harold's flying us to Kansas City and to Spain for the holidays, He wants me to work Christmas."

I stuff food into my mouth before he can make me repeat myself, offering a sheepish grin.

"Are you fucking kidding me? And let me guess, you already agreed. Fuck. Do I even get a say in the matter? How long? When? You know I have to fucking work. You said you weren't going back to work until Le Salon was ready." He's white knuckling his fork as he growls at me.

I swallow the food and frown down at my plate, pushing the paella around.

"He wants me to do a soft open for Le Salon. We're bleeding cash and the Scapelli Christmas—"

"No! He doesn't own you. You're not doing it. You're fucking going to be with me on Christmas."

"Yes, I am. You know how important Le Salon is to me. It's not Harold asking me to do it. It's me wanting to do it. We both know I get my way with him. We need the money, Mick. You told me to find a way to fix it. Working *is* fixing. That's how I make money, remember?" I look Magellan square in the eyes in my defiant anger the beast flares to life as he stares back at me.

It doesn't matter. I'm sleep deprived, my boobs hurt, my ass is sore, and I'm fat. I inhale sharply to provide the grand finale of my tantrum. "Fuck you and your fucking suit and perfect fucking hair with your awesome fucking car where you get to go talk to grown-ups all day and I have to fucking toe the fucking line to make your fucking parents who aren't even here happy!" I snatch our plates as I stand, regardless of him being finished, and I storm over to the sink and clank them into it without care.

I follow this display with stomping back over to Castian, who starts to blubber. I unclasp his highchair, wipe his face with the bib, and toss it onto the table like a gauntlet thrown in challenge. My display completes as I scoop up Castian and escape to the kids' bedroom with him; not looking back to see Magellan's reaction.

Bedtime is a few hours away, so I plop down on the floor to play with Castian until he gives me sleepy yawns. When the shower kicks on in the other room, I puff like a dragon snorting and purse my lips. I refuse to cave and apologize. I don't care how much trouble I'll get in. While I'm his submissive, I'm also his wife. There's a time to roll over and take punishment, and a time to tell him to go fuck himself.

In the time it takes me to get both the kids put to bed I've cooled down and am mildly fretting walking into our bedroom. I decide to weasel out of punishment by digging into the closet in the kids' room for the "accessories" I wore on our wedding day. Several minutes of quiet shuffling and rummaging in the tiny space wins me getting all the items I want. The clasps around my already tender nipples brings tears to my eyes and mildly arouses me, knowing he will be tempted to play with them. I follow this with fishing out the matching lingerie. After inspecting the frilly piece I'm not convinced I can get it on., I pull the closet door to and strip down.

I wriggle, squirm, and wriggle some more. I work and work until it happens, the terrible Velcro-like sound of me tearing the lacy fabric, because I'm no longer the size I was on our wedding day. Even though I was pregnant at our wedding, I was smaller. "I really am a fucking cow." This is where the dam breaks. My sobs are muffled by my hand over my mouth, and I sink to the floor, half-naked. No longer looking forward to making up with Magellan, I pull the closet door closed. Pulling knees up I allow myself to ugly cry.

My mind races about all the food I need to throw out, how many days can I go on only water, and sleep an hour less each night to get an extra workout in. I can't make the tears stop and I hug my knees tighter. I'm convinced Magellan no longer finds me beautiful and wants to leave, which is why he's being such a dick.

There's a gentle rap on the door, "Can I come in?" Magellan asks quietly.

I wipe my cheeks with breakneck speed and try to get myself under control. I'm humiliated and want to find a cave to hide in, because I'm convinced that I look like a troll. "No, go away." I reply like a petulant child.

The door opens and I scrunch up my face as Magellan steps into a closet that isn't large enough for me, my wedding gown, and him. He pulls the door closed behind him.

"I told you to go away," I mutter at him and cross my arms like a petulant child.

"Uh-huh, and now we're in here." He shimmies around me and does this weird catcher's squat until he forces me forward, allowing him to sit. He wraps his arms around me to pull me into his arms, holding me against his chest. "What's going on, Hope-Marie? Talk to me. I'm here for you"

"No, you're not. You're angry and hate everything I do. How I look. I'm a fat cow and can't do anything to make you happy. You're mad at me because I wanted to work and feel beautiful again. I broke the lace because I'm still a fat cow." The tears come harder and faster as I can't speak without hiccupping between the words. His arms tighten around me and his fingers dig into my soft skin.

"You," he pauses, "are an angel. You are perfect. You are beautiful. You are amazing. If anybody's a monster here, it's me. I know I shouldn't let those fucks at the office get in my head like that," he sighs. "I'm sorry."

"You're just saying that to make me come to our bedroom to dominate me. The cuffs won't fit either. Mooooo."

His body stiffens, and he shifts me around to pull me into a passionate kiss. Once he releases me, his lips brush against my earlobe before he nips it. "If you are such a fat cow, could I do this?"

He hoists me off the ground like I'm no heavier than the lingerie I tore, presses me against the wall and reaches down between us to push his pajama bottoms to the floor. His lips find mine again, swallowing any protest I might have had as he thrusts into me.

His hands cup my ample ass until he's satisfied with spearing me onto his cock. He reaches between us and twirls a finger around the chain to give it a firm tug, causing me to moan, and my toes curl from the mix of pleasure and pain.

"Silence," he commands. "You're not allowed to speak until you can praise yourself." He bites my earlobe as he thrusts harder. "And I'm going to keep teaching you how perfect your body is until you praise yourself." He devours my lips again in a forceful kiss while he pounds into me.

Ghost of Christmas Past

I bite my lip to keep from making a sound. He releases my nipple chain and his hands rove back down until he cups my ass again, forcing my legs to part more with each thrust. His hot breath tickles my collar bone followed by a faint bite against the crook of my neck. My eyes close and I arch off the wall, trying to impale myself further on him. I can't remember the last time he touched me like this. Nor can I remember the last time he drove into me like I was the last woman alive. I bite my lip harder with the effort to keep from moaning. My fingers run through his hair as I cling to him, the pressure of my orgasm threatens to send me into an uncontrollable mess.

The banshee wail of hunger tears through our moment as Helena demands my attention.

I'm ripped back to the devastating reality of our current existence from the memory of a hot and steamy night in my crappy little apartment two years ago. Our precious baby girl shrieks in her crib, unaware her parents are attempting to fornicate in the closet.

We slump in silent defeat. He throbs inside of me and I pulse around him.

God, I don't want him to put me down. I hold my breath, praying Helena soothes herself back to sleep before he loses interest.

His hands press firm against my ass, and I tighten my grip around his waist.

She wails again, and we have lost all hope for a grand finale.

Magellan helps me to my feet as he gently brushes his fingers along my nipples to release them from the little gold chain.

I gasp and bring my hands up to cover my breasts. He's close enough his smug grin makes me giggle. Over the next few seconds we contort and twist with grunting and giggling when we spill out of the closet, presentable.

Magellan kisses my temple, then heads out of the room while I scoop up Helena from the crib. He wouldn't hold me to silence while tending to our children. I settle into the rocking chair and let the little banshee latch on, turning her into a leech with razor-like gums, not saying a word.

When I walk into our bedroom I detour to the bathroom to clean up my breasts from. I pause, looking in the mirror to take a moment to take stock of myself. At first, all I see are large, aching breasts with angry red nipples. Followed by the fading red stretch marks and the pudgy love handles of my body recovering from having an infant. My hips are wider and softer. I'm in no way fat, or ugly. I'm willing to bet my porn money men would find me hotter.

I brush my fingers over the hickey, reminded of Magellan pounding me to remind me how sexy I am. I blow hard breath out of my nose as I let go of my anger. I understand his frustration at not being brought into the loop. However, I'm not beholden to him on decisions regarding Le Salon.

He makes decisions all the time without asking me.

I rub my hand over my face as I internally behave like a child. I miss the fun-loving days of misadventures and no responsibilities. With a frown, I turn to my torn lingerie. What I thought was completely ruined turns out to only be a popped seam, something I can fix. I wriggle out of it and toss it into the hamper on my way back into the bedroom. Without a word, I crawl onto the bed and over Magellan, purposely dropping my weight on him to pin him underneath me. I give him a big cheesy grin and finger wave.

He laughs as his fingers trail along my sides, not reacting to my full weight resting on him. "Ready to be a good girl and say something nice about yourself so we can talk like grown-ups again?"

I'm sorely tempted to bite him in response. While he smiles up at me, the serious anger brewing like a good stew in his eyes causes me to keep my sass in check. "I might be even sexier as a milk momma in porn."

He blinks as he tries to process whether I'm being naughty or nice. A devilish smirk crosses his face, and his hands slide between us to cup my breasts firmly.

I gasp and writhe on him like a worm on a hook trying to escape the pain. "Mick," I whine, "I just cleaned them up."

"And? Maybe I like you dirty." He smirks as he rolls us over.

I part my legs.

While he nestles between them he doesn't reward me with his lovely hardening manhood he keeps selfishly tucked in his pajama pants. He leans down and gently kisses against each breast before he props himself on his forearms for the grown-up talk. "Now that I have your undivided attention," he grins, "Fine, work Christmas," he grumbles. "It would have been nice if you had talked to me first. Now I have to explain to my mother why you aren't there. You know how she likes to feed you.."

"I'll be there on the twenty-sixth. I didn't promise Harold New Year's." I nestle under him and bring my hands up to run my fingers through his hair. When he nuzzles my hand I smile.

"You better, or you're getting doubly punished when I get home." He lightly bites the heel of my palm.

"Oh? And how would you doubly punish me?" grinning up at him.

Magellan kisses me tenderly. "I more than want to," as he grinds against me. "We have already stayed up too late, and I have to head into the office early tomorrow."

I pout as he rolls off me and turns off the lamp, thrusting us into darkness.

December 25, 1985

Le Salon's halls are decked out with all the Christmas cheer a girl could ask for. There are men everywhere flirting with half-naked women. Drinks flow, the food is decadent, two of the four salons are open for entertainment. The public salon currently sports three young men and two new strippers from the Oyster for people to interact with. Near the entrance of each room stands a man dressed in leather pants and straps to keep the patrons from getting too naughty with the staff.

I have never hated Harold more than I do as I stand in my lavishly designed salon. My feet hurt, my tits are sore, and the prick I have bent over the pony is too drunk to consent. This leaves me standing here cooing to him in French with an occasional smack on his bare ass with my riding crop.

He's thoroughly enjoying himself as he slurs and shakes his ass like a dog wagging his tail, "Peas Miss-ress, have me 'nother!"

When he's finally escorted from the room, I wipe down the pony. I'm thankful these sessions are only thirty minutes. I look down to check my costume for the next session and part of my costume is damp. "Fuck," I mutter. A quick glance at the wall-clock and I step into the antechamber of the room. Thankful no one can see me like this, I retrieve the pump from my duffel bag. With an easy motion, I free my breasts from the leather top and remove the gauze taped over my nipples to help stop leakage. The men fawning over me for the past few hours has staved off the feeling of being a fat milking cow. I hum quietly as I pump both breasts and relax as the pain ebbs.

I'm never letting Magellan put his dick in me again.

I store the little pouches of milk in the mini-fridge I made Harold add to my salon. One baby wipe to my breasts later lets me apply new gauze and tape and pull my top back into place. I preen in the full-length mirror; touching up my lipstick, gently adjusting my face mask, and give my ponytail a quick tug. While I may not feel sexy, I look sexy. When I emerge from my milking station to let the next client into the salon, I am not alone.

I'm looking at a ghost. He has broad shoulders nestled in a perfect black Italian-made suit. The scent of Colombian cigars and bourbon fill my nostrils. A mix of excitement and fear washes over me as Big Tony Scapelli has come back from the grave like one of Scrooge's ghosts. My fingers curl tighter around the riding crop. Every muscle in my body tightens and my stomach churns. I freeze like the Gazelle I am.

Read The Room

I swallow hard. If this is Tony Scapelli, I'm going to beat him with this riding crop for making me believe he was dead. My brain struggles to process who would be here if this isn't him, looking like he belongs in a speak easy. I cautiously ease forward when the door to my salon bangs open and two drunken men stumble in.

"We are here for our session, Mistress!" They shout in unison.

When I don't reply instantly they stop looking at me and turn their attention to the mysterious man in the sharp Italian suit. All merriment stops as the men's gazes ping-pong between the man and me. Their exaggerated behavior of turning and bolting from the room causes me to snort in laughter and breaks the tension that had been building.

The man on my chaise chuckles.

I take a deep breath and press forward with all the confidence and grace of Giselle. The closer I get, the more I realize this isn't Big Tony. Mistress Giselle wouldn't care, and to stay in character, I bite against the inside of my mouth; not wanting this man to see my disappointment.

His eyes never leave mine as I approach, and his angry expression seers into my soul.

My gaze reluctantly pulls from his eyes and trails down his body.

He leans back on the chaise with one arm draped across the back, revealing he isn't armed. He raises a brow at me with a stony expression.

The silence in the air is as loud as the music thumping in the cabaret outside my salon.

He measures me like a predator does its prey before it attacks without moving a muscle.

Maybe it's the long night of irritating drunks, or being tired enough from traveling I can barely stand, but I can't take the deafening silence. "'ave you been a good boy?" I coo to him in my French accent. "Or do you need punishment?" I slip into the comfort and safety of Giselle to keep from freaking out in front of this older version of Tony. This is Antonio Scapelli Senior, Big Tony's father, a man I've only met once before in my life. He was present the day Tony's will and testament was executed.

He does not respond at first. Instead, he takes a sip of the drink in hand.

I lift my chin, staying in character. The show must go on. "Answer me," I demand as I crack the riding crop against my thigh.

His expression darkens. He sits up straighter and sets his drink down. Shifting his weight forward, as if he's ready to lunge at me.

Everything in me screams to turn and run. I've seen the grief-stricken look of a man ready to burn everything into oblivion because he lost someone he loves. I pause, forcing myself to calm down and focus on him. If he plans to kill me, running will do me no good. No one here will stand against this man, not even Harold.

Like the moth ever inching toward the flame, I move to stand in front of him. This is a man who knows exactly how to control the situation and he's unphased by my antics. Standing before him, I bring the edge of the riding crop up to his chin to lift his gaze. I don't command him again, and he has still said nothing.

The seconds tick by like hours as we stare at each other.

His hair is slightly disheveled, eyes are bloodshot, and from here I can smell the alcohol on him like it's his cologne. His fine lines give way to silvering black hair, and his body is fit for an older man. Tony definitely got his looks from his father. Tears cling to my lashes and I break first, turning away from him momentarily.

With a few easy steps, I reach the toy table where I gently set my riding crop down. I take my time removing my mask and retrieving my silk robe. If he does intend to murder me, I don't want to be Giselle. I want him to see Hope-Marie. My hands tremble as I tie the robe closed and I flex them until I'm confident I can turn to face him without impersonating a leaf on a windy day.

I swallow hard and sit on the chaise, keeping my back straight, crossing my legs at the ankle only and resting my hands in my lap, clasped. Maman would be proud at such a lady-like posture. I wish he didn't scare me more than his son did.

He remains silent, observing me.

Unsure of what to do, I lower my gaze. I unclasp my hands and play with the hem of my robe as if it were the most fascinating piece of fabric ever. My voice waivers when I speak. "Thank you for throwing such a wonderful party to help Le Salon." I have no idea what to say to him.

He gives me a practiced smile that doesn't reach his eyes. "My son definitely had fine tastes. You are an exquisite young woman." His heavy Italian accent rumbles like Magellan's Roadrunner as bitterness fills his voice.

I sit up straighter, as if that were possible, and clasp my hands again to keep from fidgeting. My muscles ache from being poised like a gazelle who faces a predator. "Thank you. What can I do for you, Mr. Scapelli?" I have never been a patient person, and if he intends to hurt me, I would rather not drag this out.

He raises a brow and takes a sip of his drink without responding.

I resist the urge to fidget under his scrutiny.

"I came to see what you have done with my son's blood money. If you are worth his life." He sets his drink down with a clank on the side table and drums his fingers on the arm of the chaise without ever taking his eyes off me.

I flinch like he slapped me and open my mouth to explain that I never thought it would go that far. I could lie and say I had no idea he would be in danger if he helped me. If I were Mr. Scapelli, I would be furious with that bullshit. "Tony was the strongest person I knew. They had already destroyed my husband, and I knew Tony would protect me, and by extension, Magellan. I never thought he would die. Not after how Harold built him up. I thought he would go and stomp them out. Make them hurt how they hurt Mick. And... And... Oh God," I cover my mouth to smother the sob into my hand. Guilt hits me like a Mack truck.

Tony Scapelli is dead because of me.

He shifts forward, close enough he could easily grab hold of me. "We both know the smartest play would have been for your man to sell it and run."

I frown and replay the events that took place in my mind. The helpless rage at being afraid of my then fiancé bubbles to the surface. The countless nights I spent pacing the apartment near the phone when he worked late or didn't come home when I expected him.

My temper flares to life like a Phoenix out of the ashes. "No." I shake my head. "You don't get to blame me for Tony's actions. I ran to Tony, willing to give him the world and destroy mine. He and Meg threw me out. Left us to fend for ourselves. We spent months of our own money and time rebuilding that place. All the while, realizing that I meant nothing to your fucking son that I would have given the world to if he hadn't tried to rape me! We would have sold it to the first person who walked through the door when we put it on the market. That first person turned out to be your son, who *chose* to give my husband the out. He bought it for a hell of a lot more than it was worth eight months *after* I asked him for help."

My body shakes with the burning fury of my anger. I clench my fists and level my gaze on him. "So no, you don't get to sit there and give me that shitty look. I lost the man I fell in love with to thugs like you. Tony got himself killed doing whatever the fuck he did. Forgive me, Mr. Scapelli, if I don't bow down and grovel to you because you're shitty that your son made the choices he did. I'm not the one who killed him. He was a grown ass man that made grown ass choices and that's what got him killed. You and I both know that when Tony put his mind to something he did whatever the fuck he wanted. Or do I need to fucking remind you of the contract you had to pay for because of his choices?" Tears stream down my cheeks, and I can't decide if I want to slap Antonio Scapelli or to get up and walk away. My chest heaves, and I wipe my cheeks on my forearm. Any hints of fear have been snuffed out by the blazing fire of my anger.

"Do you have children, Mrs. Lacienda?" His tone is quiet compared to the rising pitch of my speech.

I freeze in place and my heart begins to jack-hammer. The pendulum swing back to fear is like a tidal wave of ice on the flames of my anger. My hands ball into fists and the adrenaline surges as I'm on the precipice of fleeing the room to call Magellan to verify they are safe and sound.

"I... have... two, a one-year-old, and a two-month-old." I grind out, trying to force myself to remain calm. I'm silently thankful they are at the vineyard in Spain while we have this conversation.

He slowly reaches out and cups my chin in his hand.

I close my eyes, praying to God to watch over my family when I'm gone.

He pulls me forward. "Then love them," he says as he places a kiss on my left cheek. "Cherish them." He turns my head to place another kiss on my other cheek. "Raise them to be the light in this world." He places a final kiss on my forehead before he releases my chin.

"You are everything I could have hoped for in a woman for my son. Never lose that feeling you just had. It is the same for all parents, regardless of which station in life they live. You are a good woman, Hope-Marie, and were deserving of my son's love." He gives me a morose smile before he stands and leaves my salon.

Pomp & Circumstance

May 1986

"Why are we attending Columbia University's graduation?" Sophia Scapelli eyes her husband next to her in the back of their limousine.

"To show support to a family friend." He replies patiently as he pats her knee.

"Which friend would that be?" She swats his hand away and huffs.

"I thought I told you this already," he sighs. "Do you remember that girl, the one our son left the townhouse to?"

"The whore?" she stiffens.

"Not whore, dominatrix. There is a difference, my love."

"The dominatrix that got our son killed." She says the words with the bite of an angry Italian mother still in mourning for her baby boy.

"She did not get him killed, Sophia." Antonio inhales sharply as he corrects his wife.

"That isn't what you said six months ago." She crosses her arms and reminds him of their youngest child getting ready to throw a tantrum.

"I've had a change of heart. That girl is as much a victim as our son was."

"You slept with her," her voice rises in anger.

"I did no such thing. She's young enough to be our daughter. I talked to her. The only reason she went to our boy is she was terrified her man would be killed. She ran to the one person she knew could protect him." He chuckles. "As she put it, our boy was a grown ass man making grown ass decisions. As much as I hate that thought, she's correct. I'm choosing to focus my hate on the person who deserves it, the figlio di puttana who pulled the trigger." He hesitates as he looks at his wife. "I want you to see what our son saw. She has made something with the gift of life our son gave her. That, my beautiful wife, is worth celebrating." He reaches out and brushes her cheek.

She pouts at him, not ready to relinquish her anger towards this girl that got her son killed.

Staying awake during the ceremony takes all my effort. This long and boring process of calling each student's name, shaking their hand, and having them walk across the stage into their new lives is one of the most archaic celebrations of achievement I have ever seen. Then I walk across the stage and the rousing chorus of "Awoo" fills the fieldhouse and I can't wipe the smile off my face.

My husband convinced my sweet little Castian to shriek it like he's being murdered.

By the time I reach my family, I discover the reason the Awoos were louder than I expected is that my parents snuck a few of my siblings into the ceremony. What surprises me most is the adorable young woman hanging on Joe's arm, and the look of sheer twitterpation as he gazes back at her. I can't help myself and I tease him. "Guess you don't need the rest of my movies."

"Nuh-uh! Nope. You already promised autographed copies," he says.

"You're in movies?" The stars in her eyes blinds me. "Wait. I thought that was the other sister. Not the singer one. The one that married the sasquatch."

I snort with laughter and Joe coughs as he blushes. "Yeah, Joe. Why didn't you tell her I was in movies?"

Joe leans in close and motions for the two of us to lean in, pausing for dramatic effect before he whispers, "You remember the movie you said you liked? You know, the one with the whips and chains at that school." He whispers conspiratorially in our pow-wow. Before she responds, he slips his hand over my eyes, blocking half my face.

"You're Giselle?!" she squeals.

Everyone in the Tri-State area hears her as all eyes turn to us. Thankfully, they don't linger when nothing happens, and she turns as red as a tomato.

"I'm surprised at you, Elijah. I never once thought you'd use my movies to get a girl." I flash him a devilish grin and cross my arms in my sarcastic disapproval.

Joe smirks and shrugs. "*She* chose it off the shelf." He juts his thumb at his girl.

She slaps his arm hard enough to draw the attention of the people around us again. Then whisper-shouts at him, "You never told me it was your sister! That... It's... We... YOUR SISTER!"

I'm worried she might faint where we stand.

Joe gets a wolfish grin and pulls her close, nuzzling her before he coos. "And you liked it. Awoo."

Thankfully, I'm saved by this awkwardly intimate moment by the last person I ever expected; Antonio Scapelli Senior.

He has a twinkle in his eye when he says, "Pardon the interruption, Mrs. Lacienda. My wife and I wanted to congratulate you. You've done well for yourself." He holds out a small, gift-wrapped package, bound by a ribbon matching Columbia University's school colors.

I take the gift as if it will explode in my hand. When I'm not blown to smithereens, I look around to determine if anyone will stop me from unwrapping it. The fountain pen nestled in vellum is as exquisite as the wooden box holding it. I fling myself against Antonio and hug him tight. "Thank you, it's wonderful."

We're interrupted by the gentle cough of Mrs. Scapelli and I turn, without hesitation, and pull her into a tight hug as well. She gently pats my back and extricates herself. "You never said she was a hugger, Antonio."

He clears his throat and smiles, "As I said, congratulations, young lady. You have done well."

"Of course she has done well! She graduated Cumma Suma Mumma whatever. Never can remember what that phrase is. Either way, I'm proud of her. Who's your friend, Hope-Marie?" My father's ever-cheery voice fills the area and I could not be more embarrassed.

I panic. Every mobster scenario plays through my head as I hear Mr. Scapelli ask me if I have children in my salon again, and I look from Papa to Mr. Scapelli and back.

Maman is on Papa's arm, smiling from ear to ear. I don't think I've ever seen her this happy. I pivot in place, trying to pull myself together. As if I've been put in slow motion, Mr. Scapelli reaches his hand out to shake my father's hand.

Is this where I learn my father is also a mobster?

My eyes narrow and I keep my gaze laser-focused on Papa. There's no way I would ever believe my father could be a mobster. He's like G.I. Joe on steroids, all good and no flaws.

"Antonio Scapelli, Senior." He greets my father formally.

"Name's Wolfe, John Wolfe," Papa smiles and shakes his hand with a sturdy grip. He always loves the James Bond joke. If it isn't a Music Man reference, it's James Bond.

The two men smile at each other and Mr. Scapelli asks, "Weren't you in the House for a while?"

"Surprised a big-time New York gentleman like yourself would recognize a small-time congressman from Missouri." Papa has a goofy, proud smile on his face again.

"I don't track all congressmen. Your stance on civil rights definitely caught my attention. It's a shame you could not stay longer."

"Well, thank you kindly. How do you know my girl?" My father never elaborates that he didn't stay longer because of my mother's complications with giving birth to Joe, then to me.

My eyes widen to the size of silver dollars and I stare at Scapelli, willing him not to give anything away without saying a word.

Please don't tell him about Tony and me.

Or that you came to my salon.

Or that I perform kinky sex acts on rich and powerful men.

"Her husband sold my son a café in Brooklyn after your daughter provided a compelling case to purchase it." Mr.

Scapelli is a master at spinning the truth he wants people to believe.

"Good to know she's as charming as ever. She sells you one café, and you fall in love with her. You comin' to the party?"

"Papa," I whine, my cheeks turning pink.

"No, thank you, Mr. Wolfe. My wife and I wanted to congratulate her. We have another engagement to attend. It was a pleasure meeting you." He pauses to take Maman's hand and kiss the top of it, "and your lovely wife." After, the Scapellis take their leave.

Papa pulls me into a bear hug. Once he releases me, he chuckles. "He seemed nice enough. Glad you're making friends out here. Your Mom and I always worry you might not be okay out here in the big bad city. You know that, right?"

I don't correct him regarding my relationship with the Scapellis. "Yeah, I do, Papa."

"There's the girl of the hour!" Harold's voice roars over the other people conversing around us.

I smile brightly as the shy two-year-old buries her face against Daddy-Rittendorf. We all love that nickname for him around the Oyster and Le Salon.

"Harold Rittendorf, CEO and President of the Rittendorf Modeling Agency." He snatches up Papa's hand and shakes vigorously. "Hope-Marie's boss."

Stella and I exchange bemused looks at Harold's behavior.

"Harold Rittendorf." My father's entire posture changes. His grip tightens on Harold's hand, and he puffs up to square his shoulders. "Hope-Marie has told us exactly who you are." He takes a small half-step forward and appears to grow in height as well. The smile on his face is his politician smile.

I hold my breath and raise both brows, expecting my father to deck Harold where he stands.

"John," Maman coos as she deftly extracts Harold's hand to shake it herself. "It iz a pleasure to meet you, Monsieur Rittendorf."

Harold gets a child-like grin on his face as he darts his gaze to me before turning back to Maman. Giselle's French accents sounds remarkably like Maman. "You must be her mother. You have done a wonderful job teaching her French. I'm most appreciative of her skills."

If Harold weren't holding a toddler, he would be on the ground with the death stare my father gives him.

"Hi, I'm Stella," Stella steps between Harold and my father, trying to diffuse the situation. "Hope-Marie's truly an inspiration for everyone she works with."

My father deflates back to his plucky self, and he shakes her hand appropriately.

Arms wrap around me from behind, hoisting me in the air, squeezing me and spinning me around all at once. The faint scent of motor oil and leather permeates the air and I squeal in delight, "Billy!" At least my pole turning skills are useful as I squirm in his arms to return his hug.

"Hey, pip-squeak. When are you gonna feed me? I thought these things had a party. I got the twelve pack, where's the beef?" He releases me to my feet. I love he's smiling and relaxed. He must have left the kids with Gruncle, the pet name given to their mother's uncle.

"I got that covered!" Harold proudly chirps.

"I bet you do," Papa grumbles.

"MOMMY!" I barely catch my son as he flings himself from Magellan, slipping out of his arms like a greased pig.

"Oh, you're getting too big," Papa crows as he plucks Castian from my arms.

I open my mouth to warn him and Castian screeches, "NOOOO! MOMMY!"

"Castian," I scold, "You know better. Be nice to Abuelo Wolfe. He has missed you." I try not to laugh at the cutest pout that forms on his face. He looks like Magellan when he doesn't get his way.

Speaking of the devil, he slides up alongside me and pulls me into a soft kiss. "Hey. Ready to blow this popsicle stand? We should probably get going if we want to beat traffic."

My stomach growls like I swallowed a lion.

Without missing a beat, Magellan retrieves a cookie wrapped in a napkin from his pocket.

"You always bring me the best presents." I devour the cookies, much like the apple he gave me in Paris.

"You probably should have saved one. Those were Castian's."

He lowers his voice to keep Castian from hearing us.

"He's with Pop. He'll never know." I stuff the napkin back in his pocket to hide the evidence.

Magellan laughs, pulling me into a sweet kiss before handing me Helena to put in the car seat.

27

Let Them Eat Cake

I never thought a bouncy castle could be this much fun. Harold went all out for this party. I'll have to get him a nice gift. The bright colors and wiggling clown face draws Castian in, and as soon as he sees it, all of us are chopped liver. He wriggles his way out of pop's arms and eagerly bolts to the enticing castle.

Magellan holds our precious princess and smirks at me. "Go on," he nods.

Seconds later, my stilettos sit neatly next to Castian's cute tiny sneakers, and I'm wriggling through the entry way he happily tumbles through. I get onto my knees inside and hold his hands as he bounces with all his might.

He doesn't get far until I bounce opposite him. Then he soars up enough he lets out a glee-filled shriek to rival his Awoo from earlier.

My brothers are outside the bouncy castle as they watch us through the mesh netting. The two of them enjoy a beer while I entertain my son.

"A bouncy castle!" One of the girls from the Oyster squeals.

The next thing I know there are four of us and Castian bouncing without a care.

Castian shrieks with delight every time he soars in the air.

Each of the women fawn over him as they bounce him from one to the next like they're passing a doll around.

I bob to the edge and see Harold and Magellan has joined my brothers in overtly staring at the bouncy castle full of women. The shit-eating grins on Billy's and Joe's faces says they're enjoying the show.

My eyes catch Magellan's gaze and he watches only me with a devious expression. He motions for me to get back to it and I blush as I head back into the fray.

"Best hundred dollars I ever spent," Harold crows and motions with his glass of whiskey.

"What are you boys... looking... at," my father's voice slows as he falls in line next to Billy. Then there are five men gawking at the beautiful young women bouncing and giggling as they play pass-a-toddler.

"Ow! Hey! What was that for?" Joe's voice squawks.

"Shit pop! How can we not stare? Look at them." Billy protests at the same time as he motions with his beer towards the merriment.

"I raised you both better than that." My father grumbles. His eyes have not left the bouncy castle either.

I laugh and after a good ten minutes of bouncing like a fool, I wiggle my way out, taking Castian with me. The whining awes from the other women make me chuckle.

The bouncy castle soon fills with other children and strippers.

Castian pouts and whines until I set him down next to Rebecca, Harold's daughter. He takes one glance up at me, then runs away from her like she set him on fire.

She squeals and chases after him.

I glance over at the line of men seeing only my family enthralled.

Magellan has wandered away to the food table.

Harold avoids my father like the plague as he mingles with other guests. His animated way of storytelling holds my friends and family captive almost as much as the glorious display of bouncing strippers.

I spot Maman sitting under one of the pop-up tents with Helena nestled against her chest, fast asleep.

Magellan snuggles me from behind, offering me a plate of food.

I'm starving and immediately pop a mini corn dog in my mouth.

"Do you know how fucking hot you are?" He purrs the question in Spanish in my ear.

My cheeks flush pink and I can't reply as he timed it perfectly to wait until I had a bite of food in my mouth.

He eases his arm around me and pulls me back against him, placing a tender kiss on my neck.

I settle comfortably into his arms and enjoy the moment, swaying to the radio playing in the background. We silently watch our family and friends enjoy the afternoon. I wriggle my bare feet in the soft grass, envious of Harold and Stella's home with a yard. Our two-bedroom apartment feels like a cramped box in comparison.

Harold approaches us after extracting himself from the Bennetts.

Mr. Bennett had just explained to Harold how he was in the war with my father.

I chuckle as the expression on Mr. Bennett's face is the exact face my father gets when talking to Harold.

"There's the woman of the hour! How are you doing, kid?" Harold crows.

"Great! We should get one of those for the Oyster." I motion to the bouncy castle.

"Stella said I couldn't," Harold sulks like a child before he mutters, "Drunks and vomit."

Magellan and I laugh.

My gaze shifts to see Stella ushering a disgruntled Castian and Rebecca away from the treats table. Based on the brownie smears all over their faces she's too late to prevent over-indulgence. She has the kids well in hand, so I leave them be.

"Any plans now that you're a bona fide graduate?" Harold clears his throat to draw my attention back from the brownie thieves.

Harold has been asking me for a couple of months to perform the Giselle show for high-priced bachelor parties.

Other than Christmas, I've held firm in not performing as Giselle anymore. The problem is Harold keeps asking. He makes me feel like I can't say no, which leads to fighting with Magellan.

Magellan stiffens behind me.

I focus on Harold, wanting to punch him for bringing up business today. I have a small window of down time before I start my residency, and plan to use that time to finish getting Le Salon ready. We still needed bartenders, dominants for the public rooms, and to teach the staff the difference between working in the cabaret, the salon, and the Oyster.

"What do you want her to do?" Magellan's Spanish accent sneaks out when he growls the question, showing his irritation as Harold's demand for my attention. The way Harold asks me for things rattles the beast's cage.

"Come work the old show for a couple of bachelor parties. You know they always go over well. Everybody makes money, and--."

"She doesn't need the money, Harold," Magellan barks.

I raise a brow and shift to put Magellan in my line of sight. His eyes are slits as he stares at Harold. The muscles in his neck twitch as his hand tightens on my hip.

Harold may not realize he's waking the beast.

The last thing I want at this party is for my husband to lose his cool and beat one of my closest friends. "We'll talk it over, and I'll let you know when I come in for the bartenders."

"Well, I kind of need an answer by tonight. I have a bachelor party booked in the VIP room tomorrow." Harold sounds sheepish as he pressures me to answer now.

I know him better than that. He's being a dick and all it's going to do is put me in a bind.

So much for soothing the beast back to sleep.

Mick's grip digs into me, making me purse my lips and suck in a sharp breath through my nose. I could kill Harold for doing this. He damn well knows he's being unreasonable and that my work ethic won't allow me to leave him hanging. "I'll think it over."

"All I can ask for," and Harold flounces away.

I turn in Magellan's grip, hoping to soothe him, and not cause a scene at my party. I have no intention of discussing Harold's request until we're on our way home.

Magellan shoves away from me. "We both know you'll do what he wants no matter what I say. You'll do anything for

Harold. I wouldn't be surprised if you two cooked up this plan."
He storms off.

I stand perfectly still, white knuckling the plate he brought me. Tears well in my eyes and my nose burns with the effort to not start crying. Magellan's icy response makes me feel small and rejected. I can't think to form words, or respond. I want to run after him and beg his forgiveness, and to tear him a new asshole for being as unreasonable as Harold.

Magellan scorches the Earth with how fast he reaches the beer coolers. He snatches one up and takes a healthy swig, not even bothering to inspect the aftermath of his outburst.

My lip quivers and I suck in a few more sharp breaths to keep from turning into a blubbering mess. An arm wraps around my shoulder and I swear to God I'll stab Harold in the neck with this fork if it's him.

"Hey, everything alright?" My father pulls me close for a hug. He has a knack for swooping in and being the big damn hero, especially when it comes to me. Everyone in the family jokes that I'm his favorite.

I shift my plate around and take the moment to hide in his embrace to compose myself. "Yeah, Papa, just work stuff."

"Okay." Papa's tone holds the hint of doubt. "You know you can tell me anything, right?" He reminds me for the second time today.

"I know, Papa," as I plaster on my show smile. "Everything's fine, I swear."

"Good. Because I have a three-year-old who needs his mama, stat."

I follow my father, setting down my plate. Even with being hungry enough to eat a whole steak, my appetite is gone. Magellan's fury is enough to make me want to run to the nearest bathroom and vomit. As we make our way to my son's location, I scan the crowd. No one appears to be lingering on what happened.

We find my darling son standing at his full height, puffing up against a formidable foe, Aunt Stella, in front the cake table.

"Me cake!" He whines up to her as he crosses his arms.

"No, mister. You had at least four brownies before I caught you. This is your mother's cake. No one gets cake until she does."

"NOW!" He shrieks at her.

"Castian. That is not how you ask for things." I scold him and step alongside Stella to show him I'm not having that kind of behavior..

"Cake," he mewls back, and pulls out the cute defense. His lip juts out in the biggest pout I have ever witnessed. He then realizes Aunt Stella said no cake until I got some and he lights up, exclaiming, "Mommy cake!"

"Mhmm. We need to take a sweets time out. Mommy will get a toothache." I couldn't eat a piece of cake right now with how twisted my stomach is from Magellan's wrath.

Castian, in proper three-year-old fashion, rips himself from my hand and throws himself to the ground, kicking and screaming in an ear-splitting tantrum. I lean down to soothe my little lion cub when his father roars to life.

"That is not how you behave in public! Stop that noise this instant and get off the ground!" Magellan shouts in Spanish.

Castian is having none of that and wails louder.

Magellan barrels across the lawn, snatches Castian up by his forearm, and hauls him off to the side. He pulls out a chair and flips Castian over his knee in a fluid motion. Then proceeds to spank him hard.

I flinch with each smack to his bottom.

Castian shrieks in a mix of fit and terror.

Magellan rights him and carries him to a table as far from the fun things as possible. He thrusts him in the chair with a great deal of force. "You will sit here until you learn how to behave in public. Do not leave that spot, or I'll really give you something to cry over." He jabs his finger in Castian's face with such aggression, I'm worried he might hit Castian again.

When Castian whimpers and shies from Magellan, he storms back to where he left his beer.

I'm frozen in fear. Flashes of the night Magellan had me slammed against the wall and his brother pulling him off of me dance in my mind. I can't breathe, and the urge to vomit is even stronger than when Magellan walked away from me.

Magellan locks gazes with me. His jaw twitches as he snorts, daring me to defy him in public.

I lower my gaze in submission. My cheeks flush hot with shame. Now everyone knows how awful a parent I am along with being a horrible wife.

Can't Win For Losing

The surrounding crowd falls silent, watching my life fall apart on Harold's lawn. The murmuring is like Def Leppard music cranked to eleven. My gaze lingers on Magellan, pleading for him to turn around and apologize.

Stella's hand gently rests on my shoulder and I lift my chin, putting another fake smile in place, I do what any person does in this situation, make light of it. "Now that the entertainment is done, it's time for dessert!"

The crowd chuckles and I help Stella cut the cake.

"I got this if you want to check on Castian," she whispers.

I nod and ease away from the group encircling the cake.

Castian is in the exact spot where Magellan left him. His little gaze darts to see where his father is. He does not dare move. Daddy threatened him with more spankings. The tears have stopped as he sulks in the chair with his arms crossed.

"Hey, buddy."

He doesn't say a word, crawls into my lap, and buries his face against my shoulder.

I pet down his back to soothe him, holding him close. This feels like we're both in timeout with how his father circles the beer cooler, ignoring us.

My father is with Magellan, talking to him. His expression is drawn into a frown and he is gripping his own beer tightly.

I wish I could hear what Papa is saying. I kiss against my son's temple and silently pray that whatever Papa says doesn't set Magellan's temper off further.

Castian's breathing steadies. He squirms in my lap to sit with his back to me and watch the partygoers. We remain in silent the entire time people usher along the cake table.

Maman approaches with Helena. Her little fist is in her mouth while she makes tiny whines of protest at its lack of nutritional value. She takes Castian by the hand after handing me Helena.

The trauma of Daddy spanking him is forgotten as Abuela Wolfe takes him to get a piece of cake.

I step into the house with Helena for some much needed privacy. Left alone, I let the tears come. I had not expected today to go like this. The quiet ticking of the clock in this sitting room is calming. I half expect Magellan to come blazing in to have out the fight he wanted to have in the yard. My body won't relax and Helena gives a disgruntled gurgle from me holding her too tight.

"Sorry, princess," I coo as I wipe the tears from my face. I don't want my make-up to run too much, or my face to be blotchy when I return to the festivities.

Helena happily resumes her meal with her chubby little fist pressed into my breast.

I hate that I'll cave and will do the show tomorrow. I had wanted to truly talk to Magellan before I decided. Lately, telling him anything related to work leads to a fight. My anger at Harold ambushing me when he knew I couldn't truly discuss it causes me to tense all over again.

Helena feeds until she drinks herself into a stupor, her little mouth making a faint sucking motion without drawing anymore milk. I shift the burp rag onto my shoulder and tilt her up to lean against me. With a firm pat against her back, I coax out the air bubbles in adorable little belches. I'm not ready to go back into the party and face all the people with a lie on my face. I take time rocking my baby girl and calming my frazzled nerves.

The serenity of being alone allows me to focus on Magellan's behavior. His position on Wall Street is stressful. He won't talk to me when it comes to the office. His friends call less frequently, and when they do, it results in Magellan growing more agitated. He likes to be in control. He has a very set way of doing things and since 'The Incidence' there has been a lot of chaos in our lives. He hasn't brought up going to the PTSD sessions with the veterans in months. Today's incident is the most violent outburst I've seen from him in some time.

I hate that I will have to confront him on Castian's behalf. He went too far. I refuse to let him hurt our children how he has hurt me. Unable to find an excuse to hide any longer, I fix my clothes and return to the party.

Papa swoops in and takes Helena from me with all the skill of a man who has raised twelve children.

I'm left standing alone once again. A smile dances across my face as Joe and his girlfriend duck into the bouncy castle together.

Billy holds court at a table full of strippers, regaling them with his glory days on his bike. His handsome, sun-kissed features give nothing of the trauma he's suffered away.

Harold and Stella sit under the pop-up tent, Rebecca nestled in Harold's lap, happily sucking soda through a straw.

Maman and Papa approach me with the baby in her carrier and Castian in Abuelo Wolfe's arms.

"We're heading to zhe hotel. It has been a lovely soiree. You can pick up zhe children tomorrow." Maman gives my arm a squeeze and gentle smile.

"You're kidnapping my kids?" I raise a brow at my parents.

"A healthy marriage can always do with a night without children. Why do you think we kept sending you off to camp?" Papa gets a twinkle in his eye.

"John," Maman gasps in mock surprise.

"Madelyn, you damn well know those nights were the nights we got the best damn sleep. Summer camp was *your* idea." He wriggles his brows at her before leaning in to give me a hug. "We're proud of you. You and Mick enjoy yourselves."

I return his hug, then hug myself as I watch the circus of the Wolfe family leaving.

Billy shouts across the lawn, "Hey Elijah, hurry it up, or we're leavin' your ass."

Joe and his girlfriend tumble out of the bouncy castle a disheveled mess. Harold will have a heart attack if he finds out what they were doing in there.

As if on cue, my family's departure creates the mass exodus of the party.

I move to the nearest table, stacking plates and cups to pick them up in one fell swoop. I'm avoiding being alone with Magellan. I haven't seen him since I disappeared to feed Helena.

"You put that down, young lady. This is our party for you. You're not cleaning it up. Shoo." Stella swats me away from the table.

Rendered useless, I head to the bouncy castle to get my shoes, the lone pair of heels left. Concerned Magellan left me here, I bite my lower lip, scanning the yard for him. I don't have to search long as he is coming to me. I stand up straighter and brace for whatever he might say next.

His expression is stony and distant. He says nothing as he passes me, cutting me as deeply as his jab earlier did.

Falling in line behind him, I feel more like a kid busted at a party than a college graduate.

"Hey, wait up," Harold calls as he catches up to us.

Magellan pauses and turns to watch the two of us as I turn to face Harold. His expression still holds that stony ambivalence.

The added pressure of not wanting to say the wrong thing to make him even angrier feels like I've been set on fire.

"Got an answer for me?" Harold looks hopeful.

"I'll call you in the morning to let you know. We never got time to discuss it. You should have a backup ready." My tone is even when it comes out of my mouth, for which I'm thankful. I don't want Harold to question if I'm alright in front of Magellan. I also don't want to push Magellan further by making him think I'm happy with this situation either.

"Oh. Okay then. Make sure you do. Congrats again, Hope-Marie. I'm proud of you."

I squeak as he invades my space and pulls me into a quick hug. I keep up the fake cheery disposition until we're alone in the car. I don't dare look at Magellan. Instead, I focus on putting my heels back on and I stare out the window in silence.

Not a single word is spoken between us the entire car ride home, nor as we take the elevator up to our apartment. I watch the little dial tick up until we reach our floor and I step out in front of him, fishing the keys from my purse. I hope all he wants to do is take a shower and go to sleep. He ruined today with his temper. I'll forever look back on one of my crowning achievements and think of how he treated me.

We go through the motions of stripping down and we both get into the shower. I could have waited to take my shower, but I want to have this conversation uninterrupted.

He leans forward in the shower/tub combo and rests his hands against the wall to let the water drench his head.

I gather up the washcloth and Zest soap to lather it up. Starting at the center of his back, I trail the rag down his spine. "About tomorrow…"

"I already fucking told you to go. What else do you want? My permission to fuck Harold? Sure. Go ahead. Then you'll really be his whore."

"You know what, Mick? Go fuck yourself. I can't win with you. I don't tell you when I make a decision that is good for my business, I get in trouble. I try to include you and I get in trouble. It's bullshit! What you did to me today was shitty. What you did to Castian is even shittier. Heaven forbid I try to talk to you like a grown-up. So, yes, I'll be fucking working tomorrow to help generate traffic for my business, and to help Harold out. How dare you fucking call me a whore! I have never, not once, been unfaithful to you! Fucking wash yourself, you fucking prick!" I shout at him and jab my finger in his chest. "Don't fucking follow me."

I throw the rag with the soap bar down and step back out of the tub. I snatch a towel off the rack and storm out of the bathroom to dry off in the other room. I would normally fret and panic that I upset him. Tonight I don't care. He called me a fucking whore. He can do whatever he wants. I'm not his whipping girl. I have half a mind to march back in there and shout that at him. That will only result in apology sex. I don't want him to touch me. I haven't felt this alone in our relationship since the night after he discovered I was a stripper.

After I towel off, I throw it into the hamper, despite wanting to defy Magellan and leave it on the floor for him to pick up. My fit gears up as I jerk open the dresser to grab pajamas, followed by yanking my pillows off the bed to storm out of the room. I slam the bedroom door behind me on my warpath to the living room, taking out all my frustrations on the inanimate objects between our bed and the couch. The pillows hit the couch and I dive onto it, pulling the quilt draped over the back over me. The finale of my tantrum comes with me burying my face into my pillow to sob properly at my life falling apart.

Oh, You Got Trouble

I don't bother with checking on Magellan when I wake up. The sun creeps over the horizon. It's normal for the two of us to be up this early; me with the kids, and him getting ready for work. I bite my lip, and can't help thinking how hot he looks in his suits.

No! I'm mad at him. No sexy wall street fantasies.

My body aches from being curled on the couch all night and my breasts hurt with the need to expunge the milk. I wander into the kids' room like a zombie and hook up the breast pump by feel, not even bothering to turn on the light. I half expect Magellan to appear to make up with me. That's our thing lately, and I'm tired of it.

When I get the first pouch filled, I adjust the contraption and switch over to the other breast. The relief is instant. I never felt more like a cow than I do while pumping. By the time I'm finished, Magellan still hasn't shown his face. He's going to be late if he's still sleeping.

With the milk deposited into the fridge, I head into our bedroom. Silently, I ease open the door to peek in. When I don't see Magellan sleeping, I furrow my brow and push the door open more. No sounds from the bathroom either. His wallet and keys aren't on the dresser.

"Hrmph." He didn't even bother to wake me before he left.

He must still be angry as well. I slip into the room and leave the door open as I make a break for the bathroom. Seconds later, I'm standing under a hot stream of water, letting the tension and stress from yesterday wash down the drain. With no one here, I linger under the hot, pelting water until the hot water runs cold. Then I mad-dash wash myself. I should have taken a bath instead. The hot water worked its magic and relaxed my muscles.

Twenty minutes later, I'm hopping onto the train to head to the Oyster. While I'm heading the wrong direction for the morning commuters, the subway car is packed. I stand to be closer to the door when the train stops. My heels barely touch the stairs as I trot up them. A quick glance at my watch and I know I have time before Harold starts the auditions. I duck into my favorite bakery to grab us all breakfast.

Mac's standing outside the Oyster's door, keeping the lookie-loos out. "Morning, ma'am."

"Mornin,' Mac. Want breakfast?" I open the box to reveal the pigs-in-a-blanket stuffed inside.

"Don't mind if I do. You're here early," he says between bites.

"I'm helping with auditions, and Harold said he had a bachelor party tonight." I thought it odd that he's having one tonight. We're normally closed for business on Mondays. This client must be big money for him to agree to this. Harold's stunt yesterday is going to win him a hellacious talking-to when I get upstairs. I'm not one of his girls anymore. I'm supposed to be his business partner.

"Yeah, I saw you and Mick's thing yesterday. Is that what pissed him off?"

"Something like that. I don't know, Mac. Everything I do is wrong when it comes to Mick these days. I mean one minute he's the man I love and married. The next minute he's cold and cruel. The third he's a raging monster. Got any insight in that man-ape brain of yours?"

Mac snorts his laugh and nearly chokes on the bite of food as I unload on him. "Oh, honey. Every marriage has its rough spots. You have to power through. If that boy hurts you, you tell me. I'll straighten his ass back out. Don't matter the shit he's been through. You don't hurt women."

"Oh Mac," I lean up and kiss him on the cheek. "You're the best."

"Uh-huh. That's why I get double," as he snatches a second pig-in-a-blanket.

I leave Mac to his breakfast and trot up the stairs to the studio, where Harold and Stella prepare for auditions. The small line of girls I pass give me a mix of curious and distrusting looks. A year ago I would be more inclined to explain who I am. Today, I'm more likely to bite their heads off for looking at me wrong. I shake my head as I open the door to the studio at the top of the stairs and pause when Stella barks at Harold.

"You should let this go already and turn it into a restaurant. We can't afford all this." She yanks her notebook out of her bag and tosses it on the table.

"They're not staff, they're dancers, gig workers. They only get paid when they dance." Harold protests as he gently takes her tossed aside items and rights them for her.

"Or when they train. We still have to clothe them. Plus, your bleeding heart will give them all the benefits they could ever need." She brandishes a pen at him like a sword.

"Which is why they won't leave us," he says with a smile.

Harold's ever-optimistic reply makes Stella groan.

"Even if they're bad dancers, they know better ones. They paint us in a positive light and bring the better dancers seeking the perks of working for the Rittendorf Modeling Agency," He sprawls his hands like he's displaying the name in lights. "At which point I can downsize the chorus line."

"Or, you know, we could not try to be the Rockettes," I chime in.

"I never once said, Rockettes," Harold grumbles.

"Take a chill pill, Harold. I'm teasing you. We only need eight girls, not sixteen, and we can fill it with single acts as needed. I brought breakfast." I set the box of food on our table and Stella happily dives in.

"I can count on you for tonight?" He smiles at me like a small child trying to cheeser-smile their way into contraband cookies.

I roll my eyes hard at him. "Yeah. I'm in, but this is it, Harold. No more Monday nights. No more, you're my only hope.

No more of this "one more time" business." I exaggerate with finger quotes. "I'm done doing the Giselle show. Mick's not even speaking to me because of the stunt you pulled yesterday." I plop into the folding chair next to Stella and snag a pastry.

"What? You can't mean that. I'm counting on you for the new Monday nights. I can't run it on Sundays. I already have a new act for the VIP room on that night." He feigns being the wounded savior.

"Goddamn it, Harold!" I shout at him. "I'm not fucking working on Monday nights. I'm already here six days a week running Le Salon. I'm not your golden goose anymore." Of course, I'm the one who feels guilty when Harold wilts like a scolded puppy.

"Just thought it was a... fine. Tonight only." He mutters.

"You thought it was what?" I growl. This is bullshit and he knows it.

"I thought it was a perfectly good business opportunity." He still sulks.

Staying mad at Harold is like trying to herd cats. I adore the man, and he has done right by me from the start. Even with me wanting to ring his neck for trying to force me back into the VIP room.

"What do you mean you're working six days a week?" His kicked puppy act disappears as he rounds on me, back to the man in charge. "You're not supposed to be working at all. Where's Mistress?"

I rub my nose in response, not wanting to get the other woman in trouble. She's been calling me to meet with the contractors, handle paperwork for new employees, and sign off on all the deliveries. She only cares for the B.D.S.M. lifestyle. I hadn't told Harold and Stella because I assumed she had. By the look on Harold's face, I see that I have made an ass out of myself.

"Well... She's... I," sputtering for the correct words.

Stella saves the day by interjecting, "Harold, that woman wants nothing to do with running a business. She wants to be a dominatrix. The only reason she even agreed to this was to get more money out of her private clients. She's been pushing all her responsibilities onto Hope-Marie for the past two months."

The tension between the three of us is thicker than fog rolling in from the harbor. Did Harold think I'm some wanton sex-kitten, lazing around the house, waiting for my man to get home? I have slept less than three hours a night, between homework, work, and taking care of the kids. I have no interest in adding to my life any of Harold's money-making schemes.

"You know what? We'll talk later. I want to see women with extraordinarily little clothing on, bouncing their tits for all to see as they try to dance, okay?" He rubs his temples as he slumps into his seat on the other side of Stella.

"Okay," Stella and I say in unison, like we're talking to Castian and Rebecca.

The first batch of girls are ushered in.

We watch in silence as they're taught the routine we want them to perform, followed by them performing the routine real-time. I jot down the ones I like and we have them run through the routine a second time. The three of us compare our notes and dismiss more than half of the dancers.

"Great! Ladies, you will report for your new hire orientation on Friday and start rehearsing on Monday. Congratulations."Harold cheers as he dismisses our new cabaret dancers.

Not So Easy Rider

The music rocks the main stage of the Oyster. The girls dancing are new, or desperate for cash. I've been in their shoes, desperate to make money I picked up every available minute of time Harold dangled in front of me. Hell, I'm still here, working on my day off. I frown as I realize I'm using work as an excuse to not confront Magellan. My heart isn't in this tonight. With each step up to the VIP room, the night Mistress Giselle was born comes to mind, and guilt wells, For the first time since I met Magellan, I wish things had been different between Tony and me.

I meet my submissives outside the VIP door.

Mac grins when he sees me.

I give them a once-over and while they are beautiful, they aren't Dallas and Baby. Once satisfied with their inspection, I turn them around, grab them by their leashes, and tuck Hope-Marie deep down to let Giselle come out to play. As soon as Mac opens the door any hints of not wanting to be here disappear behind my coy smile and arrogant strut.

"Oh, fellas! You're in trouble now." The DJ shifts the music to my theme song, Sweet Dreams, and the men whistle as they settle into their seats. It never fails, one of them tries to touch one of my girls.

I smack his hand with a riding crop.

His punishment is to get on his hands and knees and carry me the remaining ten feet to the stage like the bad dog he is.

"Kiss my heart." I command when I finally ease up off him.

The men cheer and clap as he behaves, and I allow him to return to his seat.

I spank and tease the two women with me until I guide one to lap-dance for the groom, while the other girl mischievously sneaks off to entertain one of the other men. The few minutes of the song for the groom's lap dance gives me a chance to set everything up for the real part of his bachelor party. I get the chair settled front and center, and I nod to the DJ who fades out their music.

"Zhat is enough play time wif zhe young man. Bring him to get his punishment for being such a wicked boy." I have perfected the French accent at this point and am still wearing the show smile when one of the men shoots up out of his seat like a rocket. At first, I'm worried I'm going to have to handle an unruly drunk.

Then our gazes meet.

Billy Wolfe's blazing anger leaves flames in his wake as he barrels toward me like a freight train.

"Since you 'ave been such a good girl, you may spank him." I hand the riding crop over to one of the submissives, and I quickly move to intercept my brother before he can make a scene in front of the other guests. "If he isn't properly punished when I get back, you vill be."

The men roar in excitement.

I exit the room with Billy on my tail.

He growls, "What the fuck do you think you're doing?" He grabs my forearm and whirls me around.

I'm forced to hold him to keep from losing my balance.

Mac steps forward, ready to clean Billy's clock.

I shake my head no and wave him off.

"You vill unhand me zhis instant." I try to jerk free of his grasp.

"Stop it! Fuck! Are you fucking serious, using her voice for your whoring?" Billy switches into French to yell at me.

I bite my lip hard to keep from laughing at Billy until he calls me a whore. The ringing slap that connects with his face is loud enough to make Mac take pause.

"I'm not a whore and you will behave or I'll have Mac throw you out. This is my job, Billy. She doesn't own this accent." I switch to French as well.

"She's our Goddamn mother and you showing your tits with her voice is not okay, Hope-Marie!"

"Giselle," I correct.

"No. Your fucking name is Hope-Marie." His chest heaves with his deep breaths. His fists curl and uncurl as he struggles to keep his temper in check. I half expect him to turn into the Incredible Hulk before my eyes.

"No, you bull-headed pig. My name when I'm working is Giselle, and I'm from France. You want all these horny bastards to know my real name? Follow me home and fuck with my family?" I jab my finger in his chest as I yell back at him. The words are out of my mouth before I can catch myself and immediately I regret speaking them.

Billy knows all too well what an obsessed stalker can do to a man's family. One destroyed his by causing Frankie, his wife, to take her life. He visibly flinches, deflating. The cloud of guilt and sadness washes over his face as his shoulders slump in defeat.

To my defense, my nerves are frazzled from fighting with Magellan. "I'm a fucking adult who makes damn good money entertaining men with kink play. This party alone probably makes me more than you'll make in a whole fucking year. You are not going to ride in here on your righteous high horse and call me a whore or degrade what I do for a living. I didn't fucking see you complaining yesterday when you ogled my friends like they were play-things for your enjoyment. Or let's talk about how you abandon everyone when the going gets tough, leaving the rest of us to pick up the pieces of your fucking mess!" My voice reaches the fevered pitch of a woman who is at her limit.

He stands perfectly still with his arms now crossed, watching me, silent as a crypt.

The longer he does it, the worse I feel for blowing up at him. It's not his fault, I'm pissed at Magellan.

"You..." He lets the word hang as the gears turn behind his eyes. "I was going to say you need to get laid, but we both know that isn't a problem."

I could kill him for the smirk he gives me.

"So, now, I'm going to say you need get drunk off your ass. Tonight, after work. You," he flicks a hand towards me, "and me." He flicks the hand back to himself. "We're going out and getting you slammed. I won't take no for an answer, you hear me?"

"Fine!" I huff at him like a small child. "I'll have to call Mick. Do you mind? I need to get back to work?" I motion to the VIP room.

He narrows his eyes and clenches his jaw, nodding.

I shove by him and strut back into the room to finish the show.

After the show finishes, I change and go to find my brother.

He's sitting at a table, enjoying the girls on stage shaking their tits for any wayward souls who ventured into the bar area from the party. He gives me a once over and downs the drink. After standing he drapes an arm over my shoulder and walks me out without a moment's hesitation.

"Hey, wait, I need to call Mick still." I whine as I try to wriggle free.

"Already called him. He knows who you're with. Besides, I thought you were a grown ass woman who didn't need anyone's approval for what she does?" He tightens his grip and cocks a brow at me with a smirk.

I want to smack his smug look off his face as we exit the club and get in a cab.

Billy takes us to a place where you need a tetanus shot to enter. He doesn't allow me to say a single word until I've had at least four shots.

My cheeks are flush and my lips feel puffy when the interrogation begins.

"You wanna tell me what's going on?" His graveled tone reminds me of the Billy I knew as a kid, before he met Frankie.

"Nope," I shake my head like a toddler emphasizing their answer.

"Then we need another round." He taps the bar top.

The portly, balding man grunts as he fills the shot glasses.

"Bottoms up," Billy motions before throwing one back.

I eye the amber liquid with a dubious look. When I try to snap my gaze to Billy laughing at me, the room feels like I hit a fast spin of a tilt-o-whirl.

"You men think you can always tell me what to do!" I brandish my finger at Billy.

"You parade around doing whatever you want, whenever you want. Heaven forbid I try to do something for me, or to help you. Then it's all anger and yelling. I know it's all my fault. And now I'm an ugly cow. Moooooo! Even cows have feelings." I pout at the shot glass.

"The more I try, the more he hates me. He's mad all the time. I can't do anything to make him happy." I snatch up the shot glass and sway before I down it.

"And then you," I point the glass at Billy.

"And then me. Kid, what's going on with you and that prick of a husband of yours? Last I checked, he loved you to pieces. Is he not taking care of you? Need me to go teach him a lesson?" He gently takes the shot glass from me and orders us coffee.

I cut him the dirtiest of looks as I jut my lip out to pout. Perched on a barstool in skin-tight pants and an oversized shirt, my hair still curly and fluffy around me, I believe I'm the first woman in this place in a long while. Turning my alcohol blurred gaze from Billy, I inspect the room. There are only a handful of men in here, each grizzlier than the next. They're paying me no mind, which is a blow to my ego.

Why aren't they looking at me? Do I look fat? Or worse, is there spit up on my shirt?

I fidget and teeter on the stool.

Billy's strong hand rests on the small of my back, stabilizing me. "Drink up," he commands as he turns me to face the bar.

"See. I've lost it. I'm not sexy anymore." I bemoan.

"Hope-Marie, you get that bullshit out of your head." Billy barks at me. He's been through much worse than I have, yet here he is trying to help me out while I get upset over some old creepy men not fawning over me.

"I don't know." I throw my hands in the air dramatically. "He won't talk to me. He's pissed all the time. Everything makes him fly off the handle. Anytime I bring up the club he gets pissed. If I mention Harold, he flies off the handle. And yesterday..." I try to wipe the tears away as I cry.

"I got you, Kid." His arms are strong and warm as he cradles me against his chest. He waits for the waterworks to simmer down before shoving a cup of coffee into my hands. Once satisfied I'm not going to topple off the barstool, he fishes out his cigarettes. He taps them on the counter, fires up the one that slips from the pack, and takes a long drag before he continues.

"Frankie and I had our issues," he says before he takes another hit off his cigarette. "I would trade this silence for the worst shouting match we had in a heartbeat." He stares at the drink on the bar as he taps the ashes from his cigarette into the ashtray. "Kid, if you love him and he loves you then there's always time to work this shit out, okay?"

"Okay," I sniffle. With a shaking hand, I wipe away the tears. The coffee's bitter and disgusting.

The face I make when I take a swig causes Billy to laugh hard and long. "C'mon, Princess, let's get you back to Prick Charming."

Grand Preparations

July 2, 1986

From the bachelor party to Le Salon's grand opening, I barely have enough time to sleep let alone pick more fights with Magellan. We're in an awkward routine of him working during the day, and me at night. The hours we spend together with the kids focus on eating or our children.

I put extra hours in at the club to get my body back. Stella started a work-out regime to help girls keep in shape. While the Rittendorf Agency wants its girls to be healthy, they have to be in demand as well. Today, I'm in a leotard and tights, leg warmers included, and my unruly blond hair is pulled into a high ponytail.

Castian sports a headband and wristbands made of terrycloth, causing his dark curls to spike upward.

Helena bounces eagerly in her technicolored contraption.

I've given up on following the routine and have taken to dancing around the living room with Castian.

The squealing laughter of both children and the ridiculous counting from Jane Fonda on screen makes me laugh.

Castian stops moving, staring behind me like a cat looking at a shadow demon over my shoulder. His adorable smile washes away, and he fidgets.

"Mommy. Stop. You are going to get a spanking," he whines.

"What? No baby. We don't get spankings for exercising." I completely misunderstand him.

Castian's eyes dart from me to behind me again. I can't understand why he would suddenly be afraid. I finally look over my shoulder to see what he's afraid of.

Magellan stands at the door, stepping out of his dress shoes while he loosens his tie. As he comes forward, he rolls his sleeves up.

Castian comes closer to me, putting me between his father and him. He shifts his weight from foot to foot, preparing to run for the hills.

"Come on, buddy. We don't want to get behind." Magellan wiggles his hips from side to side as he brings his hands in the air. He looks ridiculous, but it does the trick.

Castian lights up and looks to me for confirmation.

When I mimic Magellan, he resumes his running around.

Magellan gives me a sad smile. He doesn't stop dancing. The hurt ghosting across his face speaks louder than Jane Fonda's inane counting on the television.

I guide Castian over to dance with Daddy while I pick up Helena.

The four of us dance our hearts out until we reach the cooldown and Jane Fonda folds herself in ways no human should.

I stop the tape and rewind it, leaving it for the next day.

Castian runs off to change out of his "sercise" clothes, which is him throwing the headband and wristbands into his toy box.

I shift Helena and slide up to Magellan to steal a quick kiss. "We're still good for you watching the kids tomorrow, right?"

"No." Magellan goes stiff. When he speaks again, his jaw is clenched. "They revoked my request. Said I needed to be in the office tomorrow to handle some delicate clients." His tone rises in anger.

Not wanting to lose the happy moment, I steal another kiss from him. "That's why you make us the big bucks. I'll see if Stella's sitter can watch the kids. If not, I'll take them with me and sick them on Harold." I smile, in hopes of my joke lightening his mood.

"Hrmph," he sulks, and the mention of Harold makes him

narrow his eyes at me as he puts distance between us.

Instead of fighting with him, I coo at Helena. I know he doesn't like me taking the kids to the club. I don't either. "We could see if Tristan is in town, if you prefer they stay here." As much as I'm irritated with whatever is going on between Magellan and Harold, I don't want to upset Magellan further. Offering my brother as an alternative is an olive branch.

Confusion replaces irritation on his face and he waves his hand as he dismisses my suggestion, "We both know Tristan is on the vineyard begging my parents for money."

"No. Not your Tristan, my Tristan." I giggle, still focused on Helena.

"You mean the Tristan that couldn't be bothered to show up to your graduation? Even with living in the same city?"

"Not fair. He was working in Utah that weekend."

He chuckles and shakes his head. "Yeah. See if he can do it. I don't like the kids at the club."

"Deal." I hand him Helena as I pick up the phone on the wall, dialing Tristan's number.

"Hello, Wolfe Residence," he says after a few rings.

"Hey, my favorite brother."

"No. That's Joe. The only reason you call me is you want me to cook." Tristan chuckles.

"That's not true. I'm not calling you for food today."

"There's always a first time for everything. What's up?"

"My babysitter bailed at the last minute."

"Can't I'm busy tonight."

"Well, good thing it's for tomorrow."

"Can I bring a date? And how long?"

"As long as you don't have sex in my apartment. It's from eight in the morning until Mick gets home."

"Are you sure we can't have sex on the couch?" he teases.

"Yes, Maman would kill me if I let you. Plus, you'll scar the kids."

"Fine. If I must. See you tomorrow."

"Oh, and will you cook them lunch?"

"See! See! What did I tell you?" He teases me. "I'll make sure you have leftovers."

"Great. Helena is still on breast milk. It's in the fridge. We are shifting her to baby food. If you don't like the jar stuff, you need to mash anything you give her."

"You don't get to tell me how to make baby food. Mash anything... What kind of cook are you?"

"A bad one." I laugh. "I'll see you in the morning. Thanks a million." I put the phone on the wall cradle. "Tristan agreed to watch them until you got home," I say, even though he heard my side of the conversation. I want his approval.

He shrugs like it was nothing. "Looks like we need to get started on dinner."

"I got it. You spend some time with Helena and unwind." I motion for him to go sit down as I pull out the food I had planned to make for dinner.

<hr>

July 3, 1986

I'm at the bar in the cabaret, going over the final punch list Mistress and I created. She's on stage as our staff files in for the big team meeting before we open. I'm unbelievably nervous. My brother really came through at the last minute.

Hopefully, Magellan will relax as the kids are taken care of and he can focus on work. He has been such a brute lately, that I'm worried he's not okay with Le Salon and is working up to asking me to leave.

The hours dedicated to getting Le Salon off the ground, coupled with my upcoming residency leaves me little room for my family. Magellan and I are ships passing in the night. What little time we do spend together we're fighting. Tristan has his own life and can't drop everything to watch my kids. The two sitters we have tried were worse than me leaving the kids in Harold's office at the Oyster.

I'm a horrible wife and and mother.

Mick's working and it's enough. I could quit.

And be nothing?

Why does it have to be me that stays home?

Mick can quit his job, take care of the kids. I'll make all the money!

"This is prostitution," Mistress's voice carries across the room as she strokes the young man on stage.

The groan from the staff member on stage causes me to whip my head up. The poor fool who thought he would get the better of Mistress is at her mercy, and by his compromising predicament, has learned his lesson the hard way.

The other employees shift in their seats. Some are enjoying the show, others are squirming in their seats.

Mistress has been hands-off with getting Le Salon started, leaving most of the staffing choices to Harold, Stella, and me. She can be intense when people first encounter her. "And this is domination." She demonstrates the difference which causes her victim to blush and groan more.

She uses the riding crop to thump his ass lightly and send him back to his seat. "Know the difference. Any of you that gets busted for prostitution will put us all in jeopardy. We are not a whore house. We are a cabaret and BDSM club. All of our members will sign a consent form as they enter, and it clearly states that you are only present to guarantee everything remains consensual. You are not there to satisfy their sexual needs. Are we clear?"

"What about you and Giselle?" One of the women calls from the crowd.

"What about us?" Mistress says as she shrugs.

"Isn't what you do, prostitution?" She presses.

"No. Not at all. We are paid to provide an experience for the members who book our salons. We won't be having sex with our clients. Being dominated does not always involve sex. Hope-Marie and I'll be running private salons. The rest of you have not been trained to engage in such sessions."

"How do we handle tips and cash they throw at the stage?"

"This is a cabaret, not a stripper stage. That should have been clarified to you. Your salary is adjusted for lack of tips being paid. If someone gives you cash, great. Do not disrupt the show to accept it. Is that understood?"

"What if someone gets handsy?" Another woman asks as she raises her hand.

"If anyone touches you that you don't consent to, immediately notify security and the member will be escorted out.”

I listen and make a note that we might need more security for tomorrow. With tomorrow being the Fourth of July, people might be squirrelly from partying too much.

After her thrilling discussion on consent, she sends everyone to get into their costumes for final inspections. She hops down from the stage and heads in my direction.

I check off 'pep-talk' on the list and gather the paperwork to head up to the office.

“Harold and I had chat regarding your schedule. That man’s insane for scheduling you like that. You need to work on your boundaries with him. Tell him to find a new golden goose, or you tell your husband he's in a harem. Either way, be the one to set those boundaries. Your marital issues are starting to affect me, and I’m not getting into your weird shit. Got it? Oh, and, you’ll have six clients, not twelve.”

“Six? What happened to the rest of them?” I’m trying to do the math of the cost of sessions lost while standing in front of Mistress like a student caught without a hall pass.

“I comped them a cabaret show for tomorrow and booked them on Saturday and Sunday. I want to discuss Devon Wilcox. He’s your third appointment tomorrow.” She motions for me to follow her.

“The stock guy?”

“Yeah. Listen. I’ve known him since he came into money. He’s one of those that has no limit.” A smile dances across her lips that suggests a fondness for Devon I’ve never seen from her.

“What do you mean no limit?” My grip tightens on the paperwork in my hands and I swallow hard. If he thinks he’s getting sex from me, we’re going to have issues.

Maybe this is a bad idea.

“Meaning, he will never use the safe word, even if you physically hurt him. It will be up to you to keep him in line with safety. Don’t let him push you into extreme behavior tomorrow. Got it?” She brandishes a riding crop at me.

“Got it. He won’t get upset will he? I mean if I don’t go as far as he wants.” I pseudo hold my hands up in surrender, not wanting to feel the sting of her riding crop.

“Nah. He’s a submissive to the core. He will love that you

limit him. Weird kind of mental torture kink. You'll like him. Give me all of this and get out of here. That hot Spaniard of yours is waiting at home." She takes the punch list and my pen before motioning for me to get lost.

"There's too much to do." I bite my lip, and hold on tighter to the paperwork.

"I got it. Go home. Harold will have my ass in a sling if you get overtime on your first week." She waves dismissively.

Sergei Vasiliev

I wish I had half the confidence to tell Harold no as Mistress does. Her quip related to choosing between Harold and Magellan has gnawed at me like a puppy chewing its way through a bone. I don't want Magellan to feel like he's the third wheel in our marriage. I also don't want disrespect Harold. Without him, I would have gone back to Missouri, never met Magellan, and probably be a miserable waitress in my uncle's bar, or worse, a farmer's wife.

I make the most of my night off by heating up the amazing dinner my brother prepped for me. Then by treating the kids to ice cream and park time while Magellan and I snuggle on a bench. I wish our lives could be like this all the time. I'm selfishly enjoying an evening without fighting and not confronting him with our issues. Our relationship isn't healthy for the kids. Castian frets anytime Mommy and Daddy argue. He's having nightmares, not to mention being clingy with me whenever Magellan is around.

Mistress is right, and I'm putting my foot down from now on. Harold will have to understand my family comes first. The idea of confronting him leaves my stomach feeling like someone's playing the bongo drums on it. I would do anything for Magellan, and if that means I have to walk away from everything I've built, I will. I hope it doesn't come to that.

Today is not the day I will confront Harold. I'm barely able to keep the meager breakfast I scarfed on the train down without having to deal with the fallout of setting boundaries. I'm jealous Magellan gets to spend the day with our kids doing all the fun things in Central Park, then to watch the fireworks. I packed all of their favorite snacks and made sure Magellan had plenty of milk and diapers for Helena.

I sulk as I wait for my first session to begin. Perched on my "throne" in my private salon, I rest my hand on my chin. I would much rather be swirling sparklers, eating cotton candy, and running around with my little lion.

My first client is Sergei Vasiliev. He runs an empire of restaurants, car services, and sponsors immigrants from Russia, among other Eastern European countries. On paper, he's a wealthy businessman with deep pockets and a penchant for pretty blonds. Mistress hinted that I need to impress him, or it could hurt our client list. The idea of a single man making, or breaking, my business frightens me. I'm supposed to be the one in power. What kind of man is he that even Mistress seeks his approval?

The man that walks into the room is tall, broad shouldered, in a tailor-made suit. His blond hair sits neatly combed back in a single ponytail at the base of his skull, revealing gentle baby blue eyes. He reminds me more of a Viking than a businessman.

He gives me a once over, followed by a smile. He neatly hangs his suit jacket on the hook by the door before he makes his way to the small bar I have available. After pouring himself a drink, takes a seat on my chaise, and leans back to relax.

I say nothing, more nervous than I was the night I dominated Tony Scapelli. My stomach twists and turns with the mix of fear and excitement. What if he doesn't play along? What if I don't like it? I make a show of walking down the steps from my throne and towards the Viking businessman like I'm rocking the runway in Paris.

My black leather corset is cinched tight, and the silky material covering my breasts shifts with my movements. Even my fishnet stockings are perfect. My mask is an intricate mix of silk and lace, tied neatly under the ponytail of blond curls. I think I look more like a Playboy Bunny than a dominatrix.

The appreciative sigh from Sergei boosts my confidence. He takes a sip of his drink, never taking his eyes off me.

I use the riding crop to lightly spank his thigh. "I did not give you permission to drink anything," I purr in French.

A slow grin forms on his porcelain expression and he sets his drink down. "Forgive me, Mistress. I don't know all your rules." He replies in fluent French. The way it rumbles off his tongue could leave a girl wanting him to read the phone book to her.

"First rule. Tell me your safe word."

"Rubies." He rolls with his heavy Russian accent.

"Bon. Second rule. Refer to me as Mistress." I'm nervous and miss that he already did this.

"Yes, Mistress." He chuckles as he already complied with this request.

"Final rule. You vill enjoy yourself." I flash him a smile.

"Yes, Mistress." His voice softens and sets his drink down.

"Since you were such a bad boy, you vill remove your pants and shirt. Stand in zhe center of the room and wait for your punishment."

He stands and begins to undress. His compliance does nothing to calm me. He's massive compared to me. Even in my five-inch stilettos, I'm a good eight inches shorter than him. Up close I can see he's more Harold's age than mine. By the thickness of his accent he hasn't been in the States very long.

While he undresses, I saunter to the table of toys. These few seconds perusing the items laid out for my use allow me to get my nerves under control. He has paid for a mild package of play, which includes a little restriction, and spanking. Nothing humiliating, or degrading. Part of me wonders if Mistress threw me a bunch of softballs today to test I could manage being a dominatrix and not play at being one in the VIP room.

"Good boy," I coo as I approach him. "Put your hands behind your back." He complies and I bind them with the scarf. He gives them tug and I spank his thigh, "No. Stand still."

"Yes, Mistress," his voice is husky and thick. His mischievous smile fades when he sees the blindfold.

I raise it up, hesitant with how his shoulders square and he lifts his chin. When he does not stop me, I lean in close and tie it firmly above his ponytail.

He leans in an inhales, his frown fading. His body remains tense, like he turned to stone when I removed his ability to see.

I spank him again, "What did I tell you?"

He grunts. "Stand still, Mistress."

"Oui," I say as I trail my fingers along his bare chest. His skin is a mix of soft and smooth with calloused scars. I ease back and brush along his chest with featherlight touches and smile as his skin goosebumps.

The rise and fall of his chest quickens and his hands are clasped tight enough he could bend steel. The longer I touch him the more his body relaxes. His muscular thighs twitch with the desire to shift his weight.

My fingers dance along the intricate patterns of his tattoos and scars, allowing him to know my location as I admire his beautiful body. I take my time, as I gauge his comfort level. This is as much for pleasure as it is pain. "Remember, you may use your safe word at any time. Are you ready for your punishment?"

His lips tighten to a thin line, and he flexes his fingers, testing the scarf again. His manhood grows firmer to bob to life. His shoulders relax and his breathing steadies.

I can relate. When Magellan leaves me tied up, the anticipation is as exciting as the reward.

"I am ready, Mistress." He stills.

"Bon garçon. Thank me and ask for another." I flick my wrist with the riding crop resulting in a loud crack against his ass.

"Mhmm," he groans and tenses as he struggles to remain still. "Thank you, Mistress. May I have another?"

I reward him with five total swats before I remove the blindfold. "You may kneel and kiss my heart."

He blinks several times once he can see again. He pulls his gaze from me to inspect the salon. His breathing is rapid and light again. As I raise my riding crop at his hesitance in obeying me, he kneels.

The beautiful sight of this massive man kneeling before me, his cheeks flushing pink as he he gazes at my red leather heart, causes me to bite my lower lip in anticipation.

He smiles as he tilts his gaze back up to meet mine and he leans in to place a perfectly centered peck against me.

I reward him by leaning forward and untying his hands. "Bon garçon. You may crawl back to the chaise and enjoy your drink."

His chuckles and makes a show of getting on his hands and knees, his manhood still fully saluting me. His graceful movements remind me of a tiger. Instead of sitting in the chase, he kneels on his calves to reach for his drink.

I tease him and spank him several more times, making him always thank me by kissing my heart. The tiny red light above the door flickers to life, alerting me to end the session.

Mac's ingenious idea prevented my salon from being ruined by a clock.

"You may finish," I coo to him, brushing my fingers along his cheek.

"Thank you, Mistress."

To my surprise, he does not finish and rises to his feet. I gather up the toys we used and return them to their homes.

"How do I schedule more time with you?" he asks as he gets dressed.

"You can let zhe girl at zhe main entrance know you wish to book time avec Mistress Giselle."

"And do you do more than we did today?" His shoulders are relaxed, and he's paying me little mind while he focuses on buttoning his shirt.

"Zhere are different packages you may purchase, oui." Excitement rushes through my veins like the first big drop of a roller coaster. The idea he likes what I did and wants more makes me giddy. I struggle to keep Giselle's cool and indifferent expression.

"Then I hope to enjoy you again, Mistress." He smoothly pulls up my hand and kisses the top of it before he leaves my salon.

I quickly finish cleaning up and take a break to pump milk. Sergei's behavior while blindfolded bothers me. It was like he expected something terrible to happen to him. I make a mental note for his next session, not wanting to create a situation where he does not get pleasure from his time with me.

The Dove That Got Away

When Sergei Vasiliev called her, she had half a mind to run for the hills, abandoning the misfits of Le Salon to their own devices. She was never going back to the lifestyle that comes with a man like Sergei. Refusing him could have dire consequences for those around her. While he is the sensible brother, she would not mistake his gentle tone for weakness. She deliberately scheduled him with Hope-Marie, hoping Sergei would get the message and leave after his session. Seeing his man, Boris, at the base of the stairs, tells her she isn't going to be that lucky. With a small nod, she passes him up the stairs to her office.

Easing the door open reveals Sergei sitting in the leather chair in front of her desk. He looks as handsome as ever, and angry. He has a drink in hand and he's facing the door. Her pulse quickens and her hand tightens on the doorknob. With a deep breath, she lifts her chin and struts into the office.

He rises to meet her, and they kiss each other's cheeks. "Ah, Katya, you look lovely."

"You don't look too bad yourself, Sergei. I take it you were not satisfied with Giselle?" She lingers in his embrace.

"Oh, no. She's charming. Very acceptable. I wanted to see how you're doing." His eyes flick down to her perfect, pouty lips.

Katya quirks a brow, snorting at the idea he would only be

checking on her well-being. "You know very well how I'm doing." She breaks the tender moment by stepping back.

"You wound me. Here, I thought we could share a drink as two old friends. Especially when one of those friends vanished in thin air." He brings his hand to his heart for effect and juts his lip out like a schoolboy trying to get to third base.

"Ah, I see." She pours herself a healthy drink and refills his before she takes her seat behind her desk.

"Quite an adorable business you've built. Your protégé did not disappoint. Her nerves almost got the better of her." He chuckles as he takes his seat.

"I can imagine. She's an excellent actress." Katya smiles from behind her glass.

"That was all an act? I seem to recall a rather heated discussion regarding it being a lifestyle." Sergei's brow raises in suspicion that the pert little blond was not a dominatrix.

"Oh, she lives the life, just not how you think." She sets her glass down.

"She's quite the precious little dove."

"She's not a dove, Sergei." Katya's voice grows cold and firm as she stiffens in her seat.

Sergei coughs at her rudeness. "I see. I'm not here to talk about your little dove, my Katya."

"*Your* Katya?" Her voice waivers. Her gaze darts from him to the door, contemplating still running. She could get past Boris before he realizes he needs to chase her. She could duck out of the kitchen entrance. Her chest rises and falls as fear holds her in place.

"Yes, my little dove, while you may have flown the coop, it has been in my best interest to guarantee your cage stays open."

Katya's gaze turns back to Sergei, and her blood runs cold. She has not been called a dove since she was cast aside ten years ago. "No. Nyet. I got myself out after you sold me to that pig! I extorted the money from his father-in-law, and I took care of myself when I was discarded into the streets of New York. Not you."

"Who do you think chose the pig that would make all your wishes come true? I listened, my Katya, and I gave you exactly what you asked for." Sergei's voice softens and his turns his gaze down to his drink, drumming his finger against the rim. He avoids looking directly at Katya to keep her from seeing the hurt in his eyes.

"Why are you here, Sergei?" Katya's voice cracks as her fear threatens to strangle her. With one word, he could pull her back into that life.

"I came to see where my dove is making her nest." He takes a sip. "Much to my surprise, I have found you merely flew to a new coop. Was I such a monster you forsake my gifts?"

"Sergei, quit being dramatic. It's my money that helped open this business. That's all this is, a *business*." Her nostrils flare as she dismisses his insinuation that she belongs to anyone anymore.

"Are you certain, my Katya?" He reaches into his suit jacket and fishes out a small manila envelope he slides across the desk.

Katya snatches up the envelope, revealing several photos of Harold with Scapelli Sr and Scapelli Sr. with Hope-Marie. Harold's holding his daughter in the pictures, and Hope-Marie is hugging Antonio Scapelli with a gift in her hand. Katya sets the photos down gently and frowns. Her fingers drum lightly over the turned down images.

"I'm not in anyone's coop, Sergei." She leaves the envelope on the desk.

"Perhaps. I thought you should know whose circles you fly in. Be cautious, my Katya, if the wrong people see this, they won't be as understanding as I am." Sergei stands, finishing his drink before he sets the empty tumbler on her desk. "I'm in town for a while. Should you need to talk, you know how to find me. Be well, my Katya." He leaves without waiting for a response.

Larry, my second client for the evening, paid for the premium package. For his hour he wants to be handled roughly, verbally berated, and humiliated. He pays the premium price to include pegging. He's a plastic surgeon, has a wife, three children, and two dogs. He drives a cherry red Lamborghini, and even put in the notes that he prefers his women to be fully shaved.

Guys like what they like. If they had to spend half as much time as women do shaving, they would quit demanding it. I'd like to see Larry spend thirty minutes in the shower doing the flamingo razor dance. Larry cares very little for anyone else's feelings, based on the chicken scratch I had to decipher on his session details form. He also indicated that his Mistress could not be older than twenty-five, and that he liked it rough.

He enters the room and grins when he sees me. "Hey doll," he cracks like he's a gangster from the roaring twenties. I rise from my throne and slowly stalk toward him, letting him get a full drink of my body before I crack my riding crop in the exact position Mac told me would drop a person to their knees.

"What the fuck?" He grunts as he hits the floor.

"Vhat is your safe word?" I demand, brandishing the riding crop again.

"What the fuck do mean, safe word? This isn't what I paid for!" He reaches up to grab my wrist. "I'm going to show you what happens to whores that get uppity."

I crack the riding crop between his shoulder blades. "Non! You must give me your safe word, or zhe session is over. I am not your whore. I am your Mistress. Be a good boy and tell me zhe answer before your punishment gets worse." I move behind him, using the riding crop to put pressure between his shoulder blades and push him forward. The effort is to keep him on his knees. If he does not comply after this, I'll end the session and call for Mac.

"What? Do you mean that bullshit they made me fill out on that form? Who the fuck needs a safe word for you to lay there and take my cock."

I restrain from hitting him for being a dick. "Malcolm," I shout.

Mac enters quickly. "Yes, Mistress?"

"Zhis man doe not want his session. Please see him out and credit him half back. He is no longer welcome in Le Salon."

Mac, without hesitation, jerks the man up to his feet.

"This is bullshit! I paid for this whore for a whole hour! She's going--."

"Boy, you need to shut your mouth before I decide to teach you the proper way to talk to a lady," he says as he drags Larry out of the room.

I grumble and bile builds as my anxiety ratchets to eleven. If I have many more clients like Larry, we won't make any money. I'm more dreading explaining myself to Mistress. She's the one who drilled into me that consent is critical. Since my salon is pristine and I have time to kill. I head to the bar, hoping watching the cabaret and a stiff drink will calm me down.

At the bar is a young man with his back to the cabaret. His shoulders are wide, and his neck's thick. His sandy blond hair is neatly pulled back in a single ponytail. The suit he's sporting fits perfectly, even though his arms are as large around as my thigh. While he is casually sitting at the bar, he keeps glancing over shoulder in the direction of the door.

"Dobryy vecher," he says with a nod. He raises his glass to me in salute before downing the shot and motioning for another.

The girlish giggle that escapes me is in no way appropriate for Mistress Giselle. I have no idea what he said to me, but he could read me the phone book and I would die happy.

What is it about men with accents?

"What're you doing out here, Giselle?" The bartender distracts me from the Russian meat candy.

"I would like a Tequila Sunrise."

"Okay, one Ginger Ale coming up!" He flashes me a cheeky smile.

I crack my riding crop against the bar. "Zhat is not vhat I ordered!"

"Harold's policy, no drinking on the job!" He points a finger at me after he sets the unopened can on the bar.

"Harold iz not zhe boss of zhis bar." I snap at him like a child.

"Yeah, and neither are you, short stack."

"Zhis is my club, and it's Mistress to you." I rest my hand on my hip and narrow my eyes at him, putting forth my best effort to be intimidating.

"My apologies, *Mistress*, here is your drink." He hastily puts together a drink and sets it in front of me, taking the Ginger Ale away. He wanders off to serve customers at the other end of the bar.

I take a sip and sulk, as my drink is a Shirley Temple.

"Hrmph," I grumble as I turn to watch the show. I'll correct this error after hours with Harold and Mistress. The cabaret is cringe worthy. None of the girls are in sink. Their dancing lacks a stripper pole, making me wish I had focused on Mr. Too Sexy next to me instead of the girls on stage. I glance at the glass in front of him, jealous he gets to enjoy alcohol during this entertainment torture.

"Do not even think it, little dove, you're not getting my drink."

His English with the rolling weight of his Russian accent sends shivers down my spine. "I vould never steal your drink, Monsieur."

"Mhmm. Perhaps not. You would definitely talk me into buying you one." He cocks a brow as he gives me a side glance and a smile.

"Hrmph!" It's petulant, and the way he eyes me makes me feel like I'm a teenager trying to sneak into this club more than the club's owner. I sulk and turn my attention back to the stage.

"Why do you keep watching them, little dove? They are horrible."

"I'm zheir boss. Zhey are horrible."

His brow furrows as he turns his attention fully to me, giving me a more thorough inspection. "If they were dressed like you, at least that would be enjoyable."

"If zhey were dressed like me, it would be a lot more expensive for you."

He laughs a full-on belly laugh. "Oh, little dove, you're most adorable."

I smile, despite feeling like a failure. His appreciative once over and compliment has me blushing.

"That is a good color on you." He glances over my shoulder. "Unfortunately, duty calls." He slips a bill under the edge of his glass and eases off the barstool. He crosses the room and falls into Sergei's shadow.

I turn back around as the bartender approaches and slap my hand over the money, not letting him take it.

"That looked cozy," he says as he wriggles his brows at me.

"Nothing there. He could not afford me. I would like some tequila in zhis drink." I point to my Shirley Temple. "I'll deal with Harold." I remove my hand from the money.

He walks to the wall of bottles behind him and makes a show of hovering his hand over each bottle before he grabs the cheapest stuff we offer. When he comes back to me he dramatically holds the bottle over my glass, stares deep in my eyes, building the anticipation of my request. When he tips the bottle for less than a one count, he smiles at his handy work and turns his back to me to return the bottle to its home.

"Asshole," I grumble.

"And proud of it!" he calls back.

I shake my head and resume watching the girls on stage flounce on stage like strippers pretending to be dancers. We're going to need a choreographer, a stage manager, a dance instructor, and director to make Harold's dream come to life. We're never going to make this cabaret work.

Devon Wilcox

Unable to continue to watch the train wreck of our cabaret show, I wander back to my salon. For the rest of Larry's session and my built-in break I enjoy the peace and quiet. The lack of children, husband, or anything else needing my attention allows me to re-center and focus on the task before me. By the time Devon Wilcox comes strolling in, I have regained all composure and quietly wait for him on my throne.

Our discussion about his lack of boundaries only mildly concerns as she assured me his is submissive. His suit is high class Armani. His dirty brown hair is sleek and clean cut. I imagine he would have curls if he didn't put as much product in it. What surprises me is how young he is. He can't be much older than me.

Is Mistress setting me up?

I sit with one leg over the other, lightly bouncing my riding crop, as if I'm bored.

He crosses the room to set his jacket and tie on the back of the chaise for guests. Just when I think I'm going to have to school him on the proper greeting of our session, he timidly approaches my throne and kneels. His head lowers and his palms rest on his knees.

I'm pleasantly surprised and relax my shoulders, happy not every session will begin with punishment. I linger on my throne, waiting to see if he will react.

Devon remains as still as a statue. His chest rises and falls quickly. His fingers flex on his knees. Not once does his lift his gaze, or move from him position.

I make a point of slowly uncrossing my legs and easing off my throne. My heels tick lightly with each step down to his level. As my riding crop brushes against his chin, I tsk at him. "Do not look at zhe floor, my pet, unless I command you to."

He eases his gaze up to meet mine, and murmurs, "Yes, Mistress."

He has the prettiest green eyes I have ever seen. His boyish features are handsome and he's clean cut to the point he could be a model. I trail the riding crop down his neck and back as I circle him. "Tell me your safe word, pet."

"Uncle," he says.

I swallow the giggle bubbling up. Him crying uncle is funny any way I look at it. "Good boy, get on your feet and remove your clothes. Once zhey are neatly put away, stand in zhe center of the room. As a reward for being a good boy, you may have your choice to be blindfolded or not."

"Blindfold me, if it pleases you, Mistress." He stands and his pants are already bulging from his hard-on.

He must have a thing for French accents.

I nod and saunter over to the toy table, grabbing the blindfold, a small container of ice cubes, and a collar with a leash.

Devon makes quick work of his clothing, immaculately folding them before placing them on the shelf.

When I turn around, I bite my lip hard to keep from gasping at the fact he has no underpants. I cock a brow, making a point of looking at his manhood before I meet his gaze again.

"I apologize, Mistress," he covers himself. "I'll put my pants back on. You said to undress."

I could ogle this man the rest of the evening. Then we'd get nothing done. I shake my head no and hand him the cup with the ice cubes in it, then the blindfold, forcing him to cover himself with a single hand.

"You may use your safe word at any moment." I flick my wrist to leave a sting on his thigh. "I did not command you to cover yourself up."

Devon sucks air through his teeth before he shyly lets his hand fall to his side.

I admire his erection, and the pink blush creeping over his body. "Such a good boy," I coo as I take the blindfold from him. I secure it over his eyes, then take the cup back. I secure the collar around his neck, letting his erection brush against my stomach.

He straightens his posture when I tug the leash tight and force the collar to turn around his neck to follow me inspecting him.

Once behind him, I pull the leash to force the collar to constrict his neck. "Do you vant to touch yourself?" I step up on my toes to press close and whisper in his ear.

Devon's muscles ripple with tension, and he shifts the cup into his left hand. "Yes, Mistress."

"Do you deserve to touch yourself?" I reach around to trail the riding crop down along his chest, allowing him to feel the soft leather ever approaching his rigid member.

"Only if it pleases you, Mistress," his reply comes husky and soft.

"It does, I vant you to insert zhe ice cube and hold it. Zhen you may stroke yourself." When he hesitates, I bring the riding crop back and crack it hard against his ass.

He whimpers, and he retrieves an ice cube from the cup to bring to his mouth.

"Non. Zhat is not where I want you to put zhe ice, my pet." I give him another light swat on the ass with the riding crop.

His cheeks flame red, and he swallows hard, before he widens his stance enough to accomplish the task.

I ease back, allowing his collar and leash to slack.

He reaches down and behind himself until he slides the ice between his cheeks to insert it.

"Hold it in place while you stroke yourself."

"Yes, Mistress," he gasps.

I walk the rest of the way around him to watch him stroke himself.

His hand curls around his shaft and he pumps his fist too fast for my liking.

"Slower," I command.

His fingers flex and he gently works his hand along the smooth skin and engorged head, making a show of going slower for me. Deftly, his fingers rake the pre-cum into the action. After several minutes, Devon is breathing harder. "May... May I cum?"

"Non," I say, and leave him alone while I retrieve the dildo noted on his sheet as his favorite. The ice cube should have melted by now. I'm worried he'll hurt himself with this thing. It would hurt me if Magellan were to shove it in my ass.

"Mistress," he whines.

"Non. If you cum, I'll make you clean it up avec your tongue and zhen make you sit quietly for zhe rest of zhe session." I'm glad he can't see me grinning.

His hand slows more.

I place a few dabs of lube on the dildo, satisfied it, and the ice to numb him will make this less painful.

He struggles to not ejaculate into his hand and whines

"Stop stroking yourself and hold your hand out, my pet."

He immediately complies, causing his throbbing cock to twitch with the need for release.

I curl his fingers around the base of the dildo and move behind him again, pulling the leash tight. "On your knees."

With more grace than most dancers, he lowers to his knees again.

"Part them further. I want you to fuck yourself until you release."

He eases his knees apart, bringing the glistening dildo to his ass. His lips part and breath comes heavy. He wiggles the tip between his cheeks. A groan escapes him when he finally gains ground and he plunges the toy in.

I'm mesmerized, holding his leash. His body teeters with the motion of rocking the dildo inside of him. His movements are like one of those mer-people in the tanks at restaurants. "Zhat's it, harder. Show me how much you like zhis."

Without missing a beat he pumps harder. He keeps his grip on his thigh tight enough the skin reddens around his fingers, not stroking himself like the good boy he is.

"Lean forward and put your palm on zhe floor." I step closer when he obeys and run my fingers through his hair.

His forehead rests against my leather heart, and he moans.

His nose presses against my thigh and the flame of his cheeks is warm against my exposed skin.

I'm weirdly aroused by watching him. I would never ask Magellan to do this to himself. He would be more likely to have me masturbate for him.

"Cum for me, my pet." I purr.

Devon's moan is loud as his body spasms with his orgasm.

I keep petting him and allow him to compose himself with his face buried against my thigh. "You have been such a good boy. Would like to be rewarded with a spanking?"

"If... It pleases you, Mistress."

"It does. Remove zhe toy." I take the dildo from him when he complies and set it on the table, leaving him in front of the mess he made. I pick up another, less in length, but larger in girth, and drip a dollop lube on it. It has straps with a ring at the end of each one. When I come back in front of him, he's still on all fours, breathing hard. "Give me your hand."

He raises his right hand, his movements less graceful as he attempts to compose himself.

"Insert zhis as far as it will go. Zhen use your fingers to slide the rings over your cock." I knew this one wouldn't work while he was raging hard, so I needed him to burn through his early erection. My original plans for this session involved spanking him around the room with this toy in place, and his cock tormented by not being allowed to grow to full attention. With the early onset of his erection, I'm proud of myself for improvising.

Devon's hands tremble, causing it to take a few tries to get the rings over his semi-hard shaft. As soon as they are in place, he leans back on his thighs and moans softly with the dildo pressing into him and holding tight.

I touch his shoulder, a wooden paddle in my hand. "Present your beautiful ass to Mistress, my pet."

His ass goes high in the air and his cheek touches the floor with his palms flat to either side.

How he missed the mess he left on the floor, I will never know. The puddle lives untouched in the gap between his person and the floor. I rub the small of his back gently to guide my hand to prevent hitting the hard part of the dildo. With a tug, I pull the strap tight, forcing his cheeks around the other straps and making him moan. I forget to tell him to count, or thank me before I rear back to paddle his ass.

Devon groans under me with each slap against his ass. He shifts and pushes back against the strap-on tethered to his hardening cock. He never once lifts his head from the floor.

The red light flicks on alerting me we only have a few minutes left.

"Cum for me, my pet." I spank him harder.

He rewards me with a guttural moan, then squirting from his throbbing cock.

Thankfully, we thought of clients needing to clean themselves up and built a small cleaning station behind the privacy screen. I reach down and release his cock ring from his softening manhood before I gently tug the dildo free.

He whimpers and his ass puckers from losing the thick dildo from between his cheeks.

"Kiss my heart, my pet. Zhen you may clean up. Our session has come to an end."

Obediently he leans forward, and kisses the red leather heart centered over my sex. "Thank you, Mistress," he murmurs.

In For a Penny, In For a Pound

Harold enters his office with a bounce in his step and a smile on his face. Between the new clients, people's curiosity of the open kink rooms, and the new girls on the stage, he considers Le Salon's opening night a raging success. When he sees Katya sitting in a chair in front of his desk with a bottle of vodka and two glasses, his good mood immediately turns. This woman is a huge pain in his ass.

"Sit down," she commands. She causes the glass to clink against the bottle as she pours them each a shot. "Why didn't you tell me you're a Scapelli?"

"Because I'm not." Harold takes his seat and narrows his eyes.

"You're a liar, or a fool, Harold Rittendorf."

"Hrmph," Harold crinkles his nose and crosses his arms defensively. "I'm not a liar."

"Then you are a fool. Either way, you will be letting me out of my contract and I will no longer be working here."

"What? Are you insane? I'm not letting you out of your contract. What in the hell has Scapelli done? These are my clubs, not his." Harold shoots out of his chair like a rocket.

Mistress throws the photos on the desk with a snort at Harold's antics.

He glares at them as if they might explode in his face. "Ah, well. That's different." Harold rubs the back of his neck, his indignant fury knocked out of him. "I'm... Family, not Business." Harold relaxes into his seat and crosses his arms, refusing to elaborate further. He's angry. Someone's trying to sabotage Hope-Marie's club before it even has a chance to make him money. "Listen, I run a clean business. I take care of my girls, and that includes you. If someone is threatening you..."

"Nyet," she replies. "I'm family," allowing her Russian accent to surface. All the work of the last fifteen years trying to hide any part of her Russian heritage tossed down the drain. Sergei's message is loud and clear. If she intends to keep being free of the life she was born into, she needs to stop fraternizing with the Italians.

Harold's brows raise in surprise as understanding washes over him. His shoulders relax and all the aggressive posture to fight her fades, leaving the slender man to slump in his seat. "Damn. And there's nothing we can do to fix it?"

"Not without you renouncing your family and joining another."

"I didn't get out of the business to hop back into another family's business, and if I'm reading this room the same applies for you. Besides, your family dabbles in business I can't accept in good conscience." Harold places his hand on his heart in a melodramatic fashion. He snatches up the poured vodka and offers the shot glass in toast. "It was good while it lasted. To Family."

"To Family."

Their glasses clink and each of them downs their shot.

"You're going to kill the Salon. She's not ready to run it," Harold says after several beats of silence.

"She will do fine. She's ready and she will get her own clients." The smile Katya gives Harold doesn't reach her eyes.

"Hrmph. We'll see. She's got a lot on her plate." Harold sulks in his seat.

"Are we good?" Katya purposely ignores his antics.

"Yeah. I'll have my lawyer draw up the paperwork and have it couriered to you."

Katya gives Harold a sad smile before she leaves his office.

"Of course, she's a Russian dove," he mutters. He rubs his

hand over his face and glances at the clock. It's too late to tell Hope-Marie tonight, as she's already gone home for the night. He pours himself another shot and winces as it burns his throat.

"What do you mean, she's gone?" My head swivels between Harold and Stella, trying to understand what they're telling me. "We talked last night, and she said it was a great night. She's not gone. Stop screwing with me, Harold, I can't take it."

"Listen, kid. I mean, Hope-Marie. She's out. It's a done deal. She wanted out of her contract and had a damn good reason. You're going to have to step up and fill in her position. We need a manager over there."

"I can't be here more than I already am. Mick'll be pissed. The kids need me. I start school in September." The tightness between my shoulder blades grows as all my plans go up in smoke.

Harold and Stella exchanges looks.

Hers says she expected this conversation to go exactly as it has.

His looks frustrated.

"Kid, You got this. We'll schedule your clients around your school schedule. You can delegate the management stuff to people you trust, and we'll work out your salary to take care of Mick and the kids. I need you, Hope-Marie. You're my only hope for making this thing work."

"Hrmph," I cross my arms. "I have to talk to Mick."

It takes one week to see that all the clients we had lined up were here for Mistress, not me, or the rest of the club. Devon Wilcox is my only client, and he upgraded himself to the most expensive package we offer. The man has single-handedly paid payroll this week.

Harold and I sit at my desk as we go over the books for Le Salon.

The etched frown on his face ages him. "There's not enough

cash to keep it open. We need more clients, or you have to do the show again. We have enough for payroll this week. If we don't bring in the whales, Le Salon is going to be out of operating cash."

"How much?" I chew on my lip to keep from vomiting. We've put in all this work for nothing. I'll have to go back to being a stripper, and who knows how Magellan's going to handle me going back to work under Harold.

"You don't have it, kid."

"How much?" I growl at him, irritated he pretends to know my finances.

"We need three hundred thousand to get us through the end of the year. Three-fifty if you hire the choreographer and stage manager." Harold waves his hands over the notebook pages where he did the math a few minutes ago.

"How soon do you need it?"

Harold stops fussing over his accounting book and looks at me with a suspicious gaze.

I hadn't discussed my inheritance with him. My maternal grandmother was holding hostage money that belonged to my mother. She was punishing my father for marrying Maman until she passed away recently. All eight of us born to Helena Wolfe inherited millions.

Eugene has been managing it for me to diversify my folio, or some other such nonsense.

I need Le Salon to succeed. I can't go back to being a stripper. Whatever happened between Harold and Mistress makes me angry. I can't control it, so I'm going to solve the problem I can control, funding Le Salon.

"How soon do you need it?" I repeat my question in a firmer tone.

"How fast can you get it?" He keeps eyeing me as if I had told him I was having Tony Scapelli's love child.

I pick up the phone and dial Eugene's number.

After a few rings, he answers, "J.P. Morgan, Eugene speaking. How can I help you?"

"Hey, Eugene, this is Hope-Marie." I twirl the cord around my index finger as I talk.

"Hello, Mrs. Lacienda. What can I do for you today?"

"How quickly can I get three hundred and fifty thousand?"

"Based on the investments you requested, I could get you one-fifty immediately, and the rest would take a week. Why do you need three hundred fifty thousand dollars? Are you alright?" The concern in Eugene's voice is touching.

"I want to buy into a business venture with Harold Rittendorf and am verifying I have the cash." I try to keep the panic of losing Le Salon out of my voice.

"You are getting this arrangement in writing, correct? Cash business deals never go well, Mrs. Lacienda."

"I promise, Eugene, I'll make Harold dot all the Is and cross all the Ts."

Harold huffs as if I had insulted him directly.

"And Mr. Lacienda is aware of your transaction request?"

"I want to take it out of the second account. Don't touch the shared money." My stomach knots and I death grip the phone cord. I don't want to talk to Magellan when it comes to Le Salon. He'll yell at me, or worse, make me quit. I hold my breath when the line goes quiet.

"Ah, okay. Well, that will be trickier. You can get fifty on that, and the rest in fourteen days."

I pull the phone from my ear and ask, "Fifty tomorrow, and the rest in two weeks. This makes me a partner, and will get us afloat?"

Harold stares at me, opening and closing his mouth like a fish out of water. He nods.

"That'll be perfect, Eugene. I'll stop by in the morning to pick up the check and sign the paperwork."

"I look forward to it," Eugene disconnects.

Harold regains himself, "How in the hell do you have that much money to throw around? And why the fuck are you still working here? I know your porn shoots were hot. They weren't that hot, and you still haven't gotten paid for two of them." He brandishes a finger at me like a parent scolding a child.

I don't need Harold reminding me of the pending lawsuits from those disasters, and rub my temples to not get worked up again. "Why don't you let me worry about my money's sources and you get your lawyer working on the contracts to make Mick and me full partners in Le Salon?"

"Or, kid, hear me out. You take that damn money and go live happily ever after. I take the Salon and make it whatever I want. That's a lot of cash, Hope-Marie."

I watch Harold in thoughtful silence. I could go live the easy life. I would have time to finish school, take care of the kids, and make Magellan the happiest man ever to walk this Earth. I'm going to give myself an ulcer with how much my stomach gets twisted. Failing at this endeavor is not an option my ego can handle. Not to mention, life with Magellan doesn't feel like a sure bet anymore. What if he walks out and leaves me with the kids? Then where would I be?

Magellan adamantly refuses to move our money from Eugene to his company. He has grown more agitated with each passing week. He won't include me in what's going on. The stress causes his temper to flare up in the weirdest of places. He blew up at Eugene a week ago, firing him, and forcing me to re-hire him.

If I walk away now, I have nothing to show for all my hard work other than a couple of porn movies, and a few photo spreads in Frederick's of Hollywood. I need to stand on my own two feet and show everyone the path I walk is the one I'm meant to be on.

"Harold, I'm in. I was in when you pitched it two years ago. I'm going to be in until it burns to the ground. My pop raised me to work hard and the good Lord knows if I leave this club to you, it'll just be another strip show with a bunch of VIP rooms." I flash him a smile to let him know I'm teasing him.

"You're only half right. Another strip club with a bunch of VIP rooms and a *cabaret*." Harold grouses, a grin splitting his face while he makes jazz hands to emphasis cabaret. "Okay, I'll let the paper pushers know and get you two proper ownership of this beast."

Breaking Point

After I get Harold the first check, and we make it through payroll, I forget the rest of the money and throw myself into finding clients. I go through every single one of the men Mistress had originally booked me and try to woo them into giving me a chance. Phone call after phone call results in varying forms of rejection. The only client I don't have to call is Devon Wilcox,

He upped his sessions to three times a week.

Devon is a weird little duck. He's not submissive when outside of our sessions. He's a cunning broker, who has more money than sense. He absolutely forbids me from offering my services to any of his co-workers, and after seeing what firm he works for I can understand his reluctance. The owner of Devon's firm holds ultra conservative views and would end Devon's career in a heartbeat.

My advisor at Columbia keeps pressuring me to get signed up for my residency and to confirm I've filled out all the paperwork properly. Said paperwork sits neatly in a folder on my desk at Le Salon, next to all the bills and receipts for the club. The knot between my shoulders won't let go, and my head is pounding.

Magellan is an absolute bear when he comes home, to make matters worse. Whatever is happening at his office is escalating his bad behavior at home, driving a bigger wedge between us.

As if the universe thought I needed more to handle, I'm late. I try to tell myself stress causes lateness, but I know better. The Wolfe family is supercharged in the procreation department.

Magellan and I can't handle a third kid right now. We barely handle the two we have. I can't think of how to broach the topic with Magellan. Our fairytale life is turning into a nightmare.

Maybe Harold's right and I should walk away to live happily ever after with Magellan and the kids. There is no shame in that, and I have enough money we could live comfortably on Magellan's income.

My stubborn pride makes me physically jerk at the idea that just ran through my head. I shake my head as I step off the elevator on our floor. I put the key into the lock, turn, and ease open the door, expecting the warm scents of dinner to greet me. What fills my nostrils is the scent of whiskey.

Helena's shrieking.

Castian's little voice is trying to soothe her.

My first thought is something has happened to Magellan. "Mick?" I call as I close the door and drop everything I had in my hands. I come around the corner and skid to a halt.

Magellan is red-faced, sitting with papers in his hands, an open bottle of whiskey on the table, and his glass empty in front of him.

My eyes narrow and my fists clench. He's fucking drinking while our children need him. "What the fuck are you doing?" I growl.

Magellan's head snaps up from the paperwork like I struck him and he's out of the chair in the blink of an eye, causing it to crash to the floor. His pupils are dilated, and the features of his face are sharp. When he focuses on me, it's not the tender gaze of a loving husband. The hateful glare staring up at me is 'the beast'. There is no reasoning with the beast.

My heart pounds in my chest and all I can do is flail backwards as he rushes forward.

The last time I saw the beast, Magellan's brother had to pull him off me. There's no Tristan Lacienda to save the day today and we have two small children I pray don't come in here to see their father like this.

"What the fuck am I doing?" his Spanish accent is thick, and he gets spittle on my cheek as he brandishes the papers for the money I asked Eugene to get me. "What the fuck are you doing? What is this money for? Where did you get this kind of cash?"

I'm too slow to respond.

He shoves me against the wall.

I grunt in pain. I need to keep his attention on me and hope to God he wakes up from the monster version of my husband.

"It's for Le Salon. Mick, I forgot to tell you. We've been busy. Mistress qu--."

"THAT FUCKING CLUB?" He roars in my face and shoves me again, bouncing me off of the wall. "You are giving that fucking asshole more money? For what? So he can have you fuck those men? You've finally decided to be his whore!"

Tears roll down my cheeks. I'm caught between rage and fear myself. Magellan is supposed to be my knight in shining armor. He's supposed to love and cherish me, to keep me safe. He promised me my career wasn't an issue, that it turned him on knowing men could look and not touch. I'm too afraid to answer him.

His hand closes around my throat, and he thrusts me against the wall again, lifting me off my toes with it and banging me hard enough the phone falls off the receiver hanging next to me.

I struggle and claw at his hand, kicking at him. "Mick! Stop. Can't. Breathe." His thick fingers around my throat are heavy and unmoved by my delicate manicured nails scratching and clawing at them.

As he leans in his hand tightens around my throat.

My air supply dwindles. He's going to make his children orphans by killing me and going to prison. I pray to God Castian doesn't come into the room.

"You are *mine!*" He screams at me in Spanish as he dents the wall with my body.

I close my eyes, the light dots dancing behind my eyelids. My hands falling away from his death grip on my throat.

God, please help me. Give me the strength to survive.

"Rocks," I rasp our safe word, forcing my body to lax and show submission. There's trust in a relationship like ours. One that hinges upon respecting each other's boundaries while exploring different methods of bonding. I have trouble with boundaries, like Devon Wilcox, and I had been using our bondage play to placate the beast before we had Castian. Using our safe word is the only thing I can think of to reach him. I know my sweet, loving Magellan, has to be somewhere in there, and will stop before he kills me.

Air rushes into my lungs, and I sink down the wall. I don't dare open my eyes for fear he's standing over me still seething. I flinch when the bedroom door slams closed. Slowly, I open my eyes. All I want to do is curl up and cry. My throat throbs where his fingers were.

Get up. We can't stay here. Get the kids to a safe place.

I push myself to my feet, trembling. My knees wobble with the effort, and I cover my mouth to keep from making any sound at all. Shock is trying to set in and paralyze me. The only force driving me forward is that I need to get our children to safety. I take shallow breaths as it hurts too much to breathe, or swallow. I scoop up the papers he flung all over the floor, trying to keep from drawing him back out of our bedroom. Leaving them on the counter, I go into the kids' room.

"Mommy's here," I coo to Helena. "Castian, be a big boy for Mommy and get your adventure bag." My voice is wispy and my throat hurts with each word. My hands are occupied with Helena, otherwise they would be visibly shaking.

"Mommy?" Castian's little voice whimpers up to me as he peeks out from under his security blanket.

"It's okay, baby. We're going to see Uncle Tristan for a few days. Mommy needs to take care of Helena and needs you to be her brave little lion, okay?"

"Okay," he sniffles before he scurries out and rushes to hug my leg.

The tears roll down my cheeks and I take the moment to hold both of them close. I kiss Helena's temple while I run my fingers through Castian's hair. I turn my gaze to the ceiling to rein in my emotions. I have to be strong for the kids, even with wanting to curl up and hide in their closet. I'm beyond thankful Magellan did not take his anger out on either of them.

"Let's get your adventure bag." I gently nudge Castian.

He reluctantly releases my leg to do as I ask.

Every muscle is on fire. I'm afraid of what might be waiting in the living room while we pack Castian's things. I take his adventure bag, along with the diaper bag, and ease to the door. Relief washes over me that Magellan's not in the living room. I keep Castian close as I guide him to the door. With no signs of Magellan I snatch the paperwork, my keys, and let the door slam behind us.

When the doorman in our lobby sees the three of us, his expression shifts from smiling and jovial to somber and frowning. He opens his mouth, as if he wants to say something, then closes it. His eyes are laser focused on my neck, causing me to blush in shame and tilt my head down, nuzzling Helena to hide whatever he sees.

"Could you hail us a cab?" My voice is still raspy, and I'm not sure I could raise my voice without losing control of my emotions.

He nods and picks up the phone at the desk. He even holds open the cab door for us as we nestle into the back seat. "You take care, Mrs. Lacienda..." He hesitates, again acting as though he wants to comment, then shakes his head and closes the door rough enough I jump.

"Where to?" the cabby asks.

I give him Tristan's address. My brother won't turn us away. I only hope he's in town and that he doesn't ask me a lot of questions. I thought of going to the Rittendorf's. With Magellan's behavior that would only add fuel to the fire. With the pain in my throat, I worry that I should go to the hospital. From my experience with Big Tony, there would be questions there too. The last thing I want is a three-ring circus that comes with a visit to the emergency room.

The tears won't stop flowing, and I'm forced to wipe my cheeks again when Castian's tiny hand squeezes my arm. "It will be okay, Mommy. I make it better." His sweet face looks up at me and it breaks my heart how much he looks like Magellan.

"Yes, you do. Don't ever change, my little lion." I pull him close.

When we step out of the cab at Tristan's building I have to buzz his apartment to get in.

"Wolfe residence," Tristan's tinny voice chirps in the speaker.

"It's Hope-Marie. Can you let us in?"

The door locks disengage and I usher in Castian. Tristan lives in a walk-up, causing us to trudge up the endless flight of stairs until we finally reach his floor. The door's open and he's on the phone while poking his head out of it. His brow is cocked in question to our appearance.

"Thanks. I know it's super short notice. We need a place to crash for a few days."

Tristan nods and closes the door behind us while he continues his conversation. "Listen, Harry, I need to go. I'll call you when I get there." He hangs up. "Where's Mick?" His gaze trails over me, then over Castian.

"At home." I rasp.

"I see." His gaze levels on me again and he looks exactly like our father when he's upset.

I resist the urge to fidget under his scrutiny.

His expression is drawn into a frown and he keeps looking at my neck. "You can take my bed. I'm off to Louisiana for the weekend. There's plenty of food in the fridge."

"Thanks. I'm sorry for busting in like this. It's...We... I needed a place to think." The waterworks start again.

Tristan's nostrils flair the same way Papa's do when he's furious and doesn't want to take it out on the person in front of him. He refrains from giving me the third degree.

I don't offer any explanation and pull my hair over my shoulder. I know it won't hide the bruises forming, but the gesture is enough to tell Tristan I don't want to talk about it.

"I need to jet. I'll call you when I get checked into my hotel to make sure you're good. You take as long as you need." His tone softens as he hauls his tiny duffel bag onto his shoulder. He pulls Helena and me into a gentle hug. "If you need me, call Harry. Number's on the fridge. He knows how to get in touch with me quickly."

I nod and set the deadbolt after Tristan leaves.

One For The Money

Tristan's knee bounces in anticipation as the cab ducks and weaves its way to his sister's apartment building. Not grilling Hope-Marie took all his resolve. The kids being with her eliminates her injuries being sustained at that club she works at. The memory of her trembling against him as he hugged her stokes the fire of his rage.

Hope-Marie is every bit the actress their sister, Eleanor, is. While she was smiling and soothing the children, he could see the broken and fearful look in her eyes. He will murder Magellan for putting his hands on her. As far as Tristan Wolfe is concerned, Magellan Lacienda has done the unforgivable and hit a woman.

"Keep the meter running and wait. I'll be right back." Tristan slides the man fifty dollars, trusting he will still be there when he returns. With purpose, he walks by the doorman and into the elevator. Tristan curls and uncurls his fists as he glares up at the numbers lighting up on the way to Hope-Marie's floor. The longer this takes, the more his anger builds. He practically leaps out of the elevator when the doors whoosh open with a ding.

He tears down the hallway like a bat out of Hell and stops outside of his sister's apartment to ring the bell. As much as he wants to bust the door down, he doesn't want to give this Spanish fuck any inkling he's in danger. The door eases open and

Magellan appears and opens the door further. "Tristan? What are--."

Tristan's fist swings and connects hard enough with Magellan's jaw he crashes to the floor. He steps in and snarls down at Magellan, "Do not put your hands on my sister ever again." Without waiting for a response, he storms back out of the apartment and slams the door behind him.

The cab ride to the airport is silent, as Tristan's temper won't relent. The more he thinks dwells on what Magellan has done to his sister, the madder he gets. He's ready to call his father on that son-of-a-bitch. "Thanks, man. Keep the change," he mutters as he steps out of the cab at LaGuardia.

He makes a beeline to one of the phone booths along the wall, and fishes out the quarter to make a call. His fingers hesitate before he drops the coin in the slot. This phone call would cause all the Wolfe men to come running to New York to avenge his sister, including Jean-Luc, who is deployed overseas. Magellan would disappear, leaving her a widow with two small children.

"Fuck," he grumbles as he puts the quarter back into his pocket. Hope-Marie would shatter if she lost Magellan, even if he's a wife-beating coward. Tristan grunts like an angry silverback gorilla at the phone before he walks away to head to his flight.

The elevator dings and whooshes open. Magellan, along with a few other gentlemen, step into the foyer of the financial firm.

"Check it out! Miss USA herself has graced us in all her glorious beauty. What a marvelous crown she wears!" Chris, Magellan's best friend turned colleague drapes his arm over his shoulder and shouts his greeting to the office. "That stripper you've been playing house with get tired of your pussy-whipped ass?"

Magellan brushes the man's arm off and cuts him a glare as he heads to his cubicle. His briefcase thumps into the corner he tosses it into as he throws himself into his seat. He closes his eyes and takes a few deep breaths. The last thing he needs is to get fired for saying the wrong thing, or giving his best friend a matching black eye.

His co-worker gophers over the edge of the cubicle

"What the fuck are you looking at?" Magellan barks.

"Shit, man, What the fuck happened? I thought you and your ol' lady were celebrating last night. Didn't she open her new club?" The co-worker holds his hands up in surrender.

Magellan inhales and exhales like he's in Lamaze class. This guy wasn't being a dick to him. "Bad fall," he lies and turns to his computer to get started for the day.

His co-worker nods and disappears back into his cubicle.

Magellan's relieved when the other man doesn't press the issue. He looks down at the picture on his desk of Hope-Marie with Castian. Her belly's round and the sundress barely covers her perfect ass while she holds their son. They're covered in cotton candy and both are laughing. He rubs his hand over his face and his chest grows tight.

He brings his hands down and stares at the deep gouges all over his hands. They're a painful reminder of his shame. How long had he been strangling her before she used the safe word? What would he have done had he killed her? His jaw aches with how hard he clamps it shut, and the urge to destroy everything in sight rages through him like a hurricane. Every time he flexes his hands the pain of her attempts to fend him off radiate up his arms. When he closes his eyes the sight of her panic-stricken face torments him.

The stress of the past several months stems from his "best friend," Chris, screwing him royally. He brought him in as an Assistant Account Manager instead of an Account Manager, which means all the commissions from the clients Magellan pulls in go to Chris and not him. This also gives Chris the power to dictate when Magellan works, what clients he gets to interact with, and how much of the commission goes to Magellan.

Today's meeting is the client that will catapult Magellan to full account manager. Chris hadn't been able to close the deal with Mrs. Hershwin and didn't think the old woman had much to offer. Magellan cultivated the relationship, working with her to discover her assets were far exceeding the type of clients Chris normally pulls in.

As much as Magellan wanted to postpone today, he can't afford to lose the client. Not if he wants to provide for his family like he's supposed to. He should have rushed after Hope-Marie and apologized. Fear he would lose his temper again if she rejected his apology held him locked in their bathroom while she fled. He shakes his head to bury his domestic disaster into the recesses of his mind to focus on the meeting with Mrs. Hershwin. Once Magellan's convinced he can keep himself composed, he gathers everything he needs to present his options and heads to the conference room.

"Oh, Mr. Lacienda!" Melissa, the front desk assistant, squeaks in her brassy Jersey accent. "Who gave you the shiner?"

He decides it is better to stick with the lie than explain that his brother-in-law beat him for assaulting his wife. "Just a bad fall," he mumbles as he passes by her.

"You should put a hunk o' meat on it to prevent swelling! I could help you with that," she bats her eyelashes at him.

"Thanks, Melissa, I'm fine." He rolls his eyes when his back is to her. Another deep breath escapes him before he pushes open the conference door and puts on his charming boyish smile. "Mrs. Hershwin, it is always a pleasure." He can't help but smile at the tin in her hands. "Are those your snickerdoodles?"

The petite, elder woman, smiling up at him with far too vibrant red lipstick against her weathered skin, brightens as he guesses what is in her tin. "They are, my boy. I thought you might like to take them to your son." She walks alongside Magellan to the table.

"You're too kind. He will love them." Magellan pulls out her chair and gets her settled before he takes the seat next to her. His gaze flicks to the door when it opens and his teeth clack as he clenches his jaw shut. Chris enters and takes the seat across the table from them, despite not being a part of this meeting.

"Dear me, Mr. Lacienda, what happened to you?" Mrs. Hershwin exclaims as she takes his chin.

"It's nothing, Mrs. Hershwin, I fell." Magellan cuts Chris a dirty look when he snorts.

"You should be more careful. You've got those babies to take care of. It would be a shame if you couldn't provide for them."

"I'm sure his wife could cover it," Chris quips, followed by smirking at Magellan.

"Enough about my family, Mrs. Hershwin. Tell me how your family is doing." Magellan tries to veer the conversation off himself and ignore Chris.

"Ruth. Please. I have told you to call me Ruth." She places her hand on Magellan's forearm and gives him a light squeeze.

"Yeah, how is your boy doing? He still teaching law?" Chris cuts in. For all of his toxic behavior out in the bullpen, he's a smooth talker with the clients. Thanks to Magellan's thorough notes on this client, he knows all of her family history and their assets.

Magellan gets the distinct impression of a predator toying with its prey by how Chris talks to Mrs. Hershwin, and he's glad he's on the other side of the table. While she fills them in on all the social escapades of her children and grandchildren, Magellan prepares the presentation. He had carefully run the numbers at least three times, and the less aggressive, more strategic portfolio would grow her fortune over the next ten years with the trust to inherit the funds and distribute evenly to the named heirs.

"That's wonderful. Let me show you this new portfolio we think your money would do the best in." Chris cracks open an entirely different presentation than the one Magellan has spread before him.

Magellan's fist clench, sending fresh pain up through his arms from the scratches Hope-Marie left. Mrs. Hershwin is supposed to be *his* account, not Chris's. The sudden loss of control causes his blood to boil and his jaw twitches from the effort to keep his temper in check. He covers up his agitation quickly with a faint smile when Mrs. Hershwin looks at him.

"Oh, I thought Magellan was handling my account." She grips her purse in her lap, frowning at Magellan.

"Well, of course he is," Chris chimes in. "He wanted to run the plan by me. That way we could make sure we found the best investment with *your* money."

Chris pops up and strolls around the table to sandwich Mrs. Hershwin between them. He proceeds with bamboozling the sweet little old lady with all the market jargon he can pull out of his ass over the next thirty minutes.

Magellan remains quiet by her side, caught between calling his friend a liar in front of a client, and potentially losing his only account to his friend's risky plan. He refuses to force Mrs. Hershwin to ping pong between the two of them. His lips purse into a thin line and his fists clench under the table the longer Chris spews his bullshit.

"Oh, I don't know. What do you think, Magellan? This sounds awfully confusing." Mrs. Hershwin turns her back to Chris.

"It will be fine, Ruth." he assures her quietly. "I'll make sure your money is handled wisely." He gives Chris a harsh look over her shoulder. This conversation isn't over and he'll be damned if he will let that prick steal her money from her.

"Well, if you think so, deary." She fishes out a certified cashier's check and lays it out on the table in front of her, between them.

Magellan's hand rests over it before Chris can snatch it up, snorting at the other man. Something is off with Chris's behavior. Magellan's not going to let the portfolio he worked this hard on to be thrown down the drain by Chris's greed.

With a few signatures and a sweet goodbye, Magellan gathers up everything, including the cookie tin to see Mrs. Hershwin out.

Two For The Show

As soon as the elevator closes, Magellan turns on Chris and barks, "What the fuck was that? The Hershwin portfolio is mine."

"You were being a pussy with those investments. As your Account Manager I made the call for a better portfolio and sealed the deal for you."

"The deal was already fucking sealed. She literally came with the fucking check. She intended to invest with us regardless of the portfolio. It just has to make money. This is a long-term investment, not a quick turnaround. Is this my fucking portfolio, or yours?" Magellan closes the distance and squares his shoulders, puffing up to intimidate Chris.

"Chill the fuck out, Mick. It's yours, man. No reason to get your panties in a twist." Chris takes a noticeable step back from Magellan.

He has to resist the urge to beat Chris with the tin of snickerdoodles. "As long as you understand that this is *my* account, we're good. If you'll excuse me, I have an exceptionally large account to create a portfolio for." Magellan brushes by Chris, deliberately shoulder checking him.

"Dick," Chris mutters as he heads on to his office.

Over the next eight hours, Magellan pours over all the portfolio options. The check Mrs. Hershwin gave him had more zeroes at the end than he expected her to invest. The last thing he wants to do is invest her money into these get rich quick schemes his colleagues are enamored with.

"Come on, man. Bunch of us are going for drinks. Let's celebrate your new account." Chris leans against Magellan's cubicle, his tie undone and suit jacket in hand.

"Thanks, man. I appreciate the thought, but I really need to get this call sheet finished."

"Dude, if you really need to finish it up, come in tomorrow. Tonight we celebrate." Chris and the three other men watch Magellan expectantly.

Before Hope-Marie stole his heart, Magellan never turned down running the town with the guys. The idea of chasing skirts and throwing back drinks pales compared to what he has with his wife. He's ruined everything. The tightness in chis chest won't let up as he's reminded again of what he's done. He's putting his nose to the grindstone to what end? He tries to shake the depressing feeling of there's no one waiting for him at home by rubbing his hand over his face. "I really want to get this right. Maybe next time, guys. Have fun."

Chris rolls his eyes, "Use the portfolio I gave you, man. The boss is hot for it. The call sheet's all filled out. All you have to do is rubber stamp it, and you'll be raking it in."

"I'll check it out," Magellan affirms. He's already given it a once-over, and didn't care for it. The returns don't add up for any person using that sheet. It's not worth the fight, so he placates Chris without committing to the call sheet.

"Whatever, man. Stay as long as you want then. C'mon guys. Let's go." Chris and his cronies abandon Magellan.

What Magellan really want to be doing is running to Tristan's place to beg his wife to come home. He can only pray that Tristan has not called the rest of the Wolfe family. Ashamed of himself, he has called no one in his family to get advice either.

With a sigh, he turns back to the portfolios. He looks at Chris's call sheet again. As he suspected, it's too volatile. The stocks are giving high reward for the moment. One downward spiral and all of Mrs. Hershwin's money would be gone. He can't bring himself, in good faith, to spend her money recklessly. He shakes his head and sets the pre-filled call sheet aside. Instead, he grabs a fresh call sheet and meticulously begins plugging in the investments to make on Monday.

The next time he looks up, the sun is threatening to peek over the horizon. His back is sore, and his muscles ache from being hunched over his desk all night. He lets out a heavy exhale and stands. After a few stretches, he gathers up all the paperwork, tucking it in his briefcase. He drops the fresh call sheet on the secretary's desk as he walks out the door.

A glance at his watch and it's six in the morning. Hope-Marie would be getting home around this time. Another pang of guilt fills his chest as he realizes he looked forward to their routine no matter how much shit was going on at work. He sulks as he passes the doorman, who scowls while giving him a nod in greeting. Once inside his apartment, he leaves the briefcase by the door and loosens his tie.

The apartment is dark and quiet. Not even the gurgling sounds of his little princess waiting for Mommy or Daddy to rescue her from her crib. Tears well in Magellan's eyes and he roughly brushes them away, refusing to let himself express the emotions threatening to rip him to pieces.

The trudge into their bedroom adds to his morose feelings, and he plops on the bed without undressing. He pulls the phone over and dials Tristan's number, praying to God Hope-Marie will answer the phone. He has to hear her voice, that she still loves him, and he hasn't lost her.

"Wolfe residence." Hope-Marie's melodious voice fills his ear.

Magellan smiles at the sound of his wife's voice. Then he freezes, unsure of what to say to her.

"Hello?" she says after he says nothing.

"Hey, it's me." Magellan palms his face at how dumb he sounds.

"Hello, Me. What can I do for you?"

The hesitation in her voice gut-punches Magellan. He chuckles at her joke, thankful she didn't hang up on him. "Uhm...how have you been?"

"Mick, it has been less than twenty-four hours since I left. What do you want?"

Magellan's heart sinks, and his shoulders droop, convinced

she hates him. "I wanted to apologize. I'm sorry for hurting you." Silence fills the line, and the tension is thick between them.

He wants to add excuses and make her promises that he'll be different. His chest is tight as he clings to the receiver, trying to silently beg his wife's forgiveness across the line.

"You've said all this before, Magellan."

Her words pierce his heart. He thought he was past being this monster. He has hurt the most beautiful woman in the world, the mother of his children, and by the sound of her voice, he will never have the chance to fix their broken relationship. He breathes harder as he struggles to not completely unravel on the phone.

"There's no excuse and I mean it this time. Is there any way I can fix this?" He begs.

Silence fills the line again.

Magellan hates he can't see her expression. Is she angry? Is she sad? Or is she afraid, and broken? Hope-Marie is excellent at pretending everything's fine when she's falling apart. Magellan thumps the phone against his forehead, trying to calm his fraying nerves down as she lets him stew in the awkward quiet of not communicating with him.

"Do you want to talk to Castian?"

Magellan furrows his brow as she deflects his questions. "Sure, I would love that." He listens as the phone shuffles and as Hope-Marie tells Castian daddy called to talk to him.

"Daddy?" his son's voice chirps on the line.

"Hey, Buddy. Are you enjoying your adventure?"

"No. Mommy's sad," he mewls.

"Yeah, she is, Buddy. I'm trying to make it better. It will be a little bit longer, okay? You think you can be brave and strong for Mommy? You always make her happy."

"Yeah... She no let me eat cookies."

His complaint makes Magellan smile. He wishes not getting cookies could be his top concern too. "Well, I'm sure if you're a proud little lion, your mother will relent."

Castian lets out the fiercest roar he can without pulling the phone away

Magellan chuckles. "Okay, Buddy. Please put Mommy back on

the phone."

"Daddy said give me cookies when I roar!" He shouts.

Magellan laughs harder as he roars again and waits for the shuffle back to his wife.

"Daddy did, did he?"

"I believe the phrase I used was that if he was a proud little lion, you would consider it."

"I see. Well, I'll consider it."

Castian roaring in the background brightens Magellan's spirit. At least he did not hurt their son or daughter in his drunken rage.

The line grows quiet and his shoulders tense as Hope-Marie says nothing more. The two of them linger in unspoken words.

"Do you plan to go to church on Sunday?" Hope-Marie breaks first.

Magellan's heart races as he sees an opening to get them in the same place. "Definitely. I can pick you and the kids up." The longer she takes to respond the more Magellan believes she'll say no. Was she asking him because she plans to avoid him? Is she going to deny him seeing the kids? Is this his life now?

"I think that would be lovely. You can take the kids to the park across the way after and spend some time with them."

"Pick you up at eight?" Magellan doesn't miss that she said the kids and not all of them. For now, he'll take what he can get.

"We'll be ready. And Mick..."

"Yeah?" He braces for impact.

"Awoo?" Her voice waivers.

"Awoo," he replies with a smile. "See you Sunday." He hangs up and lets out the breath he had been holding. She didn't tell him to get lost, or worse, that she wants a divorce. There's hope for them yet.

Saints & Sinners

I never get to sleep on Sunday mornings. I rush home from the club, grab a shower and a bite to eat. Then it's out the door to church. Today's no different, only it takes longer to get home.

Castian fights me tooth and nail when getting dressed for church.

"Come on, my little lion, Daddy will be here soon, and he doesn't like waiting." I whine while holding his dress shirt.

The threat of Daddy being angry gets him moving. He's afraid of upsetting Daddy, and it breaks my heart.

By the time Magellan knocks on the door, we're ready to go.

Castian walks with his dad. He doesn't stop talking all the way to church. He tells Daddy of the old woman down the hall who smells funny and babysits him. That she doesn't like him speaking in Spanish. How she makes the best cookies, and she snores really loud when her shows are on. The sirens scare him, and Uncle Tristan's walls make weird noises, referencing the radiator.

Magellan is all smiles as our son fills him in on the two whole days they have been apart.

Church isn't as awkward as I thought. No one knows there's anything amiss between Magellan and I.

Magellan gives me fretful glances throughout the service.

I must not have covered the bruises on my neck as well as I

thought. Reaching up, I gently adjust my hair and allow it to cover the area that is marred from his hands. I had called Father Kelly yesterday and asked to speak with him after services.

We thank him in the procession and Magellan takes the kids across the street to the playground for the Catholic school.

I wait patiently while the good Father wraps up his service duties. When he enters the room, he motions for me to stay seated and takes up residence behind his desk. "To what do I owe the pleasure, Hope-Marie?"

"I need guidance. I mean, we do. I'm... It's Mick. He's angry all the time. Nothing I do makes him happy, and on Thursday he-," I instinctively bring my hand to my throat. Tears well in my eyes and I hiccup to keep my composure. My hands tremble again from the efforts of trying to not fall completely apart in public.

He eases up and comes to sit in the chair next to me, offering me a tissue. "Here. It will be fine," his hand is on my shoulder to comfort me. "Let's start from the beginning. You said Mick is angry all of the time. I thought he had moved beyond the anger."

"I did too," I blubber. "Then, a few months ago, when he started working at the firm with Chris, things changed." I rest my hands in my lap, looking down at the tissue Father Kelly gave me.

"School took a lot more of my time than I expected. Then Harold needed me more at the club as our business partner bailed. Mick used to be understanding when it came work stuff. Anytime I even mention Harold he yells at me. I'm convinced he hates me. What am I going to do?"

"You know the answer to that. It's in your heart."

His words are gentle, but the words are like he slapped me across the face. "No, I don't. That's why I'm here," I sniffle.

"Hope-Marie," his tone sharpens as his hand tightens on my shoulder. "God has clear roles for men and women in relationships. Men are the providers, the hunters. Their role in the family is to lead and guide the family, providing for their every need."

I open my mouth to protest, then close it, as he holds his hand up, not finished in educating me on how I am all the problems in my marriage. I haven't had enough sleep to cope with this chauvinistic bullshit. Bile rises in my throat, threatening to return the bagel I had for breakfast.

"You took a vow to cherish and obey your husband. How are you keeping your home in order if you're at school several hours a day? What kind of mother can you be to your children when you whore your body to other men? How could Magellan not be angry and frustrated? His wife allows other men to covet her. Are you performing your duties at home? Or are you fighting with him because you expect him to take over your duties while you run off with another man to create a new den of iniquity?"

Stunned by his brutal and unkind words, I don't move when his fingers brush along my collarbone. My skin crawls with goose bumps. My heart pounds from the fight-or-flight shot of adrenalin. His words sting worse than the smack of a riding crop.

"I hate to see you suffer. You are such a lovely child of God." His fingers trail over the bruising. "God sends us the messages we need to hear, even if they are hard to receive."

The pain from his caresses causes me to suck in a sharp breath, mortified that Father Kelly has called me a whore and said I deserved to be hurt by my husband. He has the gall to sit here and pet me in such an intimate fashion. I want nothing more than to run away and cry myself through a pint of ice cream with this betrayal. Father Kelly had been kind and understanding when we were going through marriage counseling.

How can he be so cruel?

"Seek his forgiveness, Hope-Marie. I genuinely believe God will forgive you for the sins that led to this unfortunate incident, and he will fill Mick's heart with peace again. Once you have resumed your wifely duties, I have faith your husband will return to you."

I swallow hard, as if I am taking the bitter pill Father Kelly's words have fed me, and nod. Tears roll down my cheeks as he crushed me with his harsh words.

Could God honestly believe I deserved to be strangled?
Has Magellan told Father Kelly he feels this way?

"Thank you," I mumble and excuse myself, using all my resolve to not bolt from the church like a gazelle chased by a predator.

I'm hiccuping sobs at the gut-punching blows dealt by Father Kelley. If I get anywhere near Magellan like this, we will have a fight. My shoulders slump as I lose hope that we'll find the happiness we had two years ago. I lean against the brick wall outside the church entrance.

Mick's sitting on a bench, bouncing Helena on his knee.

Castian runs amok on the playground. He pauses to wave vigorously at Daddy before he resumes burning his toddler energy.

Finally able to force myself to stop crying, I quickly wipe my face clean with a tissue and cross the street to the park.

"Hey," Magellan says with a gentle smile when I come walking up to the bench.

"Hey," I reply as I sit next to him and face the playground, trying to avoid giving away how upset I am.

"Everything alright?" Magellan's voice is heavy with concern.

If I look at him, I'll break down to a blubbering mess. "Mhm hmm," I nod, still watching Castian.

"Liar," he grumbles.

"I don't want to fight with you, Mick. Can we just enjoy the next few minutes without fighting, please?" My voice cracks as I threaten to cry again, desperate to not have another argument today.

"We can." He slumps against the bench, keeping his attention on our daughter gurgling in his lap.

Guilt fills me with shutting him down. I can't handle a fight with him. While it isn't his fault, I'm still recovering from the blows dealt by Father Kelly.

"You mind if I take the kids to the zoo for a few hours?' He asks several minutes later.

"I think Castian would love that. I'll catch a cab home."

"I could keep them for the night. I know you need to work."

"No," I snap harsher than I mean to. I don't want him to have the kids without me.

What happens if he loses his temper and takes it out on Castian and I'm not there to save him?

"On second thought, I should go to the zoo with you." I make the mistake of meeting Magellan's gaze.

A storm of emotions dance across his face. His posture straightens, and he grips Helena tighter, causing her to squawk in protest.

I want to tell him what happened in the church and how I'm afraid he will leave me and take the kids. His reaction to my denial of him keeping our children makes me believe everything Father Kelly said is true.

"I would never hurt them," he whispers.

"Like you would never hurt me?" The words slip from my mouth bitterly. I instantly regret them. In my tired and frazzled state I'm in no position to have this conversation with him.

His body goes rigid as he snaps his gaze to me.

I lift my chin in defiance, daring him to respond. This is a disaster and I bite against the inside of my mouth to keep from vomiting an apology to him. I reach for Helena as her squawking turns into hungry wails.

"I got it," he growls at me.

"You don't have breast milk. She's hungry."

"She's fine. I said I got it," he snaps.

I retreat, turning to face the playground again.

Helena's wails get louder,

He tries her pacifier and bouncing her. He struggles with her for a few minutes before he finally relents and hands her to me.

I snatch up the baby blanket from the bag and lean back on the bench. With an easy adjustment, I push my dress aside and free my breast for her to latch onto while I drape the blanket over my shoulder and her. I don't look at Magellan, and a frown is etched on my face as the tears cling to my lashes again.

"Maybe we should leave the zoo for another day," he says in defeat.

"Whatever you want, Mick." My voice trembles when I respond.

"I want my family to come home," he says. Without the baby to occupy his hands, he's sitting slumped forward, staring at them.

My heart breaks as I see the wounds I left. I haven't even addressed the black eye he's sporting. I can only guess that Tristan paid him a visit. We can't get through a simple conversation about the zoo. I'm not going to dig into the complex conversation of our wounds.

This is all my fault. I've destroyed our family. Father Kelly's right. I should go home with him.

I could go home with him. It would be easy. We could swipe it under the rug and pretend like he didn't almost kill me in a fit of rage over money.

What happens the next time something is out of his control? What if he doesn't respond to our safe word?

Once Helena is fed, I call for Castian and we pile into the car.

The car ride back to Tristan's apartment building is somber and quiet.

Magellan helps me with the kids when we get there and there's a moment when he's close enough his cologne envelopes me, calling to me to lean into him. I wish he would wrap me in his arms and tell me everything will be alright, and to make all this hurt go away.

He clears his throat and lowers his gaze without enveloping me in his arms. The unspoken hurt between us is crushing. He gently kisses my forehead before repeating the process for Helena and hugging Castian.

We wait on the stoop as he glumly gets back in his car, driving away.

I Got A Sitter For This

August 1986

This past month has been hell. The old woman down the hall had a stroke and could not watch the kids any longer. This forces me to bring the kids with me to the club.

All hell breaks loose when Castian spots Harold. He kicks Harold in the shins hard enough it drops the man to his knee. He follows this with a tiny fist socking Harold right in the nose. "You stole my Daddy!" he shrieks at him.

Stella helps Harold up.

I give Castian two firm swats on his behind. "You know better. We don't hit people. Now apologize to Uncle Harold." I cross my arms and try to look as intimidating as possible.

Castian's crocodile tears, quivering lip, and snotty nose tugs at my heartstrings.

All my effort is put into looking stern and holding my ground.

"Sorry," he growls like a lion.

"No. You know how to apologize."

Castian droops as I pop his balloon of violence. "Sorry for kicking and punching," he says.

"It's okay, kid." Harold tries to smile at Castian, except his expression is pinched in pain.

I would be laughing, other than Castian is showing too much of Magellan's temper.

Mac saves the day when he calls his wife Sophia to come get the kids. As she's corralling them, she volunteers to watch them whenever I need a sitter.

"What was that for?" Harold asks after the kids are gone. He rubs his shin before Stella plops a bag of ice over it.

"Mick and I separated."

"What?" Stella and Harold ask in unison.

"It have anything to do with the bruises you had?" Stella crosses her arms as she stares me down.

"It did. I'm staying at my brother's place while we work things out."

"He put his hands on you?" Harold tries to stand and winces.

"Sit down," Stella pushes him back onto his couch. "You rushing over there will only make it worse. Did you not hear what Castian said to you?"

"It's fine. It has nothing to do with you, Harold. He had another incident. Like I said, we're working things out."

"Uh huh," Stella says. "You should be working it out through a lawyer."

My heart races and I square my shoulders. My cheeks flame in a mix of rage and embarrassment. "I'm not divorcing Mick. What kind of wife would I be if I abandon him in his time of need?"

"For fuck's sake," Stella growls. "*His* time of need? He put his fucking hands on you, Hope-Marie. No. What the fuck was he thinking?"

"He wasn't. That's the point. Listen. I get he damn near killed me. He's sick, and hurting. That shit from when he was attacked has him all messed up still. He needs help, not punishment. The separation is how I'm helping me. We're not going home until he figures out how to fix his shit. Now, if you don't mind I'd like to get my work done and get the fuck out of here."

I don't wait for an answer and storm out to handle payroll in my office.

Today is payday, and the clubs are closed. I'm going through the mail when I see a small brown package labeled with only my name on it. Curiosity gets the better of me and I set aside everything else to open it first. Inside is a self-addressed envelope to a post office box, a black leather book, and a letter. I start with the letter.

My Dearest Hope-Marie,

I apologize for abandoning you at the beginning of such a promising club. Unfortunately, it was unavoidable and was the correct decision to help us both. Enclosed you will find a list of contacts I have spoken to and are open to new experiences.

Should your club prove unable to recover from my departure, drop the enclosed envelope in the mail and it will get where it needs to go.

I urge you not to put off your residency another year. Do not forgo your dreams because men believe you do not deserve them. You deserve them and more, sweet girl. Do not make me come back to New York to remind you of this.

All My Love,
Katya

I can't decide if I want to laugh or cry. I pick up the little black book and begin calling the numbers within. More than one of these are the same numbers I called in desperation a month ago, and suddenly they are interested again. At least I won't have to fire the insanely good choreographer we hired.

The next few weeks are a blur, as I have solid bookings each day. I'm so excited I want to share it with Magellan. Even with all that has gone on between us, he's my one. I want him to hear something happy for a change.

Each week we attend church together. While I dutifully attend services, I have no desire to further engage with Father Kelly. We follow that up with a day of activities as a family. I don't book any clients on Sundays, and trust Mac with keeping Le Salon in order while I'm not there.

While it isn't perfect, it's a comfortable routine for us. Magellan pulls out all the stops, taking us to all the fun family activities he can find in the Tri-State area. Even Castian is thrilled to see Daddy every Sunday now that it's "Adventure

Day".

Magellan called me a few days ago to tell me he thinks things are improving at work with his promotion. He no longer has to deal with Chris breathing down his neck.

We went to dinner as a family to celebrate and for one evening it was rock soup and smiles.

He thoroughly mesmerized Castian by showing him how to eat "rocks". Castian likes oysters as much as I do, which is not at all. I'm impressed he got our little lion to eat anything other than a grilled cheese sandwich.

The memory has me all smiles as I pick up the phone and dial our apartment.

"Lacienda residence," his voice sends butterflies scurrying in my stomach.

"Hey, it's me. You won't believe what happened!"

"Hello, Me. What?" He chuckles at making the joke I usually throw at him.

"I got this client list from Mistress, and they all booked me right up! I haven't had a missed appointment in two weeks." I hold my breath as I realize he might not be too keen on hearing this. Father Kelly's words ring in my head as I wait for his response. I try to silently convince him to be happy for me through the phone line. My stomach twists in knots and heart pounds in my chest as I expect him to explode.

"That's great news! What does that mean for the club?"

"It means I'm in the black!" I shout at him with joy.

"Well, that's always a good sign. You are now a bona fide small-business owner. I'm proud of you."

His praise sends me over the moon. For all our problems, I'm still his girl and hearing him proud of me makes me feel like I can do anything. "Hey, I have to go. I just wanted to share the good news with you. Awoo!"

"Awoo," he calls back before he hangs up.

September 1986

I've known for three weeks the answer to the question that

brought me to the doctor's office today. I wish I could say I'm overjoyed with the prospect of bringing a third child into this world. This only confirms my suspicion of my family being supercharged is more than a family joke. My mother had eight children. Maman had the twins *after* Papa had a vasectomy.

Between Le Salon and Magellan, keeping track of when I had my last period feels minuscule. When I missed again, I took an over-the-counter test. It lit up like the Empire State Building. I made the doctor appointment without communicating to Magellan there may even be a possibility of us having a third child.

While things have been great with Magellan over the past month, I'm not convinced another baby would improve the situation. He hasn't shown me he has changed, other than to always be "happy" around the kids and me. He still works at the firm with Chris. He's under pressure to fall in line with the rest of his colleagues. From what I gleaned in his mind-number explanation of how his job works, what they're doing is bad.

There have been a few heated phone calls between us where I simply hung up the phone on him. He's angry that I won't leave him alone with the kids, or that I won't let him pick the kids up from the sitter. I'm too scared he will lose his temper and take it out on Castian like he has before. We've been working hard at mending the relationship between Castian and Magellan. I don't want to jeopardize that by letting my guard down.

I bounce my leg anxiously as I sit in the doctor's office alone. My lower back hurts. All the muscles are tight, and I'd give anything for a full body massage. All the reasons having a baby is a bad idea is only adding to the tension building at the base of my spine.

"Mrs. Lacienda, congratulations are in order." My doctor enters his office and sits down at the desk.

I give him a smile back, wishing this was good news.

"I want you to start on a multi-vitamin. Your Iron is low. You'll also need to come back in a few weeks for testing. We saw some abnormalities in your results.."

"Anything I should be worried about?" I white knuckle my purse. If he only knew how much I had on my plate maybe he wouldn't have worded his request how he did.

"No. No. It's routine. If you've been sick recently, sometimes the bloodwork comes back off. Everything'll be fine. You're a pro at this now, anyway. I'm sure you're excited to tell Mr. Lacienda."

I nod, giving the doctor one of my show smiles.

He continues on with the diet he wants to put me on, along with the regime he wants me to follow to maintain a healthy weight. He then goes into his lecture on stress being bad for both the baby and me.

How am I going to handle all my new clients while being pregnant?

Will they even be into that?

Of course they will, and we'll charge a premium for it.

My inner Harold is giddy at the idea of using my pregnancy to make money for the club, while my inner Stella is rolling her eyes, worried if I'll even be able to work.

Leaving the office, I head back to Tristan's place. I'm not ready to tell Magellan. He has too much on his plate as it is. I'll tell him after I have all the follow-up bloodwork done.

October 1986

I sent the kids to spend the evening with Harold and Stella and took an egregious amount of time getting ready for this date.

Magellan insisted on having an adult only date for my birthday.

When he doesn't arrive to pick me up at seven o'clock, I worry. He's never late. It is a pet peeve of his to not be on time. My heart sinks at the thought of him ditching me on my birthday, but I'm not going down without a fight. I hail a cab and head straight for our apartment.

A million scenarios play in my mind as the cabby ducks and weaves through traffic. The first is he had to work late and forgot to call. It's uncharacteristic of Magellan. The second is he met someone else and while he set up this date, he forgot and is doing something with her. The idea of Magellan being with someone else makes me flinch like someone slapped me. He's not a cruel man, leaving me to believe that's not the case either. Which leaves that he has to be hurt, and can't contact anyone.

The longer the cab ride takes the worse Magellan's state gets in my mind. By the time we pull to the curb in front of our building, Magellan is bleeding out on our kitchen floor in my mind. Throwing an obscene amount of money at the cabby I dash out of the vehicle and whirl by the doorman.

"Good to see you back, Mrs. Lacienda," he calls as I race into the elevator.

The slow climb to our floor leaves me drowning in my conjured nightmares. "Please, God, let him be safe." I don't care if God is pissed at me for what I do for a living. I'm still going to trust he won't let anything else bad happen to Magellan.

I drop my keys twice trying to get them out of my purse when I hear a loud crash on the other side of the door. I freeze in place. Fear rails through me like a hurricane.

Is there someone in there attacking him?

Is he dying while I stand out here like a coward?

I thrust the key into the lock and find it unlocked. That doesn't bode well as I now believe there may be another person in our apartment hurting Magellan.

I step into the room, swallowing down my fear. The stench of alcohol fills the air, and the apartment is as quiet as a library. "Mick," I call, letting the door close behind me. I turn my keys in hand to have them poke out between my fingers in case I need to defend myself.

The apartment is in complete disarray. No thugs leap out as I press forward. Nor is there any sign of Magellan bleeding to death on the Kitchen floor.

He's sitting at the dining room table, in a half undone suit. His breathing is hard, skin flushed, and his muscles twitch in agitation. The bottle clanks as he pours himself another glass.

"Mick? What the fuck are you doing?" Anger washes over me like a wave crashing on the beach. I stop in front of him, with the table between us for protection, an eerie sense of déjà-vu filling me.

Worst Birthday Ever

Magellan's attention turns to me. His pupils are dilated, and his eyes are bloodshot. His clothes are disheveled and his hair sticking out, as if he has been tugging on it. His cheeks are flamed red, and he sways as he stares at me, too far gone for any real conversations.

I want to scream and yell at him and to slap him across the face. Of all the nights to pull this stunt, he chooses my birthday. I shake with the building rage, torn between crying and screaming.

"I'm a good fucking man," he slurs. "I was making them money. Good money. I made the clients happy. I did every fucking thing they asked, and what do I get? Fired!" He slaps his hand on the table, making me flinch. "That's what I get! That fucking prick didn't even stand up for me. He's supposed to be my best friend!"

His Spanish is garbled, making it hard for me to understand him.

What the hell happened?

He had said he was no longer under Chris and that he was promoted. Why would they fire him if he was promoted?

Was he lying to me? Is this why he has been this way? Has he been unemployed all this time?

"Give me the bottle, Mick. I'll make you some coffee," I say in

Spanish, and hold out my hand.

Magellan's fingers tighten around the bottle and he brings it up over his head, like a pitcher winding up. His face scrunches up like Castian's does when he's getting ready to throw a wall-eyed fit.

"You throw that fucking bottle and it will be the last time you see me or your three kids." I points at him and take the stern voice I use with Castian. I hadn't even realized he had stood up before raising the bottle in the air. "I'm not your fucking punching bag! I'm your wife!" My voice raises in volume as I'm gearing up for a tantrum of my own. I can't stop shaking, terrified he's going to beat me to death with that bottle.

Why do I get the brunt of his bad days?

I don't deserve that.

I have done nothing other than love this man.

He hasn't moved and I begin to think he might be frozen in place. He purses his lips and his eyebrows squeeze together as he attempts to process what I said. Bringing his other hand up he counts on his fingers.

"One, two," he shakes his head, as if it will purge the drunkenness.

"Castian, Helena," he repeats, counting again with his fingers. He looks from his hand to me, then to my stomach. He's still threatening me with the bottle, and has no idea how close he is to me throwing all we have worked for to the wind and leaving. "I'm going to be a daddy!" He crows in Spanish. Flinging his other hand up in a triumphant pose.

I flinch, thinking he's going to throw the bottle, then square back up to face him. "No, the fuck you're not." I roar at him in English.

He blinks, panic washing over his face like a Mime laughing and crying with his hand moving up and down. All of his emotions are exaggerated by being drunk, and he sinks back into the chair, the bottle clanking on the table like someone shot him and he's drawing out his death scene.

We can't keep doing this.

I clench my fists and force myself to remain on this side of the table, and to not run to him to soothe him. I'm not the one in the wrong here, and he needs to understand that we're in this together, or not at all. As much as it kills me to not be the source of his happiness, I remain rooted in place.

He looks at the bottle again, back to me, and he starts to cry, shoving the bottle towards me. "Please. Please don't leave me. Hope-Marie, I need you. I love you. I know I royally fucked up. I don't know what's happening to me. I get so angry and all I see are those men in the café again. And.. And... I want to provide for us. I want to make you happy and to take care of you. Please, Hope-Marie. I love you." His words are fast tumbling out and in Spanish.

While I speak fluent French, I'm still working on Spanish. I snatch the bottle before he can re-think his plan.

He holds his head in his hands, now sobbing.

I'm still angry enough I could murder something. With how broken he is in front of me it makes me feel guilty. Father Kelly's harsh words ring in my ears. I cautiously move closer until I can hold him.

He moves suddenly and wraps his arms tight around my waist.

I yelp in surprise, but don't pull away. With a shaky hand, I run my fingers through his hair, letting him lean into the comfort.

"They fired me because I wouldn't buy the stocks they wanted. What am I going to do? I can't provide for you and we're going to have another baby. I'm a failure. I'm worthless. I can't even protect you," he blubbers against my stomach as he holds on for dear life.

"Mick, why don't you sleep off the booze? We'll figure it out in the morning, together." I murmur and keep petting him until he reduces to sniffling against me.

He lets go and stands abruptly.

I whimper and bring a hand up, shielding myself on instinct. When nothing happens, I lower my arm to meet his gaze.

His handsome face is drawn into a frown and tears roll down his cheeks as he stares at the floor in front of me.

I want to wrap him in a tight hug. When I ease forward, he steps back. He's too drunk to remain steady and I'm forced to grab him to keep him from falling to the floor. I'm fuming that he has ruined my birthday, forcing me to play nursemaid to an insufferable drunk.

If I had wanted to work tonight, I would have gone to the club.

We stagger and stumble into the bedroom. I only manage to get his suit jacket off of him before he collapses halfway onto the bed. I peel off his shoes and socks, tossing them aside, letting out a heavy sigh. I roll him the rest of the way onto the bed and once I'm satisfied he won't flop to the floor, I pull the covers over him. He'll sleep it off and we can talk in the morning.

Left standing in the middle of our room alone, I don't know what to do with myself. I have on Magellan's favorite dress and the heels from Tiffany's. My hair is curled and fluffy, the way he likes it. I even busted out my favorite red lipstick for tonight. My lip quivers and I cover my mouth to keep from making noise. A part of me wants to leave and have a night on the town to spite him. Other than I'm afraid it would set him into a fit when I came back.

Defeated, I perform the practiced dance of changing into comfy clothes. I toss the dress onto my chair in the corner, leaving the expensive stilettos on the dresser, . A quick stop in the bathroom and I pull up my perfectly curled hair to a ponytail. I go from sex kitten to frumpy mom in two minutes flat.

There's no way I'll be able to sleep after the roller coaster of drunk Magellan. Not wanting to be idle, I clean our apartment. He's normally the neat freak between the two of us. Our apartment looks like someone broke in and ransacked the place. The state of our apartment only lends to Father Kelly's assumptions.

I have been a terrible wife.

I cry while I clean up the broken glass from the bottle he threw before I entered the apartment. I gather up the takeout containers and trash, making more than one trip to the shoot outside of our apartment. I take my time washing the dishes. The mind-numbing task allows me to think about what to do with Magellan. Obviously, what we're doing isn't working. A plan begins to form when I put the last of the dishes in the rack. I give the counters a wipe down and sweep. By the time I've finished righting our home, I've decided on a path. All I need now is to implement it. Step one, is to give Magellan the control he needs when it comes to our finances.

I bite my thumb as I sit with the phone in my lap on our couch. Eugene had said I could call him any time. With the tension between Eugene and Magellan, I'm not springing this on Eugene. I dial the number and hold my breath, worried he may not answer.

"Hello?" his voice is heavy and cold on the phone, nothing like his normal chipper disposition.

I find it odd he doesn't specify who he is, or any other proper greeting, like this is a clandestine phone call. "Hey, Eugene, it's Hope-Marie Lacienda. You got a minute?" It's quiet on the other end and I frown, thinking I have offended him. "I'm sorry for such a late call. I can call back if it's too late."

Another long silence, not even the sound of him shuffling the phone, or breathing.

"No, it's fine. What can I do for you?" Eugene finally says.

"Have you processed the settlement money yet?"

"No. Since Mr. Lacienda tried to fire me, we agreed you would both need to sign off on any further transactions. Remember?"

"Shit. Yes. Oh, sorry! Listen. You said so long as we were smart that we could probably buy a house outright, and still have a monthly income, didn't you?"

Eugene chuckles on the other end of the line, and I blush.

I must have gotten something wrong with what he said. His money talk confuses the hell out of me.

"I said you could live comfortably if we invested the money from your inheritance wisely. You probably would still need at least one income, but you wouldn't have to work yourself to the bone. Especially after the large withdrawal you made recently. I don't feel comfortable discussing the settlement over the phone, Mrs. Lacienda. It would be better in person. Why do you ask?"

Eugene's clipped tone, and less than chipper way of speaking rattles me. I chew against my lip, worried Magellan has ruined this relationship for me. "Mick's been struggling with work. I want to talk with you both about our finances tomorrow, and set up a plan he's comfortable with and I would rather you explain all of our money to him than me trying to relay it. Do you have any time tomorrow?”

“Mrs. Lacienda, you can come see me any time at the bank. I think this is a great idea and look forward to seeing you.”

“Great. We’ll see you tomorrow.” I hang up long enough to clear the line. Then I can call home.

“Wolfe Residence,” Maman’s sleepy voice answers.

“Maman, it’s Hope-Marie. I’m sorry for calling this late. I need you.”

“What is it, my darling?”

“Mick and I... We separated. We’ve been working it out. Then tonight he...” My voice catches as I can’t bring myself to tell Maman everything.

“Has he hurt you?” Maman’s voice shifts from drowsy to razor sharp.

If I tell her the truth, my parents will be on the next plane out here and everything will be a hundred times worse. If I don’t tell her, and something terrible happens, she’ll be even more angry. “He had an episode back in July, and Tristan let me borrow his place while we work it out.”

“I see. Well, Hope-Marie you have to make a choice. If you think he is redeemable, then you must stand alongside him and help him become the man you think he can be. If he is not, then you must learn to live without him. I can’t make this choice for you. And, my darling girl, if he hurts you again, it won’t be your father, or brothers, he should fear. Do you understand me?”

“Yes, Maman.” I frown. The tone in her voice reminds me of when we were little and she wanted to put the fear of God in us. “I could never divorce him.” I add as if that would help her sound less terrifying. I would probably go back to Missouri. Divorce isn’t an option if I want to keep calling myself Catholic.

“I didn’t say divorce. I said live without. You are a smart girl. You will figure it out. You are always welcome here. Billy would appreciate the help with his children.”

I chuckle, knowing very well how out-of-control Michael and Gideon are. “Thanks, Maman. Give my love to Papa.”

“À bientôt, my darling.”

We hang up and I glance towards the bedroom. The urge to go curl into bed with Magellan is strong. I miss snuggling up to him and his arms wrapped around me. In his drunken state it’s too dangerous. If he wakes and thinks I'm an attacker, he'll hurt me again.

Instead, I grab the remote and pull the quilt over me. The couch is lumpy and cold, leaving me feel more alone than I do sleeping in Tristan's bed while he's gone. I flip through the channels twice. It's too late for anything good to be on television. I wriggle and squirm, trying to find a comfortable position, flicking the television off to stare at the ceiling.

Everything's Better With Pancakes

My nerves are shot. Every sound startles and wakes me. Fear that Magellan will attack me prevents me from relaxing on any level. I finally give up the ghost of sleep and head into the kitchen when the sun peeks through our living room window.

When I open the fridge, I'm thankful Magellan at thought to buy groceries. I pull out eggs, bacon, and milk. It doesn't take me long to get everything in order to pour the first batch of made-from-scratch pancakes.

If Castian were here, we would make animal shapes on the griddle. I pause, shrug, and start making them anyway. By animal shapes I mean oddly shaped blobs that I randomly pick an animal for it to be. A blob with three dangling parts is always an elephant. I hum as I carefully flip my puffy elephant and I bop to the music in my head.

The eggs follow the pancakes. I only know how to scramble eggs. Magellan can make any kind of egg to order, and I envy this ability. He's lucky I don't burn down the apartment when I cook. Satisfied the eggs are fluffy and well salted, I put them in a bowl with a plate on top to keep them warm.

Turning to the bacon, I bite my lower lip as I drop each piece on the hot skillet, trying to avoid being burned by flying grease. It sizzles and pops as it shrivels up and coats itself in grease. I like crunchy bacon, and since I'm better at burning things than cooking them, he gets crunchy bacon too.

"Got anything for a hangover in that breakfast?" Magellan's raspy voice carries across the room.

After jumping out of my skin and nearly toppling the bacon pan, I motion with my bacon flipping fork to the aspirin and orange juice I set on the counter for him. "Take a seat. It'll be ready in a minute." One minute really is several minutes before I bring him a plate with all my glorious efforts.

His squints, and he tilts his head as he eyes the feast. Biting my lip, I'm anxious he won't like my peace offering. Then he smiles and motions to the pancake. "Elephant?"

I laugh and nod, relaxing. "Good guess. Ah!" I squeak as he decapitates and eats the poor elephant's head.

"I love the taste of elephant in the morning. Tastes like victory." He crows.

I stare blankly at him, not getting the reference.

He pauses, staring at me and says, "Apocalypse Now. The scene on the beach with helicopters, you know?"

"I don't." I shrug as I head back into the kitchen to get my plate. I'm relieved he's in a good mood this morning and today's hangover did not go toward the angry personality his drinking can awaken.

We eat breakfast in relative peace.

He manages to devour the elephant, the rhino, and the lion with great gusto.

I struggle with how to broach the topic of where we go from here. This breakfast reminds me of our early relationship when there were no responsibilities. The pleasant and warm feeling soon fades to awkwardness as we both avoid the uneaten elephant in the room.

"You deserve better than me, Hope-Marie." Magellan looks down at his plate as he pushes syrup around aimlessly.

"Don't do this. This is the same song you sang last time. You tell me you don't deserve me. That you love me. You don't want to hurt me. Then something happens, and we end up here again. You with a hangover, and me with bruises. You damn near killed me."

Way to keep it light. Are you trying to make him Hulk out again?

He looks up from his plate and meets my gaze. The way his eyebrows squeeze together and he chews his lip make him look afraid more than angry. "Okay." He swallows hard before continuing. "What do I do different this time? Because I really do love you. I really don't want to hurt you. I sure as shit don't want to lose you, or the kids. I tried it my way, and it didn't work. So how do I do this different?"

Magellan like this is excruciating to watch. He was my savior. He has always been in control, and this is all my fault he's broken. I open my mouth to spout all the psychological babble I've learned when he flicks his fork up at me, brandishing a tiny bite of pancake drenched in syrup.

"No! This is not your fault, Hope-Marie. This is on me. I'm the one who lost control. I'm the one who put hands on you. I fucked this up. Not you." His points are punctuated with him bringing that dripping piece of pancake dangerously close to me. It reminds me of Harold waving his meatball sub at me the day I met him.

I'm thankful I'm wearing clothes that are baby tested and stain approved. I hate that he can read me like an open book, calling me out on all my fears in one fell swoop. Before I become a sticky mess, I bite the pancake off his fork and munch happily to buy myself time to think.

He waits patiently, setting his fork down to lean back and cross his arms.

"Oh, Mick," I sigh. "We're in this together. I shouldn't put all this pressure on you. Or let Harold abuse our friendship and use me as a crutch. You're right. We are going to do things differently. I want our family back together. I want to come home. I miss you. I miss the guy who kidnaps me to a Royals game because he knows I love baseball. Or the guy who tried to feed me rocks on our first date. It's all my fault you got hurt. I can't take that back. What I wouldn't give for you to never have been hurt because of me."

"What are you talking about, Hope-Marie? That attack had nothing to do with you. The café was being strong-armed for protection money. When I told them no, they beat the piss out of me." His face is pinched as he shakes his head at me.

"Wasn't it Tony's thugs?"

"Why would it be Tony's thugs? I never met the man before he bought the place. Plus, he was Italian. Those assholes were Mexican."

"Oh. Okay." I don't believe him. It had to be all my fault. Why else would someone go after Mick and the café.

Magellan rubs his hand over his face. "It doesn't matter why it happened. What matters is what I've done to you since it has happened. How do we truly move forward in a meaningful way?" He motions between us. ". You fear me. You flinch when I raise my voice. I see the way you watch me when I'm with Castian. I hate the way Castian reacts to me." He slumps into his chair, defeated. "I've fucked up this whole being a good father and husband thing."

I want to be petulant and say yes he has. "Mick, we can fix this. It won't be easy. I'm not going anywhere. I'm still your girl, and I promised forever. You're stuck with my ass, even if it is fat."

Magellan's expression darkens at my last sentence and his voice drops in tone, leaning toward his Sir voice. "First. I love your curves. Second, if I'm beating the piss out of you, I don't want you to stay. That is not a home I want for my children or my wife. My family deserves more than that."

"Yes, we do. Here's how you get us back." At least, in my lack of sleep, I came up with the plan. "You, me, and the kids, are going to therapy. Real therapy. Not Father Kelly's Catholic special." I hold up a finger for my bullet point list of rules, followed by a second. "No more alcohol. Period. Not socially, not at home, not at all. I won't drink when I'm around you, either."

He remains quiet, and his expression has gone neutral, which can be good or bad for me. What I wouldn't give to be able to have the poker face he does.

"Finally, we find you a job that makes you not want to punch everything when you get home."

"Agreed. Finding a job may be easier said than done. Those fucks probably blacklisted me. Where do I look for someone to help me?" His voice is hollow as he stares down at his hands.

I'm surprised by his full agreement. Internally, I'm squealing with joy that he agrees. I thought this was going to be a fight, and me threatening divorce to get him to comply. "What if I've already found you the perfect job?"

"Doing *what* exactly?"

I give him a wolfish grin and let him sweat, thinking of all the devious things we could do together at Le Salon. "What if I hired you to be in charge of my finances?" Before he can reject anything, I add, "Not Le Salon's finances. Harold has an accountant for that. M*y* finances. Or, well, our finances." I motion between us.

"Isn't that Eugene's job? I thought you hired him back after I fired him." He tilts his head, like a dog when they aren't sure what their human is doing.

"Well, you see. Eugene moves the money. He's not the manager of it. I have to make all the decisions and to be honest, I just go with whatever he says because I don't get any of that money stuff."

"Uh-huh. You want me to have full control over our finances, which I already do, *and* you're going to pay me a salary for it? Plus benefits? We're talking full medical, dental, the works. And that's it?"

"You won't need benefits because we can all be on mine from Le Salon, allowing us to save money there. And yes, a salary, plus the benefits are pretty sweet. I mean, you will get a full home-office plus set your own hours, and spend more time with your children."

"I see." He hesitates. "I'm going to reject your counteroffer and present my own."

Bile builds and my stomach clenches. I'm not sure what I'll do if he rejects this idea. I don't think he can handle working at a firm.

"We incorporate your finances to allow us to get proper insurance. Not that junk policy from Le Salon. Plus, my salary gets re-negotiated annually and you have to be the CEO. I'm only in charge of the finances. Deal?"

I suddenly feel like I'm getting the short end of the stick as I try to work through his angle. "Deal, on the condition that you won't drink, and that you will remain in therapy as long as it takes."

"As long as it takes." He extends his hand, "Awoo."

Baby Steps

After Pancakes, we get cleaned up and head to Eugene's office.

I'm scared this is too much too soon for Magellan. I want to fix us so much it hurts. I haven't stopped to think if this is a bad idea.

Magellan's like a hopeful puppy with the idea that if he does what I want he'll get us back.

I push all the negative thoughts from my mind and try to enjoy the excitement for our new plan. I can't stop smiling, even with being a basket of knots.

After Magellan's tantrum when he found out I used my inheritance for Le Salon, I don't want him to lose his shit over the lawsuit settlement. I don't know how much this settlement is for. It must be a lot if Eugene won't even discuss it over the phone.

This is also another secret that could set Magellan into a fit of rage. I only told him there was an issue on set that Harold's suing them for. I purposely left out the issue was them attempting to fuck me. All of the contracts clearly stated that I would not perform any kind of intercourse with a man. Had Mac not been on set with me, I might not have come away unscathed.

Magellan's holding my hand the entire way to the bank, and it's an anchor in the storm of my thoughts. If I could keep this peaceful moment going forever, I would.

Eugene smiles when he sees me. His smile fades as Magellan steps into his office with me. "Mr. and Mrs. Lacienda," he shakes Magellan's hand and ushers us to his desk. "First, I need you to sign these documents." He sets a stack of papers in front of me before he turns to face Magellan. "After our last conversation, Mr. Lacienda, I did some investigation into the money we allocated the funds to. Your assessment was completely on the mark. I was able to salvage all except five thousand dollars. I have returned the money to your cash account, and due to my mistake, I did not take my fees this quarter for managing the money."

Magellan nods. "It would be a shame for a man not to get paid for doing his job."

This causes Eugene to blink in disbelief and I freeze mid-signing to stare at my husband as if he has grown a second head.

"What? He did his job. He deserves to be paid. Hell, I want to pay him more since he chose not to get paid. That and if you had taken your cut we would have filed a complaint against you with your boss." He winks at Eugene.

"Mick," I say in the mom voice.

"I'm joking." He holds his hands up in defense. "I appreciate what you did, Eugene. Good work." It isn't an apology. At least he's attempting to get along with Eugene.

I relax and resume signing the paperwork. When I turn to the funds transfer page, I blink in disbelief.

"Hope-Marie?" Magellan's voice is laced with concern.

"Is this a mistake?" I tap the paper with the pen. My palms grow sweaty and the desire to run for the hills is strong enough I shift in my seat.

"Nope," Eugene pops the P and grins at me. "Like I said on the phone, Mrs. Lacienda, Harold's lawyers know some kind of dark magic. Congratulations."

Magellan leans in and looks at the number. He draws in a long and heavy breath before he looks up at me. His lips are tight and he squints his eyes. Without a word he's interrogating me on the reason this settlement is this large. The twitching jaw alerts me he refrains from verbalizing whatever angry thoughts crossed his mind with the mention of Harold Rittendorf.

My heart hammers in my chest, and I hope he doesn't make a scene in this office. When nothing happens, I swallow hard and quickly finish signing the paperwork.

Eugene looks between the two of us and takes the stack of papers from me. "What would you like to do with the money?"

"About that," I squeak. Magellan's piercing gaze causes me to fidget with the hem of my shirt and I don't dare glance at him, for fear I'll crumble under the anger hiding below the surface of his calm demeanor. "I've hired Mick as my financial manager."

"What?" Eugene looks devastated as he freezes mid-action and darts his gaze between the two of us. "I've always done right by you, Mrs. Lacienda."

"You have. Eugene, I don't have any mind for any of this stuff. I go with whatever you say because it makes no sense to me. Mick loves this stuff. He's great at it. And... Well... He was let go from his firm recently. I was hoping this check would be enough to buy a house, and live off the dividers."

"Dividends," both men say in unison.

Eugene visibly relaxes, and he looks at Magellan for approval of this arrangement.

"He can't fire you without my consent. I'm the CEO." I add before the two of them can get into it.

Both men chuckle.

Whatever anger Magellan had appears to have vanished with my suggestion for our finances. "The short of it is, we want to incorporate all the funds into a trust with me as executor. Your job will still be the day-to-day accounting. Any investments will be signed off by me, and I'll make suggestions on how to move the funds." Magellan confirms.

I fall quiet as the two men turn into best friends, talking financial jargon that sounds quite similar to Castian's rambling stories. By the time we leave Eugene's office, they have follow-up appointments scheduled, plans for the finances, and a decision to start house hunting before we talked mortgage or buying outright.

Eugene even gave us the business card of a preferred realtor.

January 1987

The black book has proved a Godsend. My nights are booked solid with rich and powerful men who have the wildest fantasies. Each has a meticulous profile in my office of their wants and desires. Before I started showing, I informed them of the pregnancy and to my surprise I only had one client decline sessions.

Today's session is with a man who calls himself John. I know it's not his real name. He hasn't been willing to provide that information. From our short few months together, I've learned something terrible happened with his wife. The notes that Mistress left in her book don't match with the behavior. She alluded to the fact he likes to be punished and enjoys the thrill of dancing the line between good and naughty. Yet, he has been attentive and obedient since I mentioned that I'm with child. As my pregnancy has progressed, his requests for his package increased.

If there's one thing I've learned from Harold, special requests mean more money.

He strips out of his suit, down to his boxers. His body is lean, with only the hint of softness at his hips. While he isn't sporting a washboard stomach, he is easy on the eyes. Nothing compared to my husband. No one compares to Magellan.

I gently rub my stomach as the baby has taken up soccer with my kidneys. I shift and try not to make any noise to indicate I'm in pain,

Failing at remaining quiet, he rushes to me to me, gently placing a hand on the small of my back. "Please, Mistress, sit down."

I raise a brow and allow him to guide me to the chaise.

"How may I please you, Mistress?" He kneels before me.

I had intended on spanking him while having him bent over the chaise. "You are being such a good boy. You may..." My brain freezes. This isn't how this is supposed to go. This isn't kink, or sexy fun time. What he's attempting to do is reserved for Magellan. I blurt the first thing that comes to mind. "Rub my feet."

"At once, Mistress." He shuffles on his knees to my feet and delicately unfastens my heels to set them on the ground next to the chaise. His thick fingers press into the ball of my left foot.

I moan with how good the pressure feels. Closing my eyes, I allow him to work his magic fingers along both feet.

"Does this please you, Mistress?"

Lost in the joy of relief to my aching feet, I almost break character when I speak. "Oui," I moan. I lightly swat his arm with the riding crop when he chuckles.

His fingers move along my feet and to my calves, massaging and caressing gently.

If my child wasn't causing stabbing pain in my back, I would be aroused and encourage more.

"You are beautiful, Mistress," he hums as he leans down to kiss my knee.

My eyes fly open and my body tenses. This is the most intimate I have been with anyone in months. I'm stunned by the tenderness as he continues to work his way up my thigh.

"Zhat is enough," I rasp and tense.

"Mistress, let me please you. It will be good for our baby."

Mistress taught me better than this. "Non," I growl and struggle to sit up, and fail. I look like a turtle stuck on its shell. I've lost all control of this session and veered dangerously into cheating on Magellan territory.

"Shh, easy Mistress, I got you. I know exactly how to please you and to help you relax." He coos as he crawls onto the chaise with me. His pupils are dilated, full of lust, and the raging hard-on pressing against my thigh says he's very much interested in making me feel good.

I lift my chin with a frown, bringing my knee to shift him to the side, and turn the riding crop to smack him firmly between the shoulders. "Get on your knees on zhe ground." I leave no room for argument and when he does not move, I hit him again with the riding crop. "Zhis is your last warning. Get on zhe ground."

Misguided Fantasy

John lights up at the mild punishment and quickly gets himself kneeling on the ground in anticipation.

I struggle and squirm to get myself into a sitting position again without acknowledging him. I'm angry at him taking advantage of me and pushing beyond the line we clearly established months ago. I continue to ignore him as I reach for my heels.

He perks up, leans forward, and takes my heels from me. "Please Mistress, allow me."

I snatch up my riding crop and crack it against his shoulder, intending to inflict pain. "I did not tell you to speak, or to move. Put them down."

John doesn't realize I'm freaked out by his behavior, which is my fault. We're still in session. The bulge in his boxers tells me this is more foreplay than punishment. He settles back on his calves and waits patiently. His fingers drumming happily on his knees.

I narrow my eyes and set the riding crop back down. I take my time to put my heels back on and fasten them before I silently strut back to my throne. I'm taking this moment to assess where we went off the rails and how to correct the situation. "Come, kneel before me."

He scurries over on his hands and knees like an eager puppy.

"First. Zhis iz not your baby. Zhis iz my baby. I allow you to enjoy zhe presence of my child, nothing more."

John's face crumples and his posture laxes.

I realize I have not used the safe word, and to hold his continued eagerness against him wouldn't be fair. I could end the session and never know why he crossed the line. Or I could push him and help him through whatever is going on.

He looks to the floor.

"Second," I snap my fingers to bring his attention back to me. "What did you expect to accomplish crawling on top of me?" I'm angrier at myself than I'm at him. I allowed the situation to get out of control.

"I was going to bring you respite, Mistress. You're suffering and I can ease it. Is that not what you want of me?"

"You think fucking a pregnant woman brings her respite? Get on your hands and knees." I stand up, and move behind him. "Or did you think you could enjoy your Mistress without her permission?"

John places his hands palms down on the floor. The color rises in his cheeks as I call him on his shenanigans, followed by the whisper of a smile on his face.

"I see," as I bring the riding crop down and crack it against my thigh to scare him, not rewarding him with a spanking. "Your punishment is to tell me why."

"I wanted to—."

"Do not lie to me again. Tell me zhe truth." I cut him off before he feeds me that bullshit line of respite again.

His erection fades and his gaze turns hollow as he slacks in his position in front of me. His chest rises and falls faster as he silently struggles to answer my question. "You were in distress. I wanted to do my best to help." He doubles down on trying to be my savior.

I furrow my brow as we go in circles. I shift gears and try different questions. "Why do I need to be saved?"

"That's what the father of the child is supposed to do. And I couldn't fail you, Mistress."

"You are not zhe father of zhis child." I remind him again.

"I... I know that Mistress." he sputters.

"Then what is it?" I growl at him.

"That if I didn't fail you, I could prove to myself I'm worth being a father."

His words stun me. Trying to unpack all of that is not going to happen in a single session. I move to the chaise and sit back down. "Come here and rest your head on my thigh."

I run my fingers through his hair after he complies. "Why are you not worthy of being a father?"

"Because she lost the baby." His words blow out in such a low whisper I almost don't hear them. "I put work first. I was gone in the mornings, and didn't come home until late. She tried to do too much. Complained of hurting. I didn't listen. I didn't take care of her. It's my fault our family is falling apart."

I can't imagine losing a baby. With how things are going in my life, I imagine it would destroy Magellan and me. I continue to pet him as I respond. "Listen to me. You are not going to prove your worth as a father by pampering me. I do not need zhis. Your wife needs you. She needs to hear you're hurting too, and zhat you want to be there for her. You do want to be with her still, n'est-ce pas?"

"I do now. I didn't before. I mean, we weren't sweethearts before. It was good business, marrying her. Then she made me laugh. She's the prettiest thing I have ever seen. No offense, Mistress." His shoulders shake as he breaks down further and cries against me. "And I let her suffer. She was alone when she lost our son. Doc said it was too much stress on them and our son choked to death inside her."

I want to wrap him up in tight hugs and wipe the tears away. I refrain as I don't want to send mixed signals. I set aside the riding crop and I pet further down his back, giving him a light squeeze in reassurance. "Zhen you will get dressed, and you will go to her. You will tell her everything you have told me tonight. If I find out you told her I told you to tell her, you may no longer come to see me. You will prove yourself to her." I lift his chin to force him to face me and I wipe the tears away. "You have been a good boy. Go home and show your wife the compassion you showed me today."

"What if she hates me?"

"She does not hate you," I affirm without knowing the truth. I imagine if she hated him, he would not still be married. I wish

I could ask him to bring her here and force them to talk to each other. I refrain from demanding that of him, as a wife finding out her husband has been pouring his heart out to a dominatrix won't end well. "Go," I command.

Once he gets dressed and leaves, I head into the cabaret area. The girl on stage is a fire-eater, which is a freak-show more than cabaret show thing, but she's sexy as hell while doing it, and Harold was mesmerized. I use it to fill time between the dance numbers.

The room's packed tonight. There's a group of young men in the corner booth, and at least three waitresses pause at the table.

I tilt my head, trying to figure out what is going on with that when Mac shuffles me out of the room and sends me to my office. "Harold said you've been hurting and cleared your schedule for the rest of the night. He threatened my balls if I did not put you in a cab myself. Get your pretty ass upstairs and get changed."

"What's going on in zhat booth?" I nod in the direction of the corner booth as I'm complying with his request.

"Nothing to worry about. It's a bunch of kids with too much money and not enough sense."

"Are zhey tipping the girls well? Is that why so many are stopping by their table?"

"Something like that. Get dressed." He swats my ass and I chuckle as I head up the stairs.

Mac follows me out of the building and puts me into a waiting cab, giving the cabby my address and way too much money to get me there. I grumble and sulk at Harold and Mac babying me, even if saving me the walk from the train station is worth the cab fare.

The doorman smiles as holds the door for me, "Mrs. Lacienda," he greets with a tip of his hat.

"Thanks Bill. You're the best." I call as I step into the elevator.

I quickly let myself into the apartment. Everyone is still asleep. I rarely get home before sunrise. With it only being three in the morning, I try to stay as quiet as possible. I take a quick pause to see both children are tucked in and sleeping soundly, then trudge into our bedroom. I leave a trail of heels, purse, and clothes on our bedroom floor as I carefully crawl onto my side of the bed.

"Hey, you're home early." Magellan's sleepy voice rasps in the dark room.

"I love you, Mick." I lean in and seal my declaration with a heated kiss.

He kisses me eagerly in return, "I love you too. What brought this revelation to light?"

I pout at him.

"Getting a wake-up kiss, a declaration of your eternal love, and the divine sight of you naked in my bed? I must have died and gone to Heaven."

I giggle and kiss him again as I nestle under the covers with him. " Can't a girl show her man some love?"

"Mhm hmm. Well, in that case, a guy wants to show his girl how much he loves that," he purrs in my ear as his hand glides up my thigh.

Sir & The Soup Monsters

Magellan kisses below my ear before he deftly moves between my legs.

I settle on my back, thankful for the mountain of pillows behind me to keep the baby from pushing down too much.

His lips are soft and his fingers featherlight as he moves down my sides.

The baby, as if he knows Daddy is present, starts kicking up a storm.

I groan.

Magellan swats my hands away as he brings his to my twitching stomach. The warmth blossoms from where he touches me out as he rubs in easy circles. "Settle down in there, your mother needs some attention." His voice is quiet and full of mirth.

I relax, which causes the baby to relax.

Magellan, who is kneeling between my knees, leans down and kisses my round belly before nuzzling it.

I blush and run my fingers through his hair. This is the first time we've even tried to be intimate with each other since the incident. I don't want to ruin this moment by telling him all I feel is awkward and ugly.

"You're beautiful," he murmurs as he kisses lower.

My cheeks flame red as his kisses trail further down. When I think he's going to scoop me up and shift himself to dine on the platter of Hope-Marie, he kisses lower and moves further down against my thigh. While he has always been an attentive lover, it's rare for him to dote on me like this. I settle into the pillows, and bring my hands up, lacing my fingers together under the topmost pillow to keep from stopping him. I get shy when he explores my body like this, worried he won't like what he sees, or smells. My eyes flutter closed.

His fingers press into the arch of my foot sending waves of pleasure straight up my legs to my clit.

I moan like I'm in a porno.

He chuckles. "Careful, you'll wake the kids." His fingers press firmer as he massages my foot.

I bite my lip as I moan again, enjoying this too much to care.

His works back up my calf before he turns to the other foot and starts all over again. His movements are patient and slow, drawing every tiny mewl and gasp from me like a pro.

I'm a quivering mess by the time I feel his weight settle on me and his hands cradle my ass.

When he slides into me he's as hard as stone, and fills me completely. He rocks slowly, withdrawing the full length of his manhood before he glides back in.

I roll my hips in time with him, at his mercy with how pregnant I am. "Magellan," I moan as my orgasm drives any sensible thought from me.

He rocks faster and soon erupts into me like a volcano.

Instead of collapsing against me and holding me under him, he eases himself out and moves to my side.

My body is heavy and relaxed in the afterglow as I shift onto my side, wrapping myself around Magellan like a body pillow.

He chuckles and kisses my forehead.

The few hours of sleep we get before Castian is asking for Cheerios is the best sleep I've had in months. I shift to get up.

"I got it. You sleep." Magellan kisses me before he sees to our son.

When I open my eyes again, it's lunchtime. The telltale scents of grilled cheese and tomato soup waft through the air.

Castian's shrieking giggle followed by Helena's baby laugh echo in our tiny apartment.

I have to pee like a racehorse, preventing me from laying here and enjoy the sounds. After a quick dash to the bathroom, I pull on Magellan's Columbia T-shirt and a pair of shorts. Silently, I make my way into the main room, hoping to see what has our children in such high spirits.

Magellan has them both stripped down to diapers and they are sitting at our dining room table, Castian in a booster seat, and Helena in the highchair. Both are covered in tomato soup, and grilled cheese sandwiches are broken into pieces between them.

Castian bubbles his soup between his teeth and out of his mouth, letting it dribble down his chin.

Helena shrieks in laughter. She slaps her hands in the puddle of soup on her tray, spraying them both in the red liquid.

I freeze and my eyes go wide as I dart my gaze to Magellan. Messes like this would set him off before.

He eats his grilled cheese and chuckles at their antics, sitting out of splash range.

Castian casts him a quick look.

Magellan nods, encouraging him.

He starts a new round of spit up and splattered soup.

My gaze shifts from the three of them to our beautiful towels spread out like fluffy tarps beneath our children. I bite my lower lip, dreading clean up. The towels are ruined and if the soup soaks through, it's on the carpet forever.

"Stop worrying about the carpet. I'll call your mother later. She'll tell me how to get it out. You hungry? There's plenty on the stove still." Magellan outs me from my observation spot.

I release the breath I didn't realize I was holding and nod. Moving to the stove, I scoop out a healthy helping of tomato soup into a mug and snag one of the sandwiches hidden between two plates to keep them warm. I give our soup monsters a wide berth as I sit next to Magellan.

Castian lights up when I join the party and to impress me with his soup monster skills sprays Helena directly.

Helena flinches, confusion washing over her sweet face. Her smile slowly disappears as she scrunches her face in outrage. She shrieks her displeasure as she kicks her tiny feet and waves her balled fists in the air.

Magellan laughs and leans toward me, "The apple doesn't fall far from the tree. I think she learned that from you."

I snort my soup, laughing. "What?" I mock indignation. "I never threw food at anyone."

"Dirty liar. You threw food at me at our engagement party." He smirks.

"Totally different. You deserved it."

Magellan laughs hard, wiping the tears from his eyes.

Helena settles down as soon as Castian starts his routine over, being careful to not get the soup directly on his sister this time.

After lunch, we each take a soup monster to clean. I take Helena, and he takes Castian. When we reconvene in the living room, Castian and Magellan are snuggled together on the couch, watching cartoons on Nickelodeon.

Helena and I snuggle on the other side, and in a few minutes she's sound asleep against me.

Ten minutes after that, Castian is out too.

Magellan switches it to another channel, with something to hold our interests, and I rest my head against him while he gently runs his fingers through my damp hair.

"I don't want today to end," I whine.

"You don't have to work. We can live off your dividers." He teases.

I nudge him. "I do have to work."

"Oh? Being a stripper means that much to you?" He cocks a brow at me.

"I'm not a stripper. I'm a dominatrix, asshole. And yes, I think I can help some of these people. Like, I have this one guy who is going through a lot of stuff, and I was able to help him for real last night. I'm thinking of asking him to bring his wife—."

"You are going to ask a man to bring his *wife* to a session with his dominatrix?"

I didn't think his brow could raise any higher until he asks his question. "Yes, duh," I respond like a third grader. "He has something serious going on with his wife. I think it would be good for them to talk together in a safe place."

"Wait? You talk to you clients? Other than commanding

them?"

I sigh. Of all the people in the world, I thought Magellan would understand what I do is more than kink play. "Yes, Mick. It's therapeutic for most of them to visit me. It's weird, I know. The kink lets them open up to me in ways they normally wouldn't. I can really help this guy. It's why I went to school in the first place. I want to help people. If it takes a riding crop and French accent, so be it."

His expression softens, and he gets a twinkle in his eye. "I'm glad to hear you say that." He kisses my forehead, and his tone changes, taking that deeper and commanding level that makes my toes curl. "I spoke to Columbia. You're starting your residency in June."

"What? I can't start my residency. We have three kids, and I'll already not be home at least ten hours a day. A residency is long nights, no sleep, and even less time with any of them."

"You promised you could handle both?" He's using the Sir voice.

Part of me's thrilled he's pushing me to finish school. Another part of me fears he will lose his temper if I tell him all my fears of doing too much. "That conversation happened when we had two children, not three, and I wasn't the manager/owner of Le Salon."

Panic overrides rationality and Father Kelly's words ring in my ears. My lip quivers and tears well in my eyes. "And... And... I'm already a horrible wife. Father Kelly said it was all my fault and I can't do that to you." Frantic in my response I spill the beans.

"Well, Father Kelly isn't the one who will be getting the doctorate, now is he? You will do it and the reason you'll do it is that I'll have it all under control here, is that understood?" Magellan stares at me.

I'm thankful our children are dead weight against us, holding us in place.

God, I hope I can pull this off.

"Yes, Sir," I murmur before I lean in and kiss him.

C'est Mon Salon

March 1987

I have three days to go until I'm off for a month to give birth to my little soccer player. All of my clients have been introduced to their temporary Mistress. I had to keep from laughing aloud when Devon pouted that he would not get to spend time with me for the four weeks. Harold sweetened the pot of taking shorter maternity leave by agreeing to pay for my time off.

Magellan wasn't too keen on the idea, He agreed only after I showed him how much money I bring in on my own.

I'm sitting at my desk, bopping along with the muffled cabaret music. I have gone through the payroll. All Harold has to do is sign it. Before me are the inventory sheets for the cabaret bar and kitchen. I'm on my third pass at calculating the bar's sales compared to inventory. The sales are at a considerably higher compared to the liquor inventory. Someone is over-charging for drinks, or they aren't recording the inventory properly. I sigh as it's one more thing I will have to deal with before I leave.

Stella barges into my office, letting the door slam against the wall. She throws down a tiny baggy that leaves a white puff of smoke from not being fully sealed. "Fix it or else," she barks and storms out without waiting for a response.

Stunned that Stella would threaten me I sit back in my chair, not wanting to get anywhere near the baggy. With how angry she was, I can guess it's drugs and one of the strippers was using it. That she blames me says said stripper told her she got it from me. I purse my lips and keep staring at the baggy as if it will grow a mouth and tell me where the hell it came from. Rage bubbles to the surface as I recall that night with all the servers hanging around that one table. I fish my walkie-talkie out of my desk.

"Mac! My office. Now!"

"Yes, ma'am," Mac's voice comes back seconds later.

"Close the door," I command when he appears in my office. "What the fuck is this shit and why is Stella bringing it to me?" I point at the nefarious baggy still sitting in the center of my desk.

Mac's jaw twitches like a bird on a wire. He shifts his weight like Castian does when he's been caught doing something naughty and doesn't want to fess up to his crime.

I'm furious Mac has kept me in the dark and wonder if he's in on it. "Are you fucking kidding me? You have five seconds to tell me why I don't fire your ass for dealing in my club."

"I'm not dealing. It should've never gotten to this point. I'll take care of it." He's as cool as a cucumber as he turns to leave.

I come out of my chair forcing it to scrape on the floor and storm around my desk to get in his face, only my belly and our height difference makes it difficult to look intimidating. I hate that he's calm and collected while I'm a ball of emotions.

"No, you will fucking tell me what exactly you allowed in my club, who is involved, and how the fuck it got into the Oyster!"

Mac looks down at me. He could easily toss me aside. He opened his mouth to cut me off until I mentioned the Oyster. His posture deflates, and he exhales roughly. "You know that corner booth?"

"Yeah."

"That shit came from them. Up to this point, I thought they were playing smart. A little movement of their product to patrons interested in buying. I had the bar up their prices as tax for doing business in your club. I hadn't realized it had infiltrated to the girls. As long as those boys were minding their own business, it wasn't any problem we had to deal with."

How dare Mac allow them to do this.

I uncross my arms, curl and uncurl my fingers, and shift my weight as I contemplate punching him. I swear I could power the entire city with the lightning bolt of rage coursing through me. "This is my fucking club," I shriek at him. "Don't you think I should be the one to say what the fuck is allowed? Or is this another one of yours and Harold's schemes?" I push into his personal space, bumping him with my stomach.

"Yes, it is your club," he says in tone that suggests he's talking to a small child and not his boss. Mac steps back, trying to keep some distance between us. "Your club was failing. Sales were down. The people they brought in put you back in the black." He crosses his arms and puffs up his chest, defending his choice to turn my sex club into a drug store.

I want to scream at Mac and tell him how fucking wrong he is. We would have gotten here without that shit. I know better. I can see the difference in the books. I huff and puff in front of him as I struggle to bring my temper in check.

Mac used to be a Scapelli man, and the idea of taxing the dealers is an acceptable way of handling this situation. I'm hurt he didn't trust me to talk to me with this, and listen to what I would have wanted.

"Are any of my girls in on this?" My voice waivers with the effort to not scream at him again.

"Yes, ma'am."

I should fire Mac, other than he's the best security a girl could ask for. He's fully aware of everything that has gone on and who is involved. I'll have to find some kind of punishment for him. Firing him would cause too much of a vacuum on the club's safety.

"You will round every single one up and bring them to me."

Without argument, he agrees and leaves my office.

I wear a hole in the carpet with my pacing. My back is on fire with pain, but I'm too worked up to sit still.

When Mac returns he has three Salon waitresses with him.

My office is too small for all of us and I'm forced to lean against my desk to allow them in fully.

All three girls fidget. They tug at the end of their ponytails, play with their nails, or chew against their lower lip as they dart furtive glances to Mac.

I narrow my eyes as none of them look at me, the person who has the power to fire them. "Which one of you dealt to the Oyster?"

The three of them dart glances at each other and freeze like deer in headlights.

When none of them respond to me, I give Mac a pointed look.

He steps forward, cracking his knuckles.

We hadn't rehearsed his reaction. That's why Mac is the best. He knows how to put on an intimidating show of force without me having to spell it out for him.

All three girls go white as the powder in the baggy on my desk.

Finally, one cracks, and points at another. "She did it! She's the one who gave it to Sharon."

"What?! Traitor. You're the one who gave it to Michelle!"

"Bitch! I did not!"

The three devolve into shouting, blaming, confessing.

I allow the blame game to go on long until I get the full picture of who is involved between Le Salon and the Oyster. I pick up my riding crop and I crack it against the side of my desk to end this tragedy of errors. "Enough. All three of you are fired, immediately. You will be escorted to change, then off premises. Mac will see that club property remains, including anything not officially on the menu."

All three erupt into protests at my decision. Their shrill and angry voices flood my office. Everything from begging me to reconsider to blaming me for their money troubles falls on deaf ears.

"I don't give a fuck how you feel. Your choice is to leave quietly, or to sit here and wait while I call the cops and hand your asses over for dealing."

That shuts them up.

"Get the fuck out of my club. Mac, when you're finished with them, let me know."

The four of them leave my office and I sink onto my sofa, leaning back and rubbing my stomach. I've never had to fire people before. This office is too hot. I'm sweating and the muscles on the bottom side of the baby are cramping enough, it's making me bite against my knuckle to distract myself.

With every tick of the clock I fear Mac has quit too. I figure he's having a problem with me firing them and is rounding up all his guys to walk out. I was responsible for those three people and I threw them out. Three people whose families depended on me providing for them. Three people who had potential to be more. Three people, who hate me for ruining their lives.

I ball up and cry. I know I'm stupid to feel this way. They're the first people I ever had to fire. There was no other option. If I didn't make an example of them, the rest of my staff would walk all over me.

Thankfully, none of those girls called my bluff on calling the cops. It isn't an option, as they would shut the entire club down to investigate further. That is definitely not a shit show I want. I force myself to uncurl and sit up when the door to my office opens again.

"They're gone," Mac says.

"I can't let this slide, Mac." I sigh and put myself together. "As of Monday, you're suspended for two weeks. Tonight, I need you to round up the source and get it out of my club."

"Yes, ma'am. Would you like to speak to the boy before I get rid of him?"

"You're not upset with me?" I bite my lip, afraid of his answer. If Mac hates me, I don't think I can handle it. Even if I'm madder than a hatter at a tea party.

"Ma'am. You're the boss and I failed you. I'm going to do my best to correct my mistake. Simple as that."

Mac's matter-of-fact answer surprises me. Here I am worrying if he likes me, like we're in high school, and he's doing what he should have been doing all along. I can't keep acting like I'm just one of the girls. I'm the owner. If this ship goes down, I'm going with it. I let Mac put us in this position by being a weak leader.

Maybe I'm not cut out for this.

I sigh and rub my hands on my knees. The pain in my stomach feels like someone is playing bongo drums on my ovaries. "Then yes, I want to talk to him. Next time, you come to me first, or it will be the last time you decide for Le Salon."

"Yes, ma'am." He turns to leave, pausing with his hand on the doorknob, "One small suggestion, if I may?"

I nod.

"Next time, don't show weakness to the asshole who wrongs you. We need you to be the boss, and I'm sorry I put you in this position. It won't happen again."

Business Tax

I manage to clean up and dispose of the baggy getting none of its contents on me. With my desk no longer a hazardous waste zone, I resume balancing the books. I explain the extra income in the ledger as tips and indicate how much should be added to each employee's paycheck.

One of the younger bouncers, Lou, comes barreling into my office. He's out of breath and lights up when he sees me behind the desk. "Mac said you wanted to," he struggles with the right word.

"Talk."

"Yeah. Talk. Mac said you wanted to talk to the Mexican guys."

I follow him out of the office, motioning for him to lead on.

He leads me down and out through the kitchen into the alley behind both clubs.

I pause in the shadow of the entrance, watching as Mac and guys from the Oyster brawl with the men from the corner booth. While they are putting forth a strong effort, they are no match for the seasoned and skilled Scapelli men Mac leads. When all the grunting and fist throwing is done, Mac's men strip the dealers of any product, cash, and weapons. All of which is tossed into a pile behind them.

"That is our merchandise, Gringo." The de facto leader tries to shove by Mac.

"I don't give a shit, *Ese*, consider it a business tax." Mac, being the immovable force he is, shoves back, sending the kid into the brick wall.

"Los Diablos don't pay business tax. You ain't had a problem before tonight." He spits blood. He sports a cut above his eye, and his nose is off-kilter. He doesn't appear to be harmed beyond those superficial wounds.

"Before tonight, you were smart. Tonight, you're just a dumb fuck that got me and my boys in trouble with the boss."

"Your boss is a pussy. Los Diablos own this club," another young man shouts at Mac.

"Oh boy, you are sorely mistaken if you think you own this club. The only reason you were moving your product is I allowed you to pay the tax. And the only reason you could pay the tax is 'cause the boss had bigger things than piss-ants like you to deal with."

"And the boss has decided you're her top priority," I chime in as I come down the steps, making a show of being in control and holding my head high, despite being terrified. My heels click on the pavement, and I come to a stop far enough none of the men can hurt me. Like I'm at the end of the runway, I rest my hand on my hip take up a cocked hip stance, pretending I'm not as round as a beach ball pregnant.

Mac's men part for me. Once past them they hover close enough to reinforce who they're with.

All of the booth dwellers stop fussing and gawk.

I can only imagine what is going through their minds at the sight of a five foot six blond bombshell, ready-to-burst pregnant, being called boss. I cross my arms, shifting to a superhero stance to release the pressure building in my back.

"You're one of the whores. You're not—."

Mac bounces that man's head off the brick wall behind him and it takes all my effort to not gasp in horror.

"Malcolm," I chastise. I shouldn't have come down here. I don't want any part of the violence Mac's guys are prone to. I don't know what I expected by coming out here. I've committed to be the leader. There's no turning back now. I'm projecting strength with all my might because Mac said to not show weakness.

"Ma'am," he relaxes his hold on the man, driving the point home that I'm in charge.

"You fine gentlemen are more than welcome to partake in all that Le Salon offers." I motion to the building behind me with one hand. "I will make this next part crystal clear for you. This is *my* club. I don't want that shit in it. The next time it happens, I'll not be as forgiving."

Please don't challenge my threat. Fuck. What am I doing?

"You can't keep our product," the leader growls.

"Well, young man, your choice is for me to keep this product, which allows you to run home and rethink your life choices. Or Mac can escort you back inside while I call the authorities to have you and your product removed." While I'm only a few years older than these men, I purposely pull out the mom voice to be condescending and scolding at the same time.

"She's doing you a favor, kid. Be smart here." Mac comes to my aid, putting his weight behind my authority.

Silence fills the air as I watch the man in Mac's grasp struggle to deal with his predicament.

"Junior, take the deal," one of the other men chimes in, not the guy who called me a pussy.

Junior switches to Spanish, not realizing that I understand him. "Are you going to be the one that tells El Diablo?"

A third man responds in Spanish. "Fuck, let's get out of here and come back after they're closed to steal our shit back."

To my surprise, Mac responds fluently in Spanish. "That would be the last mistake you ever make, boy."

Their heads whip to face Mac like he struck them all at once.

I bite the inside of my mouth to keep from laughing.

They fidget and Mac releases the leader, letting them make the choice of the next move.

I'm tired of this back and forth, not to mention I need to get off my feet. The cramping in my lower stomach is increasing, which makes me want to rub it. I decide what to do for everyone. "Mac, please take care of our guests and see them off property." I motion to have the "product" picked up.

Lou complies and follows me back into the building.

I have a feeling there's going to be more violence in the alley, and I don't want to witness it. "Take the guns and knives. I don't want them in the club again. I'll deal with the drugs."

"You sure, Giselle? Wouldn't want the baby to—."

"It's Hope-Marie when we're backstage, Lou. Do I look like I can't handle myself?" I snap at him.

"Sorry, Gis- Hope-Marie. I'll take care of this." He scurries to comply.

I drag the drugs into my private bathroom and bust into my first aid kit for a pair of gloves. The last thing I need tonight is a contact high. I'm hunched over the toilet for what feels like hours, tossing the small baggies out of this Mary Poppins's bag of drugs. There had to be at least three bricks worth of drugs in this bag.

While all this plumbing is new, toilets are not really designed to handle dime baggies filled with drugs. I pray the toilet does not back up. When I flush the last one down, I lean up and groan.

Everything hurts.

The sharp pain of what most people think are contractions takes my breath away. I have been through this with Castian and Helena. Number three isn't tricking me. "I know. It has been a rough night. I promise it's only two more days, then we're on easy street until you get here. First, Mommy has to deliver some bad news." I lean against the door frame and I wait for everything to settle down by practicing my breathing and gently petting the sore spot.

After weaving through the backstage of Le Salon, navigating the green room in the Oyster, I wade through the sea of drunks throwing money at strippers. This only leaves the flight of stairs I have to climb to get to his office. This five-minute trek leaves me sweating and in terrible pain again. I might have misjudged and these are real contractions. They're far enough apart there's no reason to panic yet.

"Hey, we need to talk," I say. It comes out strained when I step into Harold's office.

"You okay, kid?" Harold scurries out of his seat to come to me.

"Sarah, Michelle, Sharon, Yvette, and Drew." I gasp.

Harold stops and his brow raises. "Huh? What's up with the

VIP room?'

"Shit. Stella hasn't told you yet. They're dealing." I whimper and take a step toward Harold's couch. The office is sweltering hot and I'm panicking that I got some of those drugs on me. My heart is jack-hammering in my chest, and the pain is causing blinding white spots.

"Are you fucking serious?" Harold comes alongside me and helps me as my legs buckle and my ass hits the couch. "You're burning up, Hope-Marie. You want me to call Mick?"

"No, I'm fine. We had an issue over at Le Salon that has spilled into the Oyster." Harold's face washes with confusion, confirming Stella hasn't told him yet. "We had some guys dealing in Le Salon, and they convinced some of the staff to help them."

"And Mac didn't stop their asses?"

I laugh at Harold. For all of Harold's warts, he's sometimes too naive for his own good. "He taxed them because it was good for business." My defense of Mac suggests that I might have known it was going on and agreed, which is why Harold gets a dark look on his face, along with the disapproving fatherly look.

"As soon as it was brought to my attention, we rectified the situation. I fired my staff and put Mac on suspension starting Monday. He won't make that decision again without talking to me first. So stop looking like you're about to turn me over your knee, or cuff me to a radiator." I try to sound firm, other than this couch feels like I'm on a tilt-o-whirl and Harold's making it spin faster.

Stella, who always manages to appear when I need her, like an evil fairy godmother, makes a crack from the doorway. "She would like that too much, Harold. I'm assuming your presence here says you cleaned house."

I turn to respond to Stella, and my eyes roll into the back of my head.

Once More, Without Frostbite

Wherever I am, it's quiet and dark. The steady beeping in the distance makes me furrow my brow. I try to roll over to turn off the alarm clock and find I can't move. Panic sets in and my eyes fly open. The beeping increases in speed and I loll my head in its direction. Blinking the blurriness away, the neon numbers come into focus. I can't even reach my stomach. I lift my head and I can see my stomach still round and protruding.

"They restrained you because the doctor said you needed to stay in that position. You're safe Hope-Marie." Magellan's voice penetrates the fog.

"I'm really thirsty," I whine.

"Zhat is because you are dehydrated." Maman grumbles from further away than Magellan. "You gave us a scare, my darling."

"You're alright. You're safe." Magellan's voice is breathy and thick with his accent. He works hard to keep his Spanish accent hidden. He slips when he's stressed. "The doc went home a few hours ago, and—."

"And I'm your nurse for the evening, Mrs. Lacienda. Goodness, you have a lot of visitors. I'm Mary. How are you feeling?" The battle axe of a woman that enters the room moves by my anxious family as if there is no need for concern at all.

Trying to decide who to address first, I decide the nurse is the easiest to handle. "I'm thirsty and the baby is pushing hard against me. It hurts.”

“I know, sweetie. The doctor said this is the best position for you both. He did okay me removing the restraints once you woke up if you agree to not try to get up, or roll onto your side.”

“Okay,” I whimper.

She helps me into a more comfortable position and adjusts the bed. After making her notes in my chart, she abandons me to my family.

“What happened?” Magellan asks first. He’s staring at me like I might vanish if he blinks. His hair sticks out as if he rolled straight out of bed to come here.

“I,” I pause because I have no idea what happened. “One minute I was talking to Harold and Stella, the next I’m here. I really could use some water,” I remind them for a third time.

“Magellan, why don’t you go fetch some ice chips and a pitcher of water?” Maman may have phrased it as a question, but she’s telling Magellan what to do.

The staring contest between them makes me tense my shoulders and I suck on my lower lip, fearful they’re going to erupt into a fight.

Maman has never been this stern with him before.

Did something happen while I was out?

Magellan’s nostrils flare, and he shifts Castian to one arm.

My eyes dart back and forth between the two like I’m watching a fast-paced tennis match.

“Fine,” he grits through his teeth and stalks out of the room.

Maman sits primly in the chair, her lips drawn tight with a murder in her eyes for the next person who talks back to her. When I was little, she looked like this whenever she had to deal with my sisters, Tabby and Rachel. Once Magellan’s gone she eases up and comes to my side. Her expression softens as she reaches down and squeezes my hand.

I relax as much as I can. My back hurts like a leg cramp in the middle of the night that won’t go away. Guilt fills me as I haven’t been talking with her much since Magellan hurt me. I didn’t want to confess that I’m a failure in my marriage.

“It has been three days. Your father wanted very much to be here, but he’s taking care of the kids. Do you want to tell me what has happened between you and Magellan?”

My eyes are full of tears, my breathing hitches, and the little
beeping monitor picks up pace. I shake my head no, unable to
look her in the eyes.

"Do you want me to take you home?" Maman's voice drops
low, and knowing Maman, I will never see Magellan again if I
say yes.

"No, Maman. We are working it out. Things are different.
This," I motion to my current state, "has nothing to do with
that."

"If he puts his hands on you again, you won't have a choice,
my darling Hope."

I stare at her wide-eyed. Did Tristan told her? I'm going to
murder that weasel for ratting me out. He promised he wouldn't
and one thing Wolfes do is keep their word.

"Maman," I whine.

"Non. Zhat boy promised to love and cherish you before all of
us and God. He will honor zhose vows, or he will suffer zhe
consequences. You deserve zhe absolute best, and I will not
tolerate him hurting you."

I stiffen and ball my hands into fists in the sheets. The heart
monitor beeps faster, adding to my sense of dread. Every muscle
in my back feels like it's knotted worse than a ball of yarn a cat
has chased. "You will never talk about my husband like that
again. I'm not a child. Who I choose to stay with is my decision,
and mine alone. I told you we're working it out. I made vows
before God, too. If I abandon him when he needs me most, what
kind of person would I be? Not one worthy of much love. So, you
will treat him like the family he is, or you will hand me my child
back and go home."

Maman blinks, unmoved by my outburst. She softens and
nods approvingly as she moves back to the recliner.

I'm furious she would test me like this, which results in my
jaw clenching and me crossing my arms to sulk like a child. I
want to rant and rave at her for treating us like she has any say
in how our marriage goes.

Magellan enters the room, effectively ending any rant I might
have voiced. "Here we are." He sets the pitcher down and leans
in and kisses my forehead. "It's your favorite, crunchy ice." He
hands me the cup.

My irritation fades, impressed he manages to maneuver all this while still carrying the sleeping Castian.

He casually strolls to the empty chair by the window and tugs at it until it unfolds into a horizontal surface, laying our son down on it and ruffling his hair.

Maman who is watching Magellan like a hawk.

I snort at her, and she raises a brow at me. Instead of answering her I pop tiny ice chunks into my mouth.

"Nuh-uh. Your mother flew all the way out here for you. You are not going to give her that attitude," Magellan grumbles.

Of course he takes her side!

The silent war brewing between Maman and I immediately calls a truce as we turn our gazes to Magellan. "Hrmph!"

His chuckle at us grunting in unison breaks the tension.

As much as I would like to stay grumpy, excruciating, burning pain radiates in my back, and I gasp. The crunchy ice cubes explode in the air from me squeezing the Styrofoam cup hard enough to destroy it.

"Hope-Marie," Magellan's voice echoes in my ears, sounding far away.

"Mick," I whine as I lean back against the pillows.

The machine next to me blares like a fire alarm.

I'm blinded by the ceiling lights being flicked on. Everyone still sounds far away as I flutter my eyes closed. My stomach spasms and I groan, trying to clutch it.

"Get them out of here," Mary barks. "Page the doctor. No, no, honey. I need you to keep your eyes open. Tell me where it hurts."

Castian's crying for me. He must be with Magellan, because he sounds like he's on the other side of the world.

"Mrs. Lacienda, I need you to tell me where it hurts. Come on, sweetie, focus on me." Mary's voice is loud and warbled, like she's under water.

I groan and struggle against whatever is holding my legs down, not allowing me to curl into a ball.

"Shit. Her water broke. Get the fucking doctor in here now!" Mary orders.

My Little Angel

The room turns into a hurricane of sights and sounds. Everyone sounds garbled.

I giggle at the idea they have turned into the Peanuts parents.

My amusement is short-lived as my back spasms, my stomach cramps, and I swear I'm never going to stop peeing. Terrified as the pain grows more, I cry out.

The bed is hoisted up and positioned for me to deliver the baby and the pain fades.

Drained and weak, all I want to do is go to sleep.

"Stay with me, Hope-Marie. Your baby needs you. Come on," Mary demands. It reminds me of Maman coaxing Double Trouble into doing whatever she expects them to do.

"I just need a short nap. He'll calm down." I mumble.

"No, honey. He's coming. I need you to wake-up." Mary jostles me.

I scream again as my belly constricts like I'm being kicked from all directions. The contractions are wrong. This pain is a hundred times worse than either of my other two deliveries.

"Hope-Marie," Magellan's panicked voice vaguely registers in my mind.

"Mr. Lacienda, you can't be in here." A different male voice echoes above the others. "We'll take good care of her. Please stay in the waiting room.”

There must have been a scuffle, as everything goes on tilt, and people leave my side.

“Mick, I’m fine,” I gasp.

The beeps on the monitors are frantic and maddening suggesting otherwise.

My knees are hiked up and pulled apart. A nurse takes up residence on either side of me, cooing at me as they each take a hand.

The man standing between my legs looks familiar. His name eludes me. He’s not my normal doctor.

“Okay, Mrs. Lacienda, I need you to push,” I recognize that voice after he speaks again. My cheeks flush hot, my body tenses, and I’m struggling to cover myself. This man has been to my salon. My embarrassment is forgotten as I scream in pain and push with all my might.

“Sit down, Magellan. She will be fine,” Madelyn’s voice snaps.

“I should be in there with her!” Magellan stops his pacing to wave his hands toward where they left Hope-Marie.

“You have done enough. Sit down, you’re scaring your son.” Madelyn says as she motions to Castian.

With a snort, he sits down next to Castian.

Castian hiccups as he struggles to hold all his emotions in. Daddy looks mad. Daddy gets mean when he’s mad. He doesn’t want to get in trouble for being scared. “I want Mommy,” he mewls and squirms in his seat.

“Me too, Buddy. She’s bringing your brother to us.” He pulls the toddler into his lap and runs his fingers through his hair. “Hey. It’s okay. I’m scared too.” Swallowing hard, it’s like a knife to his chest how scared Castian is of showing his feelings.

“You are?” the dam breaks and Castian’s hiccups turn into sobs as he clings to Daddy.

Magellan wraps his arms tight around Castian and rocks him gently. “Yup. I need Mommy too, and without her I would be lost.”

"Pl...Pl...Please don't be mad, Daddy." Castian pleas.

"Let it out, buddy." Magellan holds him tighter and pets his hand down his back. His eyes lock with Madelyn and the blazing anger in her face makes him feel small and helpless as his son. It confirms what a shit husband and father he has been.

This entire situation is out of his control. He can't help his wife, who is everything to him. His son is terrified to show his emotions because of how *he* has treated him. The rage builds inside, and he closes his eyes, focusing on Castian. "She'll be okay. As soon as your brother's here, we'll see her. I promise," he coos against his son's temple in Spanish.

Castian cries and clings to Magellan for several minutes before Magellan shifts him to sit in the chair next to Madelyn. "I'm going to get us something to eat."

Madelyn nods as Castian snuggles against her.

The few minutes it takes to walk to the vending machines helps to soothe his raw nerves. He successfully tucked the rage away for Castian. He needs to release all this pent up helplessness and rage before he takes it out on his family. He closes his eyes to shove the fear away.

Hope-Marie's face fills his mind. Not her bubbling smile, or sexy orgasm face. The terrified and tear-stained face as he strangles her has haunted him since that fateful night. He doesn't know how to live without her. How could he have ever hurt his beautiful, perfect wife. What will he do if she doesn't survive this? What's happening to her is all his fault.

He leans his forehead against the vending machine, and the tears come. She has to be okay. He hasn't made up for all the shit he's put her through. He hasn't said all the words he should be saying. His fist thumps against the machine and he forces himself to take deep breaths.

The psychiatrist has him practicing breathing techniques and gave him the name of a boxing gym he thought might be helpful to Magellan. He has to pull it together for his kids. He breathes in and out like a locomotive until he's light-headed before returns to the waiting area with several cans of soda and various candy bars, dumping them into the seat next to Castian.

Madelyn doesn't approve of all the junk food. She remains quiet even with how angry she is at this boy for hurting her darling, Hope. She wants to rant and rave at him. If John knew he had put his hands on his favorite child, Magellan would be dead. The boy looks like he's coming undone at the seams. There might be hope for him yet. As much as she wants to tear into him, she reminds herself he has been through a terrible ordeal. She knows first-hand how that changes a person. She will respect Hope-Marie's wishes unless he hurts her again. Then all bets are off. "The nurse came by. Your son is doing well. Zhey have taken him to clean him up, and she said she would come back to take you to see him."

"And Hope-Marie?"

Madelyn purses her lips, staring at her son-in-law. "Zhere were complications. Zhey are working on taking care of her. She said zhe doctor will talk with you after he is finished."

Magellan's heart stops. His fingers curl around the soda can and his jaw clenches. The ringing in his ears roars louder as the urge to destroy everything around him grows.

Castian whines and clings to Abuela Wolfe as Daddy turns scary again.

"Magellan," Madelyn barks his name like a drill sergeant. She's relieved when he noticeably relaxes. "We need to talk about Hope-Marie."

"What of her?" Magellan huffs.

"Do not get short avec moi. I'm not zhe one who put my 'ands on her." Madelyn says. "Zhis is important. You need to listen to me because she will not. She is bull-headed, like her father."

"I'm listening." Magellan gulps, backing down. He readies himself for the news that Hope-Marie is leaving him.

"You are not. You will though. Sit down, and shut up." She pets Castian as she issues her commands to Magellan.

Magellan frowns. The sight of his son cowering against Madelyn douses any flames he had to fight with her. He eases into the chair next to her, gently pulling Castian into his lap to not startle him further.

" We were in zhe capital when Helena gave birth to Joseph. It was terrible. She was bed ridden, and in pain zhe entire pregnancy. John was beside himself. Unable to take zhe pain away, and unable to do anything for her. She lost a lot of blood giving birth to Joseph, too much blood. She nearly died during labor. Zhe doctor told her that she would not survive another pregnancy."

Hope-Marie had briefly told him that her mother died giving birth to her, and that she considers Madelyn her mother. He had not made the connection that Hope-Marie would have the same medical issues as Helena Wolfe.

"John and Helena tried. Zhey went against the church and she started taking birth control. John wanted to get a vasectomy. Helena refused to let him. She told him he would be able to still have children after he left her." Madelyn rolls her eyes at the memory of John telling him Helena believed he would leave her for Madelyn. "He used protection. But, as I'm sure Hope-Marie has told you, zhe Wolfe family is *blessed* with zhe gift of fertility." She flashes a smile at Magellan.

"Don't I know it. Are you suggesting I get a vasectomy?"

"Would you?"

"Not without talking to Hope-Marie." He shakes his head no.

"Hmph. You will have to be zhe responsible one. Zhat is if you wish for your wife to raise your children with you."

"What do you mean by that?"

Madelyn sighs. "I mean, Hope-Marie is Helena's daughter, and here we are, waiting to see if *complications* have killed your wife."

Magellan flinches. He struggles with the harsh words from his mother-in-law, and he shifts his gaze down the hall where he last saw his wife. He shoots out of his seat like a rocket, only stopped by Madelyn's hand reaching out to catch his wrist.

Silence fills the waiting area until Helena makes her displeasure known by shrieking. Even after a diaper change, feeding, and comfort from both Madelyn and Magellan she cries.

The distraction of caring for Helena does little to soothe Magellan's already frazzled nerves. He paces with the baby, trying to soothe her back to sleep.

She's not having it.

Madelyn keeps Castian occupied with coloring.

Neither adult wants to leave should something happen with Hope-Marie. So the quartet keep the waiting room occupied until the doctor appears at the edge of the seating area.

"Mr. Lacienda," his voice is gentle, and his expression is

somber and cold.

Magellan freezes, squeezing Helena against him. His heart bangs like a drum in his chest. Every muscle in his body braces for impact. "How is she? Can I see her?"

On The Mend

February 1987

Our apartment turns into Grand Central Station in no time flat with people coming and going, all checking on us. We have an entire freezer full of prepared meals, as no one realizes Magellan is the cook in our family. The hospital held me hostage for two weeks, then released me to light duty and bed rest for two more weeks.

Maman has been with us the whole time and has been a lifesaver as well.

I grab a shower to feel less like a milk monster. After, I'm standing in front of the mirror, trying to find any traces of the sexy body I once had.

Thank God they didn't cut Angelo out of me.

I hold my belly with my hands and suck it in as much as possible.

All that hard work gone. I'm a fat cow again.

"Moo," I whisper to the reflection, stealing a glance to guarantee Magellan hasn't heard me.

He and Maman are shouting at each other in the kitchen. They must think I'm still in the shower as they play nice whenever I'm around.

Castian's worried mewls echo into our bedroom and pull me from my pity party. He stands near our bedroom door, teetering between entering and watching the kitchen.

Magellan threatened a spanking if Castian didn't leave me alone.

Castian whimpers as he watches the kitchen. His fear of spankings out-weighing his need for Mommy.

My anger flares at the two of them causing my son this much distress. I toss on some comfy clothes and head into the bedroom. "What's the matter, my little lion?" I run my fingers through Castian's hair as he clings to my leg.

"Abuela Wolfe is mad at Daddy. Bossing him again." He hugs my leg, burying his face into my thigh.

"Ah, well, it's okay. Mommy's here, and Abuela Wolfe's allowed to boss Daddy." I clear my throat dramatically to catch their attention and cross my arms.

All arguing ceases.

I nudge Castian and let him stay close as I wade into the battlefield of our kitchen.

"Hey, you're up. We didn't wake you, did we?" Magellan asks as he pulls me into a light embrace with a kiss on the cheek.

Maman turns and finishes cooking whatever Magellan has abandoned to greet me.

"What is going on with you two?" I whisper, meaning to keep the conversation between us.

"We'll talk later," Magellan sighs. His jaw is twitching, and his muscles ripple, reminding me of an agitated animal in a cage.

"Not mad, Daddy?" Castian wrings his hands, still hovering at my side.

"No, Buddy, I'm not mad. Abuela Wolfe is being a grandma." He gives our son a gentle smile.

I purposely avoid retreating to the sanctuary of our bedroom for the rest of the day, forcing a truce between Magellan and Maman.

After dinner, Maman takes the kids and they disappear into their bedroom.

Magellan refuses to let me help him clean the kitchen.

Assured he and Maman will not start their argument back up,

I bite my lip and get an impish grin. I sneak into our bedroom and strip out of my comfy clothes. After rummaging in Magellan's dresser, I retrieve the blindfold and cuff set, his favorites of all our toys. While we can't have sex, I can offer to relieve some of that energy in other ways. The thrill of being intimate with him again makes me giddy and anxious.

Will he think I'm sexy in my fat cow body?

What if he won't touch me after what happened with Angelo?

Am I ready for this?

I pull the blindfold on, wearing it like a headband, and take the cuffs with me. I cuff my ankles after I kneel at the foot of the bed, running the small chains in a crisscross pattern. I cuff one wrist behind my back, reach up to pull the blindfold down, plunging myself into darkness, and finish cuffing my other wrist blind.

The time that ticks by starts to feel like hours.

My legs are sore, and my breasts ache from growing heavy with milk. My head tilts as I listen for any hints that Magellan enters the room. The longer I wait the more I doubt this is a good idea.

His scent suddenly surrounds me, Old Spice mixed with Zest.

My pulse quickens and I straighten my posture, eager to show him I'm willing to give this to him.

He chuckles

I blush in response, unsure if he likes what he sees. I hold my breath in response to his fingers brushing along my cheek.

"Are you sure?" His voice is husky and thick.

"I am, Sir."

His fingers brush along my cheek again and his lips are tender against my forehead before he leaves me kneeling alone again. I crane my head to hear what he's up to.

His scent surrounds me again. His calloused fingers cup my cheek and lace into my hair, tilting my face up to meet the smooth skin of the engorged tip.

The nervous energy in the air radiates from both of us. This is the first time since I walked out that we have been intimate with each other this way.

I trail my tongue along the smooth skin and swirl it around the sensitive tip, grinning at him sucking in a sharp breath.

"Don't tease, or I'll punish you," he hisses.

"Maybe I like punishment," I purr as I draw his tip in and suck hard.

"Jesus Christ," he groans. His fingers tighten in my hair and he tries to push forward.

I suck tighter to prevent him.

"Hope-Marie, suck my cock, or I swear I will--"

I relax my jaw and let his swollen shaft glide along my lips. I expect him to pump hard and fast, like he did before.

He rocks gently, letting his throbbing member escape to the tip before easing all the way to my throat. The position he holds my head in allows him easier access, and I'm at his mercy.

I eagerly suck as I gaze up at him.

"Good girl," he gasps as he continues rocking slow and steady in my mouth.

I glow with pride from his praise.

His brown eyes smolder with lust as he keeps our easy pace.

I trail my tongue along the ridge of his shaft and he bites his lower lip to keep from making too much noise. Our tiny apartment is in no way soundproof. I suck harder, encouraged by his response, and force him to speed up to keep rhythm with my mouth.

Seconds later, he's moaning my name like a prayer. He thrusts fully into my mouth as his release spills into my throat. When I think I'll pass out from lack of oxygen, he eases back.

I continue to suckle him until he pulls himself out of my mouth completely.

"I want to fuck you until you scream my name," he says as he leans down and kisses me and steps away.

I whine, aching for his touch. I thought he would tease me more, or go for round two, but all I hear is a dresser drawer open, followed by another, then another.

"Shit," Magellan mutters.

The bathroom light switch clicks on, soon followed by frantic rustling of the drawers in our bathroom being opened and closed.

"Fuck," he growls.

The next sounds are closer and angrier.

From where I'm kneeling he must be checking our

nightstands. "Sir?" I whimper. Fear wells as I can't judge how much danger I'm in without being able to read Magellan's body language.

I never should have done this. What was I thinking? He's going to hurt me.

I jump and yelp from him lifting the blindfold up and off my head.

"Where did you put the key?"

"The key?" I blink to adjust to the light. I'm trembling. "I...Uh...The last time I saw it was in your nightstand on the key chain with all the other keys."

Magellan frowns and looks around the room for any other places the keys could be hiding. He purses his lips, pulls on his robe, and leaves our room.

I furrow my brow and squirm in my restraints. Instead of telling me what's going on, he's rustling about in our kitchen like a cat burglar trying to hurry and find his prize.

He comes back holding a pair of needle-nose pliers. "Hold the cuffs tight and don't move."

"What are you doing?" I look over my shoulder.

He wedges the pliers between one of the links in the cuffs.

I buck, saving the chain from its fate, and topple forward.

He catches me before I face plant. "I told you not to move."

"Do you know how expensive these are?"

"I'll buy you new ones. Unless you miraculously remember where the key is."

"Why would I know where the key is? It's your responsibility."

"Well, darling love of my life, you have two options. I free you and destroy the poor handcuffs, or you sleep like this and I search for the key in the morning."

As if on cue, Angelo reminds us of his presence by fussing in his bassinet.

"Fine, free me," I huff and push the cuffs far enough out for him to destroy them.

He kisses my temple and chuckles.

"Don't worry, I'll find the key in the morning. Your mother won't see your jewelry. You can stay in here with our little angel until then."

He gives the pliers a rough tug. Swatting my ass as helps me up, he turns me towards the bathroom.

"You clean up. I'll get our son."

Cleaning House

Angelo squawks and whines until he's latched onto one of my breasts. His chubby little fists bang against my breast as he gloms milk from me.

I bring him to the bed and settle in against the headboard.

Magellan has a goofy grin on his face as he stares at me.

My cheeks flush, and shyness takes over, causing me to pull the sheet up.

He catches it. "No. You are more beautiful each time I see you like this. Don't hide it from me."

I let the sheet go. Instead, I pat the bed next to me. "We need to talk."

"Uh-oh," He climbs into the bed, and trails his fingers along my thigh. "That sounds ominous."

"What's going on between you and Maman?"

He sighs and turns his attention to the dangling chain from the handcuff. "According to her, I'm a layabout. She reminded me that it's the man's duty to provide for his family this morning. Then interrogated me on what I plan to do to accomplish that goal."

"Did you tell her you're working?"

He shrugs, still fidgeting with the chain. "It's none of her business."

"No, it's not. Not telling her could be why she has stayed longer."

His snorts and nods. He's still getting used to the idea of working for me and staying home. While he may struggle with people's opinions of him, I have seen a marked improvement in his personality. The sweet, loving man I met in that café shines through more each day.

"She won't accept that we're fine, and she says she's staying until the end of the school semester to travel back to Kansas City with Cosette." He finally confesses.

The despair in his voice makes me giggle.

Three adults in this apartment turns a space that was barely functioning into a sardine can.

Maman is meddling, and I'll talk to her tomorrow. Tonight, I'm happy to have a conversation with Magellan that doesn't result in us fighting, or him blacking out with rage. I look down to Angelo, who is drunk on milk and dozing while he continues to suckle against me. He looks exactly like my father, with Magellan's olive skin. He's going to be a heartbreaker when he grows up.

"We need a house," I blurt.

Magellan laughs at my random segue and kisses my temple. "Yes, we do. Not tonight though. Tonight, my amazing wife, you will rest, and tomorrow I'll free you from your bonds." He flashes me a fiendish grin as he extricates the sleeping infant. He brings him to his chest and gently rubs his back until the tiny baby releases the belching monster hidden within.

Magellan being tender with Angelo makes me warm and tingly all over, drunk on happiness.

He crawls back into the bed, nestling into the covers. I snuggle into him, and he kisses me softly.

I try to pull the covers over myself again

He raises a brow at me. "I seem to recall I told you not to hide yourself from me."

"I'm cold," I pout at him.

"I'll provide all the warmth you need." He wraps his strong arms around me, pulling me into him.

I'm up with Angelo early the next morning. The last thing I want is to explain to Maman why I'm wearing handcuffs. As the hours tick by, I huff at Magellan tricking me into staying in bed. The longer he takes, the more irritated I get that I'm still naked and cold. Well, almost. I put on a robe in case Castian comes bolting in.

Near lunchtime he comes barreling into our room with Castian hot on his trail. He turns on heel and looks down at Castian. "Go ask Abuela Wolfe. She knows where the treasure is." He shuts the door in Castian's face.

"Smooth," I say from the bed. "You know he'll still be there when you open it."

"It would appear we need to improve where we hide our toys. He'll be fine. He's convinced we have pirate booty hidden somewhere." He strides over to the foot of the bed. His gaze trails up my semi-naked body. His erection growing the longer he stares at me.

I preen at his appreciation of me.

He draws me into a longing kiss as he crawls over me. His hardened shaft brushes my thigh, making me wish I could roll him over and ride him like a bucking bronco.

"Our son," he says after stealing another kiss, "has taken all the keys and hidden them to protect the treasure from pirates."

I laugh.

"Apparently, somebody read him Treasure Island. He's convinced he has a stash of treasure chest keys."

"I thought it was a good idea when Maman asked to read to them." I bite my lip with a guilty smile.

"Turns out, our little lion has quite the imagination. And you may, or may not, have to play the damsel in distress to be saved from the evil conquistador at some point." The glint of mischief in his eyes makes my heart flutter.

I lean up and draw him into another heated kiss. Had this happened months ago, he likely would have spanked Castian, and we would be fighting as I try to defend our son.

He frees me of my jewelry, then disappears to start lunch.

I soon follow, dressed in one of his Columbia T-Shirts and

sweatpants. The cozy scene of Maman on the couch with Castian and Helena, and Magellan working in the kitchen makes me smile. I join Maman on the couch and pull Helena into my lap. This conversation is going to be hard. While I don't want to hurt Maman's feelings, I need her to butt out of my marriage.

"Maman, I really appreciate everything you've done for us."

"Of course, my darling Hope. I'm always here for you. Avec Mick not working, I'll stay until Cosette's semester ends. Zhat should be enough time for him to find suitable work."

I chew against my lower lip, and hesitate. "I love that you have been here for us. We've got it from here. If you want to stay in New York, you should probably stay at Tristan's place. He's got a guest room, and plenty of space. You'll still be close enough to help if we need you. Magellan is working, Maman, and our place is too tiny for all of us."

"Are you kicking me out, Hope-Marie?" Her perfectly sculpted brow arches in question as she ignores my last statement.

"What? No. Yes. I mean. Well, not exactly. It's just, well, too many cooks in the kitchen spoil the soup. Besides, wouldn't you want to meet Mae?" I'm playing dirty using Tristan's live-in girlfriend to get Maman off my back.

"Who is zhis Mae?" Maman narrows her eyes at me.

"You remember the girl Tristan was moon-eyed over when he graduated?"

"Zhe one with zhe Frenchman? She is in New York?"

"Mhm hmm. Living with Tristan." I nod to drive the point home.

He's going to kill me for this.

Maman watches me without any indication one way or the other if she's upset before she nods. "Perhaps zhat is a good idea."

"I love you, Maman. Thank you, again, for everything." I pull her into a tight hug.

During lunch Maman asks Magellan to take her to Tristan's place.

I don't call Tristan to warn him.

Serves him right for snitching.

While he's gone, I begin the scavenger hunt for our keys.

Castian's happily watching the Disney movie I put in the VHS player.

Magellan startles me when he gently pats my butt. I'm ass-up in the toy box sifting through the collection of toys for the tiny keys.

With a gentle tug, he guides me out of the kids' room and back to ours. "I don't know what magical powers you used to get her to go, but I want to reward you." He pulls my T-Shirt up and over my head until he has my hands bound up in it. His lips brush against my earlobe, "And to punish you for covering up." His voice is husky against my skin. He nips my neck and moves further down, his lips brush against my overly sensitive nipples.

I gasp and squirm. "Castian?"

He leaves me on the bed and steps to the door. Peeking out like we're teenagers sneaking behind our parents' backs he smiles. "We have fifteen minutes before the movie ends." He eases the door closed and wriggles out of his pants as he comes back to me.

"Mick, we can't have sex yet," I whine and struggle more against my shirt restraint.

When did he learn to tie a T-Shirt like this?

"Oh, my beautiful minx, you'll be quite capable of satisfying me without sex."

My eyes widen as he lays me back fully and brings himself up my chest until he nestles his dick between my swollen breasts. My cheeks flush hot and I arch my back, jutting my breasts up to him.

"That's it, good girl." His rough fingers massage my breasts and the mix of pleasure and pain arouses me even more. He pushes them together until he gets the friction he wants, pumping his swelling cock between them.

I tilt my head up to flick my tongue along his tip protruding through. Teasing and licking I finally get in a position where I can suck his head into my mouth while he rocks.

It has the effect I want, bringing him to climax faster.

I pop him out of my mouth in time for him to release all over me.

"Fuck, I love you," he pants above me.

"I love you, too."

"Don't move."

He kisses above my belly button before he disappears into the bathroom. When he returns he gently rubs the warm cloth over my neck and chest, erasing his dirty seed.

Dog & Pony Show

June 1987

Friday nights are always our busiest nights. Tonight is no different as both clubs are hopping. There are two bachelor parties in the Oyster, and Le Salon is packed. Tonight is the first night someone is brave enough to order the Pony Package.

The Pony Package is a double session and takes a person and turns them into a pony with a bit, ears, and hoof boots. My excitement is barely contained at the idea of meeting the person who wants to be treated like a pony. My giddiness flows into my other sessions, and I'm riding high when I walk into my salon at ten in the evening.

I stop dead when I see who is enjoying my liquor, my giddiness quickly turning into anxiety. It's common for the clients to be shown into the salon if it is ready. The person sitting on my chaise has been thrown out of this club once already. A small frown forms on my lips as I try to figure out what Junior, the ringleader of the drug dealers, is doing in my salon. His safe word makes more sense. He could be here to hurt me, or to recoup his drugs. Either way, he's in for a rough evening. I decide to pretend like I don't know who he is, and start our session. "Remove all of your clothes and stand in zhe center of zhe room with your hands behind your back."

He rises from the chaise, setting his drink on the side table.

I'm ready to bolt and scream for Mac when he eases his jacket off, followed by his gun holster. My eyes never leave him until the holster sits on the chaise over his jacket. I hold my casual stance while he removes the rest of his clothing.

He's fit and slim, still young enough he has not filled out yet. He would be quite handsome if he weren't such a menace. Completely nude he stalks to the center of the room, where a spotlight shines down.

"Good boy," I coo. My heels click on the tile floor as I approach the toy table. I have a feeling he won't appreciate being cuffed or blindered, so I pick them up first and hook them on the back of my corset before I approach him.

I ease in close as I come to face to face with him. "Put your hands behind your back to get your reward." I trail my gloved fingers down his toned chest.

His cock bobs in excitement. With a smirk, he clasps his hands behind his back, and it forces his chest out.

My fingers trail lower, dancing dangerously down the V of his muscles to taunt his already rising manhood. I brush one hand back up as I lean into him, my lips tantalizingly close to his, while I reach behind my back. I brush my nose against his, bringing the cuffs around to click them both into place in unison.

He's smiling and leaning into me until the cuffs click closed. His body tenses and he tugs against the cuffs, finding them too tough to tug apart. "What are these for?"

"Zhis is about bringing you pleasure based on your desires." I continue to pet him, attempting to soothe the wild beast while I prepare him for what he paid for. "Kneel."

He takes a second to comply, and I patiently wait for him to get on his knees. He's facing the throne, and away from the toys, and the winch behind him.

I fish the blinders from the back of my corset and bring them down to his head.

He balks and I raise a brow at him. "If you wish to stop, zhen say your safe word. You remember it, oui?"

His eyes turn to slits with anger blazing in them, and he says nothing.

"Tell me your safe word."

He snorts, still not answering me.

"If you do not tell me zhe safe word, zhis session is over and I'll have you escorted from the building." His expression darkens more and I gently pet his cheek, drawing his chin up to let him face me. "Or be a good boy and tell me zhis word, and you can get your desires."

His body twitches as he jerks against the restraints. He glares at me. His cock is rock hard and bobs angrily with his moments. He does not want to submit and doesn't want to stop either. He finally mutters, "Puta."

"Good boy. Tell me you want to continue."

He snorts and grits his teeth.

I give him as much time as he needs. Consent is critical. Having doubt and fear is normal. For most, giving this level of control to a total stranger is terrifying. If he wishes to stop, we will. He is in control of what happens to him.

"I want to continue." He shyly replies.

"Bon," I chirp, and bring the blinders to his head.

He balks again, and I lightly slap his cheek. "Non. You will wear what I put on you."

His shoulders tense, and he allows me to put the blinders on him.

I strap the binding over the top of his head to meet the strap around, followed by the strap down under his chin, to prevent shaking them off. I pat his forehead. "Stay."

"Yeah, okay." He mutters.

I lightly slap his chest. "Yes, Mistress."

He smirks, "Yes, *Mistress*," he says, mocking my title.

I let it slide as I leave him to gather the cord attached to the track in the ceiling. The system is rigged to hold up to a ton of weight and allows me to keep my pets from wandering too far from the path.

He cranes his head and cannot see what I'm doing, the blinders keeping his vision tunneled.

As I approach him from behind, "Easy, I'm preparing everything." I click the cord to the jump ring on his cuffs and take a few steps back. I press the crank button to hoist him off the ground.

"What the... Hey... This isn't comfortable. Let me down!" He growls and struggles. It's too late as he's hoisted up until only his toes touch the ground, forcing his arms up and him forward.

"If you wish to stop, say your safe word." I gather the cock harness and tail plug. I put a generous amount of lubricant on the tip to aid entering him.

He has yet to use the safe word, despite him struggling and wriggling in his bindings.

I step to his side and drape the bit over my shoulder. I ease in close again and stroke his cock.

He's raging hard, and his face burns with shame, causing him to still when I slip the strap around his shaft.

I ease the harness down until I pull his balls into their sack and ring the tail plug to his separated cheeks, lining it up with the ring from his sack to keep everything in place. "Deep breath."

"What?" He gasps as I rim him with the tip of the plug.

I get lubricant all around the hole and slightly in before I deftly push the plug into him.

He yelps and arches as I hold the tail in place for him to adjust to it. His skin flames even more red, and he's between whimpering and growling. His cheeks clench and try to push out the foreign object I'm holding firmly in place until his own muscles finally pop around the rim to hold it for me.

As this is our first session, I went with the training tail. The tiny plug may feel like it is massive. It's only a few inches in length and not wider than fat marker.

He still does not use his safe word.

With a small smile, I bring the strap up to clasp the leather collar around his neck, completing the harness to hold everything in place.

He whimpers and struggles while I retrieve his boots. His struggles win him sinking his tail inside him with no chance of falling free.

I come around to his front and kneel to grab one ankle.

He tilts his head down, frowning at me.

When I slip the first boot on and zip it into place, it gives him purchase on the ground. While he's observing the first foot, I get the second one. I thought for sure he would say the safe word.

He paid for this. Who am I to judge? With both in place, I move out of his range to gather up the final pieces, his bit, and ears.

I place the ears on first, clipping them to the blinders, then I bring the bit to his mouth. "Since you will be a good pony, you will stamp your left hoof twice for your safe word. Tell Mistress you want to continue." I watch his hotly flushed face for signs we need to stop. I pick up shame, maybe humiliation, and definitely lust. I don't see any signs of session-stopping distress in his body language.

He still does not use his safe word. "I... I...want to continue, Mistress." His words are breathy and timid.

"Good pony. Open your mouth." When he complies, I slide the bit into place, forcing it back as far as his mouth can handle and clasping it into place at the back of his head. I give him a moment to be nestled in my bosom, a small comfort for what he's having me do to him.

He nuzzles me, to my surprise.

I move around him again and grab my riding crop. When I come back, I lower the winched cord enough for me to pull his reins and force him to stand upright. There are hoof gloves for the full pony experience. I don't trust him enough to let his hands out of the cuffs. He could beat me to death with the hoofed gloves.

"You will learn to trot, my little pony. Trot." I click at him as I would a horse. When he doesn't move, I bring the riding crop hard against his ass.

He yelps and moves forward, unsure of himself. The clop of the horse hoof boots makes him groan in the bit. He takes another uneasy step, and I spank him again.

"Trot! Knees up, pony."

He stiffens and groans as the tail nestles in his quivering ass. He moves faster, bringing his knees up.

I have to stifle a laugh at how awkward he looks at first.

With each bouncing step, he moans and whimpers.

We weave around the room with me following him enough to spank him when he slows down.

Beads of sweat form on his brow, and he's panting by the time I make him stop. His cock throbs in its confines.

I give his balls a squeeze while we're standing still.

The material forms to his shape, tightening around his balls and staying in place. His cock twitches.

I run my finger along the ring keeping him from ejaculating. With a gentle stroke of his manhood, I smile at his pleading eyes. "What a good pony you are. Do you want Mistress to continue?"

He leans into my hand as I stroke him. Not once does he stomp his left foot. He rocks into my hand instead and I let him rest his head against my breasts. His groans turn into soft moans, and his rocking grows faster in my hand.

"Good pony. Trot!" I click again, removing my hand from stroking him.

He whines and follows my command without hesitation.

As our time comes to an end, I stop him where I started him in the light, and I tease him with the slow rhythmic clicks of the winch, raising him back to his toes to force him forward. I remove the harness, along with the tail.

As soon as his cock's released he spurts hot cum all over the floor.

As a reward, I gently stroke him until he stops spasming. I notice the ring left rawness on his skin and I step away to get the Vaseline. Applying enough to help soothe it. I get him out of his boots and finish by stepping in front of him again to remove the bit.

"You fucking whore! I'll kill you when I get out of these cuffs!"

I grab his chin and jerk him forward to face me, pulling him off balance and forcing him to look at me. "Non! You had every opportunity to tell me to stop, to use your safe word, and you *chose* to continue. You *enjoyed* yourself as you pranced around like a good pony. Don't you talk to me like zhat, or you won't get your reward." I shakes his chin roughly. "Do you want Mistress to give you your reward?"

Anger, shame, and curiosity flicker across his face as I stare at him. "Fine, Yes, *Mistress*," he growls at me.

I bring up my other hand and I pop a baby carrot into his mouth. "Good pony." I pat his head lightly, then I move to the door, giving it two knocks.

Mac enters and looks from me to Junior and back. He crosses

his arms and furrows his brow as he tries to understand why I called him into this session.

I release Junior from the cuffs and step back.

He spins like he's going to football tackle me

Mac clears his throat.

Junior's face pales, then burns bright with shame again. His chest rises and falls with harms out to his side like a classic Hollywood monster about to attack.

I'm thankful Mac stands as cool as a cucumber as I issue my last command to Junior. "Kneel, zhen come to me, and kiss my heart, my good little pony."

Junior's eyes widen and he cuts Mac a look before he slowly lowers himself to his knees and crawls to me.

That was stupid. You should have just told him to get dressed. Now Mac can't stop him from hurting you.

He stops in front of me and glares up at me.

I hold my breath.

Hesitantly, he leans forward and kisses my heart.

"Good boy. You may get dressed and go home."

Pushing Boundaries

August 1987

Magellan thought he had done everything he needed to do to allow me to pursue my residency starting in June. The letter I received made it absolutely clear I was only on the waiting list until January. They wrote the standard song and dance of how competitive the program is, and should an opening present itself, I would need to be available immediately.

Imagine my surprise when it actually happens.

I got a phone call three days ago, informing me my first day at Bellevue Mental Hospital is the following Monday. I pout at the ugly, functional shoes the eager clerk is showing me at Macy's. According to my advisor, the dress code is business formal.

"Thanks," I deadpan and take the bricks called pumps from her. I slip them on my feet, crinkle my nose, and whisper moo at them angrily. I'm glad Magellan isn't here to hear that, or there would have been punishment for putting myself down. I stand and attempt to walk in them.

"Oh, those look adorable on you!"

I give the clerk a side glance, disbelieving her chipper accolades.

She must work on commission.

It takes a few steps to get used to walking in anything less than five inches high, and I can feel my calves burning already. If Stella were here, I would punch her for turning me into a stilettos only woman.

"Do you have three-inch heels?" I ask. Hopeful there is something that even remotely looks stylish.

"Oh, not in that style. You said business formal. Two inches is the highest in that category."

"Hrmph," I frown in the mirror as I inspect myself in these old-lady clodhoppers. I understand no one else cares what my heel size is, and that patients aren't going to be focused on my outfit. The only thing I can focus on is how ugly these shoes make me. My legs are less shapely, and my baby fat love-handles are more accentuated, accentuating my bovine features. My shoulders droop at how fat I have gotten.

Mick thinks I'm hot.

He's biased.

These shoes do make me a fat cow.

"No. Take these back. I'll keep looking," I say as I step out of them and hand them back to the clerk as quick as possible.

"Oh, okay. Would you like to try another color?" Her expression sours.

"No. I want stilettos, black, round-toe. Four inches or higher." I bark like a drill sergeant.

The clerk's face screws up like I threw dog shit at her. "You want stilettos for business formal?"

"I do. It's my business." I resist the urge to say it with a French accent as I channel Giselle. On the inside, I want to eat my way through some Auntie Anne's pretzels because this clerk makes me feel like a hooker playing dress-up with her judgmental looks. I slip back into my casual stilettos and follow behind her.

"That's a brave decision," she retorts.

As we approach the section of heels I prefer, she turns and motions with a dismissive hand. "Here are the working...heels," her voice quivers as she struggles with what I assume is the reference to being a working girl.

My brow raises and I bite the inside of my mouth to prevent

myself from parroting one of Harold's diatribes on the definition of working girl. "I apologize for not being clear. I'm looking for the real brands. If Macy's no longer carries those, I'm happy to take my business elsewhere."

She inspects me from head to toe. Her cheeks reddening as our exchange is quickly turning into a battle.

I'm in a Royal's jersey-cut shirt, a pair of fitted jeans with the knees blown out, and a pair of red stilettos to match. My waist-length blond hair is swept into a high ponytail to complete the All-American girl image.

"This way," she relents and we turn the corner to the display wall of the heels I want.

I know exactly where the heels I like are, and what is available. At this point, it's a power struggle. This judgmental clerk, whose annual salary is likely what I make in a single session, isn't getting away with treating me like a cheap hooker. "Thank you. If I need your help, I'll ask."

Magellan comes strolling up with our tribe in tow as I'm having the clerk ring three pairs of stilettos up.

"Thank you, for being oh so helpful," I say with sugary sweetness and an award-winning Giselle smile. I take the stroller from Magellan, letting him walk with Castian.

"What was that about?" He eyes me and glances back at the clerk.

"Nothing," I sing-song with a smug smile on my face.

"Uh-huh. Well, Miss Nothing, I think some Auntie Anne's is in order."

I cut him a look, wondering how he could know I was thinking I wanted pretzels.

"Yup. Definitely time for some cheese sauce." He wiggles his eyebrows at me.

The Following Monday

My heels click steadily on the gray linoleum floor as I walk down the main corridor to the office of Dr. Caleb Lamb. I glance from side to side to see if I'm being pranked. What are the odds of being a Wolfe paired with a Lamb? Okay, I'm technically a Lacienda, but once a Wolfe always a Wolfe. "Awoo." I whisper before I knock.

"Enter," he bellows from behind the door.

I ease the door open enough to slide in and let it close behind me. The first, cursory glance of this office reminds me I'm in a mental institution and not a private office. The walls are muted gray to match the floors, and the lighting is harsh white, washing every ounce of color out. Degrees hang framed on the wall, along with his license. His desk is massive metal with the fake-wood covering plastered all over it. What catches my eye is that it is bolted to the floor.

Who would be strong enough to lift that?

"Can I help you?" The man sitting behind the desk turns his gaze to me and tilts his head to inspect me over the rim of his glasses.

I swallow nervously and clutch my clipboard for dear life.

Maybe the stilettos were a bad idea.

I resist the urge to smooth my skirt out in front of him. "Dr. Lamb?" I ask, concerned I'm in the wrong location. "I'm Hope-Marie Lacienda, your new resident."

His gaze starts at the top of my head and trails all the way down to my shiny black stilettos.

I'm used to the salivating stares of men from my days as a stripper, only he's not salivating.

My blood runs cold and I want to crawl into a hole to hide under scrutiny.

His mouth is turned down in a pensive frown, though it could be how his face is all the time. One brow slowly cocks when he reaches my shiny new shoes.

As much as I love my hair being down, I pulled it up high and wrapped it into a neat bun. I chose a simple long-sleeved silk blouse, black pencil-skirt to match, and my brand new, shiny black stilettos.

"I see," he says without any emotion. "The locker room is in the basement. See the nurse on shift, she will get you scrubs." He pauses and looks at my feet again. "And appropriate footwear." His gaze meets mine again. "Once you're ready, we'll start our rounds." When he finishes, he resumes working on the paperwork on his desk as if I had never interrupted him.

"Yes, Sir." I hurry out of there like the place is on fire, not stopping until I'm back at the reception desk. "How do I get to the basement locker room?"

"And you are?" The overweight, angry woman at the desk looks me over from head to toe. "Mrs. Lacienda. The new resident with Dr. Lamb."

"You got some ID, sweetie?"

I fish out my license and wait patiently.

She looks at me, looks at the license, looks at me again.

I smile, hoping this isn't the beginning of a battle of how I don't look like a doctor. I'm already furious at the prick from Columbia who didn't warn me of the dress code differing from in the packet he gave me. If I didn't need this residency I would give him a piece of my mind.

"You have to be escorted until you get your ID. Frank!" She shouts.

A massive man dressed in scrubs comes around the corner. "Yeah?"

"Escort Mrs. Lacienda here to the pit."

"Yes, Ma'am," he smiles at me, like a kid turned loose in a candy store.

"And keep your hands to yourself," she barks.

"You said she's a Missus. You know married women ain't my thing. C'mon, Mrs. Lasinda. We'll pick up some scrubs from laundry."

"Lacienda," I correct.

"Bless you," he says.

I laugh and shake my head. "Mrs. Lacienda. My name is La See Enda," I explain as we walk down the stairs hidden behind a door we have to be buzzed through to access.

He cocks an eyebrow and a lopsided grin forms on his face. "Yes, Ma'am."

We arrive in the appropriately named pit. This place feels like all the joy has been sucked out of existence. The walls are green instead of gray, casting a horror movie glow from the fluorescent bulbs hissing above.

Frank hands me standard blue scrubs, a pair of socks, and a pair of plain slip-on white tennis shoes without laces. "Women's locker room is over there. I'll wait out here for you. Don't be too long. I have rounds."

The dim lights and rusted lockers ratchet the horror movie vibe to eleven as I enter the locker room. I pick the best-looking one that doesn't have a lock on it and place my purse inside., followed by my clothes after I put on the uniform. Before I leave, I give myself a once-over in the mirror at the end of the row. "Ugh," I scoff.

All that effort for nothing. At least I can still wear make-up.

Frank leads me to a man named Al who happily takes my picture. "Haven't I seen you somewhere?" he asks as I stand in front of the baby-blue screen.

"Nope," I say with such conviction it leaves no room for him to think on the matter.

Al is definitely someone who would frequent the Oyster.

Since he doesn't immediately recognize me, I'm not offering anything up to him. I'm blinded by the camera flash.

"Hrmph. You must have one of those faces. You'll have to stay with someone for the day while they process this. I'll get it to Sheryl when it's ready."

"Sheryl?"

"Woman at the front desk."

"Ah, Thanks. How do I get back to Dr. Lamb's office?"

Al's face scrunches in displeasure at the mention of Dr. Lamb.

That kind of reaction triggers my curiosity. Since it's my first day and I don't want to be branded a gossip, I don't ask him his opinion of Dr. Lamb. I have a horrible feeling that Dr. Lamb is not a pleasant person to deal with. I follow Al back out of the pit to Sheryl's desk where she issues me a visitor's badge. My hand cramps at the novel I have to write just to get the temporary badge. I can't imagine which of my children they'll claim for the real one.

When I return to Dr. Lamb's office, he doesn't seem put-out at the time it took me to get ready. He gives me a cursory once-over and nods in approval. "That'll do. This way."

Shakes, Rattle, & Roll

Mac sits at the end of the bar, tapping his pen to the beat of the music.

Monday is payday, inventory, and rehearsals at Le Salon. If a girl wants to get off the pole and onto the stage, she has to put in the extra time. There isn't any overtime.

Mike, behind the bar, takes a bottle, puts it on the scale, and writes the weight. The steady clank of bottle in and bottle out is almost in time to the beat of the music. His body bops along as he works.

"So, why isn't HM here today?" Mike asks.

"Because she needed a day off from your ugly mug." Mac teases.

"That's what your wife said last night."

Mac cocks an eyebrow and grins. "Mhm-Hmm. You couldn't handle Sophia. She would break your scrawny ass in twain."

"Twain? Who the fuck uses twain?" Mike laughs as he continues working.

"I do. Especially when talking to dim-witted assholes like you."

"That's what your sister said."

"Delusions of grandeur."

"HM always says to dream big."

Mac laughs hard. "She sure does. You almost done?"

"You rush me, and I have to start over. She'll have my balls if I get it wrong again."

Mac shakes his head.

The door opens and flashes the white light of day into the dark club causing him to glance toward it. "Hey, Carrie," he smiles as he fishes out her paycheck. "Sign here."

"Where's HM?" she asks.

"Busy," he grumbles. "It's almost like you don't like me or something."

"Or something," Mike chuckles from behind the bar.

"It's weird. She's always here."

"Well, today she's not!" Mac growls.

"Jeez, Mac, who pissed in your cheerios?" Carrie pouts at him.

Mac rubs his hand over his face, realizing the lack of sleep makes him irritable. "No one. Here's your check." He watches her shapely ass as she struts back out of the club. If he weren't a married man, he would be in a lot of trouble.

Mike clanks down a soda in front of Mac. "On the house," he grins.

"Uh-huh." Mac shakes his head.

The door opens and closes again.

"Sorry, man. We're closed. Come back Wednesday." Mike rattles off like a robot.

Mac swings around to see who entered and eases off the barstool at the sight of the punks they threw out of the club at Hope-Marie's request. "Junior."

"Gringo. Where's your boss lady?"

"Doesn't matter, does it? We're closed. Get out of here." Mac motions to the door.

Junior clicks his tongue and gives Mac a devilish grin. "You see, Gringo. You ain't the one in charge. I need the person in charge. It seems you have a nasty problem."

"Yeah. You will too if you don't get your ass out of here. Club's closed."

Junior's eyes narrow and the three young men with him make all kinds of noise, "Oh, shit! Gringo's got balls. You said there was a hot fucking whore who ran this place. Not some old fucker."

Mac, who is broad-shouldered and tall, takes a moment to unbutton and remove his suit jacket, gently draping it over the back of the barstool. Scapelli men always dress to impress. He unbuttons his cuffs and rolls his sleeves up. "Gentlemen, I believe I told you the club is closed. Don't make me tell you again."

"Or what, Gringo? You think you can take all of us on?" The mouthy one flashes his shiny pistol tucked into his pants.

"No. All I have to do is beat the shit out of one of you until the cops get here to arrest you for trespassing."

Mike takes this cue to pick up the phone and dial.

Junior holds his hands up. "We're goin'. Remember, Gringo, you had the chance to play nice and pay your business taxes. It's not on my head what happens next. You tell your puta she has three days to bring her account in arrears. After that, who knows what happens?"

"Get the fuck out of here, kid, before I show you which one of us is the puta." Mac snorts.

Junior's jaw twitches.

His brother, the mouthy one, explodes and pulls his gun, keeping out of arm's reach of Mac and postures back and forth like an animal locked in a cage. "You're fuckin' lucky I don't cap your ass for what you did to my brother."

Mac crosses his arms and stands like a mountain between these boys and the stage behind him. This isn't the first time a gun has been waved in his face. Today won't be the last time, either.

Junior backhands his brother. "Shut the fuck up. We're out of here. Don't forget, Gringo. Three days." He waggles three fingers at Mac as the boys usher out of the club.

Mac stares at the door long after the boys have gone.

"We callin' HM?" Mike finally pipes up.

"Nope. She doesn't hear a word of this."

"But—."

"I got this. Not a word to her." Mac points at Mike.

By the time Dr. Lamb releases me, the sun is swathed in a hazy pink and orange as the Big Apple shifts from day to night. From the moment I returned to him, I don't think I sat down once.

We even grabbed lunch on the go.

From one patient to the next, he patiently met with, listened to, and observed each one of them. He answered my questions and grilled me like one of those terrible action film villains in the movies my sister makes.

My feet hurt. My legs hurt. My head hurts. I feel like death warmed over. As I pull into our parking spot at home, I rest my head on the steering wheel. My ears ring from the constant noise at the hospital. All I want to do is take a hot bath, and sleep for ten years.

I gather up the shopping bags from my only detour between the hospital and home. Tomorrow, I will be sporting new, pretty pink Adidas and have my own scrubs. I'm thankful there is no one in the elevator that requires my social skills. A tiny part of me hopes the kids are already in bed. As I step off the elevator, the streamers and balloons outside our door tells me the kids aren't asleep. I exhale roughly and put on the happy face because my children don't need to see their mother too tired to deal with them.

"I'm home," I call as I ease open the door.

"Happy Birfday!"

"Congrats!"

"MOMMY!"

Castian, Magellan, and Helena shout in unison, causing me to laugh.

Castian still thinks balloons mean birthday regardless of the actual celebration taking place, specifically *his* birthday.

I drop the bags in time to catch the running Helena.

Magellan smiles at me.

Castian teeters back and forth, covered in icing. "I get presents now?!"

"No, buddy. I told you. This is celebrating Mommy's first day, not your birthday."

"Okay. She gets presents?!" He hops like a bunny.

"How much sugar has he had?" I stage whisper.

"I licked the bowl!" Castian crows.

I raise a brow at Magellan, questioning his sanity in this decision of bowl-licking icing. I refuse to lose my cool over the madness of happiness being showered upon me.

That fool grins back at me as he leads me to the couch.

I plop down and am snuggled by both kids.

Magellan heads to the kitchen and I light up when I see the Budweiser in his hand upon return.

"It'll take me a few minutes to re-heat dinner for you." His words are clipped and don't match the smile on his face.

I did not even have a minute to stop and call him to tell him I would be late. My assumption of the day had been woefully wrong.

When he returns, he hands me the hot plate and takes the hyper children. "Bath time," he motions. "Mommy needs a timeout."

Both groan like he's killing them.

"Mommy just got here," Castian whines.

"Mommy day!" Helena pouts.

"Yes, she did and yes it is," he grins. "Still bath time," he says as he ushers them out of the room.

I scarf the food faster than the speed of light. I don't care what it is, even if it might be rock soup. It's hot, smells good, and fills my belly. The giggling and shouting from the bathroom makes me smile. After a healthy sip of my beer, I lean my head back and close my eyes.

"Come on, Princess. Let's get you to bed," Magellan says as he scoops me up.

I curl to him and inhale deeply, enjoying the scent of his cologne. "I'm sorry I was late. I didn't realize how long he would keep me," I mumble in my half awake state.

"Sounds like you had quite the day."

"He made me wear flats," I pout.

His body shakes against me as he struggles to repress his laugh.

"Uh-huh. At least you survived. Is it everything you hoped it would be?"

"No. It's way worse. I have to wear scrubs." My sleepy brain can't get past the superficial pieces that bother me about today.

This time he laughs "I think you need some sleep, Princess."

As exhausted as I am, I enjoy Magellan undressing me to put me to bed and snuggle to him when he joins me. "I'm not going to let that Dr. Lamb chase me off. I can still work even if I don't look pretty." I huff as I'm drifting back to sleep.

"You're beautiful in whatever you wear, even scrubs." He kisses my forehead before he turns out the light.

Reality Bites

My alarm beeps at me before the sun peeks over the horizon. I groan and smack it, rolling over to snuggle into Magellan's warmth. His hands slide over my hips and he pulls me close.

"If you keep wriggling, you're going to have *four* children," his husky voice chuckles into the darkness.

"Mrhm," I groan again and push away from him.

His laughter is rich as I stalk into the bathroom to start my day.

"I love you too, honey," he calls after me, still laughing.

I shower, moisturize, and put on foundation with some lipstick. I would never leave the house without having my face presentable. Nothing says I have to put on the church face for work. My hair is swept into a tight bun again, and I grudgingly put on the scrubs instead of the cute business attire I purchased.

"Awe, no more sexy librarian?" Magellan pouts at me.

"Shh," I jokingly chirp at him.

He lights up and hops out of the bed. "Okay. Number four here we go," he smirks as he stalks toward me, hands flexing like he's going to get me.

I squeal and hurry out of the room, shaking my head as I slip into the kitchen.

He's not far behind me and dances past me to put on the pot

of coffee. "How you like it," he grins as he sets down the cup of cream with two shots of coffee in it a few minutes later.

"Thanks."

"Knock 'em dead, hot stuff. Wait. That might be frowned upon. Break a leg? No. Still too rough."

I laugh as I kiss him to shut him up. He has no idea how happy I am to see him joking around like this, like he was before he was attacked. "Save the day?"

"Hmm. Nope. Can't do that. That's Mighty Mouse."

"Who?"

"Oh. Oh. We are definitely going to have to make you watch some Saturday morning cartoons." He turns me toward the door and slaps my ass. "Go earn me money."

My cheeks flame red and I snort my coffee at how crass he is. I'm definitely walking on air as I head to the car thanks to him.

"Good morning, Sheryl" I chirp as I walk by the receptionist when I get to Bellevue.

"What's so good about it?" she grumbles.

I pretend I don't hear her as I continue to Dr. Lamb's office.

I knock before entering, and he's already at his desk, working.

"You're here. Good. Let's get started." He stands and grabs his lab coat before ushering me back out the door.

I fall into step with him. "What time do you get here in the morning?"

"Starting time," he deadpans.

"And that time would be?" I roll my hand in front of me to indicate he needs to elaborate.

"Not relevant to you," he says as he pushes his glasses up his nose.

"I would say it is completely relevant to me, as I want to be here at starting time."

"Well, you are. Now that you're here, we can get started."

I feel like I'm playing the 'Why?' game with Castian. "That's very kind of you. If you're here at six. I'm here at six. If you're here at five. I'm here at five. Don't take it easy on me." I huff.

He pauses in our walk and raises a brow as he looks down at me. He ignores and dismisses my reply. "Our first patient today came to us last night. Attempted suicide. Age sixteen. Female.

Hispanic. No history of mental issues."

I scramble to fish out my notepad and take notes.

He checks the room before he unlocks the door, holding it for me.

She jerks against the restraints and shouts at us in Spanish. She's going fast enough I can't fully understand her.

Dr. Lamb moves further into the room, attempting to talk to her.

My head ping-pongs between the frantic girl and the cold, professional doctor.

"Please slow down, I don't understand you when you talk this fast," I say in Spanish. "If we cannot understand you, we can't help you."

The room goes quiet as Dr. Lamb takes his attention from the restrained girl to me.

The girl stops in her thrashing and wailing to stare at me as well.

I swallow hard and ignore him as I move closer to her bed. "Easy. Tell me what happened. We aren't here to hurt you." I continue in Spanish, taking the same tone I use on Castian when he has had a nightmare.

In short order, I learn that she's pregnant by a boy her father does not approve of, and that her father killed the boy. She, being the Juliet of this story, tried to kill herself as well.

I sigh and gently brush her hair from her face. "You need to relax. I need to talk with the doctor. Can you do that for me?"

She sniffles and nods.

I leave her at the bed and motion for the doctor to join me in the hallway.

Thankfully, he follows without a fight.

"She's pregnant. The father was murdered last night by her father."

"Hmm. Well, she's still being held on a psych watch. If she calms down, she'll be able to go home tomorrow."

I frown. "That won't help her. She tried to kill herself."

"How do you expect me to stop her from trying to kill herself in the future? If people are that determined, they will succeed regardless of what we do."

"We write her off because she's calm?" My voice raises with

my anger bubbling over.

"No. We give her as much comfort as we can while she's here. We're bound to return her to the world when done treating her."

"You think you can solve a teenage girl's broken heart in twenty-four hours?" I cross my arms and give him an incredulous look.

"Nope. That is not what I said."

"What you said is she's out if she's calm. Do you know how many women fake calm to get men to let them go?"

He raises his hand to attempt to de-escalate. "What I'm trying to say is that if she asks for help, I'll do what I can. Until then, we must move on to the next patient."

I open my mouth to retort, but he's already walking away.

I glance at the door to the room, then back at him walking away, and have to trot to keep up with him.

I stare daggers at him throughout the next evaluation, not paying attention at all to the patient, or his comments. This argument isn't over. We're here to help people and by God I'm not going to just process her through the system to be chewed up like a piece of bubble gum.

"What do you think of Mr. Robinson's symptoms," he asks me when we get in the hall again.

My cheeks flame red and I bite my lower lip as guilt washes over me. I was too upset from the first patient, I completely tuned out the second. My shoulders sag and I look down. "I'm sorry. I wasn't paying attention."

"I know. For the next patient," he says as he pulls out another file.

"No," I bark, harsher than I meant to. "You need to take care of the first patient before you move on. You're going through the motions and ticking the boxes on the paperwork."

His body stiffens, and his eyes narrow into razor lines as he stares at me.

If I could disappear into my scrubs, I would.

"Come with me," he growls as he turns on heel again and storms back to his office.

I march after him, rearing for the battle royale we're going to have.

*I'm defending the patients. He can't get rid of me for that...
Can he?*

I have only been here one day, but I'm not wrong. He's not helping that girl. I will face whatever wrath he might dish out, calling upon Giselle to keep me strong.

He stalks around his desk and tosses the stack of papers onto it. Then he plants his hands firmly on it, palms down. "Hope-Marie, we need to get one thing straight. I care for every patient that comes through my door. No ifs. No ands. No buts. I'll help every patient I can help. You need to understand I can only help those patients who let me."

"You literally talked over her in English when she obviously was not comprehending what you said. How is that helping? Where the fuck was the interpreter for her?"

"She's a teenager, living in New York. Of course she understands English."

"What if she's an immigrant who hasn't been here long enough to understand English?" I cross my arms and huff.

He sifts through the folder and flips open the file for the girl and reads, "Born Syracuse, New York. Attends public school and is an honors student. Knowing that, you're telling me she doesn't understand English? It takes two hours to get an interpreter here *if* they even come. We're not exactly the Ritz."

My cheeks flame again as I had not yet seen the file. I was more concerned with calming the girl down than reading the file. My work instincts to control the room kicked in. "Oh," I mutter as my anger deflates.

"What I'm trying to say is we have to use the information we're given and have to talk with the patient. If they are not willing to work with us, what we can do is limited. We're handcuffed to only treating those who are a threat to themselves, to others, or who ask for treatment. The reason she was even brought here is she was a threat to herself and was under observation. We were there to follow-up and see if she calmed to the point we could assess her further. You calmed her, which is a good first step. Questioning my motives is unacceptable."

"Yes, Sir," I murmur. This feels more like a trip to the principal's office than a discussion on the best way to treat a patient.

"Furthermore," he thumps the stack of files. "We have fourteen new patients we have to see today in addition to the patients we saw yesterday. Yes, I could spend all day with one patient and work through her problems until she's golden. Then what happens to the rest of them? Don't they deserve the opportunity for me to help them as well?" His chest rises and falls with his angry breathing. His hands curl into fists like he's resisting the urge to flip the desk.

I don't answer immediately, as my knee-jerk response is to cow down and accept his authority. I don't agree with this method. It's madness to think anyone is getting helped like this. My face scrunches as I struggle to form a response. "This isn't right," I finally say, sounding like a child.

"You are absolutely correct. It's not. Unfortunately, this is reality. We are a public hospital. We treat the public when they are at their worst and pull them back from the edge. That's our job. If they need more help, we have to commit them, which creates an entirely different world of problems. Or, they have to find someone in private practice who can treat them. We are not the solution, Hope-Marie. We are the hand that reaches out to them. Sadly, we cannot be the one who stays by their side as they heal."

My lip juts out in a pout as I never thought I would be the one who gets a harsh dose of reality. Everything has always fallen into place for me and I don't like not getting my way. My chest hurts from every muscle being tense in defending the way the world should be against this vile knight of reality. My breathing is hard, like a dragon ready to breathe fire. "Then we should get back to work," I say through gritted teeth.

"Yes, we should." He snatches up the pile and stalks back out of his office, roughly thumping the next file into my chest as he passes. "Read it to me as we walk."

The Devil Came Down To Brooklyn

The rest of my day at Bellevue goes without incident. I even remember to call Magellan and tell him I have to stop by the club to pick up the scheduling paperwork over lunch. He requested I pick up pizza as my punishment.

I never noticed how creepy the clubs are when the lights are off and no one's around. Everyone went home at least an hour ago, and I'm only here as long as it takes to get the paperwork to make next month's schedule. I get my keys in hand before I get out of the car, using the light from the car to see.

Like a small child afraid the monster in the closet is going to leap out and eat them, I race to the door and unlock it in no time flat. I slam it behind me, then lock it. I flip on every single interior light as I make my way to the stairs up to my office. My office door being open and the light left on is common. With Mac and Harold, I'm lucky our electric bills aren't in the millions.

I barrel through the door and move to my desk without going around it. The schedule requests are in a folder on the tray and the schedule sheet is on top of that. I take the inventory book and flip it around to take a quick glance. Mac would let me know if something is amiss and I trust him. I still have to check.

My office door slams shut, causing me to scream like every horror movie heroine in existence. I follow my scream by throwing the inventory book at the door over my shoulder, without even looking, and leap over my desk to crouch behind it, hoping whatever slammed my door won't find me here.

Laughter fills my office in response.

My heart thunders in my chest. Every muscle screams in response to flight or fight. I force myself to ease up and gopher-peek over the edge of my desk.

Across the room, leaning against the door, is a tall, slender man. His suit shimmers with the light. Mirth dances across his handsome face. He has dark hair, dark eyes, and a neatly trimmed mustache and beard kiss his jaw. Tattoos peek-a-boo out from under his clothes, snaking up his neck.

I swallow hard as I slowly stand.

"You don't look like an expensive whore," his heavily accented voice cuts through the laughter. "Who are you, Señora?"

What does he mean by "look" like an expensive whore?

My back straightens, and any fear I had is replaced with righteous indignation at my looks being questioned. "That's my line. Who the fuck are you?"

Mirth vanishes from his face as I bark at him. "I see why he likes you."

"Didn't answer my question, pal. Who the fuck are you? How did you get in here?" I clench my fists, gearing up to throw a proper tantrum.

"You may call me El Diablo."

I snort. "You're hardly the devil."

While he smiles at me, it doesn't reach his eyes. This man's a predator and he knows it. His cold and uncaring gaze makes my blood run cold. "Not important. What is important is whether you're the expensive whore."

"I'm not a fucking whore, you prick! That's it. I'm calling the cops." I reach for the phone.

"By the time they get here, you'll be dead and I'll be gone." He tilts his head, staring at me still. "It would be a shame to leave those three angels without their mother. Especially when all I want to do is talk."

My hand stills, and I stare back at him, measuring his threat. I'm in no state to deal with this after the day I have had. My finger hovers over the nine long enough the phone begins to make its angry noise of being left off the receiver too long. If I'm wrong and can't fend him off, making the phone call won't matter. Anger fills me again and I slam the receiver down. "Fine. What the fuck do you want, devil?"

"Nothing much. I came to collect my product."

"Your product?" I blink as I struggle to understand what he refers to.

"Yes. I believe you called it..." He pauses as if he's searching for the right words. "A business tax."

His words are like ice flowing through my veins. Junior said they are Los Diablos, and he calls himself El Diablo. I square my shoulders, leaning into Giselle. If I don't, all I'm going to do is break down and cry. If Giselle could handle Big Tony, this guy is a cakewalk. "The tax was paid. I told him he was lucky that was all I did. You want your product? Take it up with the New York City Water Board. Get the fuck out."

"Hrm," he hums as he cocks his head. "You owe me twenty-five thousand dollars."

"Listen, Mr. Devil. I don't owe you shit. Your little monsters have been terrorizing my club, costing me thousands in clients, and drinks. I had to hire all new staff because of their shit. This is *my* club, and they lost your product because of their stupidity. You want your money? You get it from them."

"Are you sure of those facts, Mrs. Lacienda? Last I checked, you were a floundering wanna-be bar until my boys set up shop. They brought the business that pays your bills. They filled your tables. They paid and drank your alcohol. One could say they are partners in your success."

Fuck him and this bullshit.

The more he talks the faster my blood thaws to a boil. I open and close my fists, wishing I had my riding crop to wipe the smug smile off his face. I could murder Mac all over again for letting those parasites latch onto us to begin with. "I don't care if I never have another customer. I'll not turn this club into a brothel for you to launder your drugs through. I worked too fucking hard to get here to have some snake charmer try to steal my club from me."

"Then I would strongly suggest you pay your tab." He pushes

off the door and opens it.

"You can take your fucking tab and shove it where the sun doesn't shine. If I see you anywhere near my club, I won't hesitate to report all of you."

He pauses and looks over his shoulder while still holding the door. "You needn't worry. If you refuse to pay your tab, the next time you see me will be your last, I promise." He pulls the door closed behind him.

My mouth hangs open, shocked he would blatantly threaten me. The hum of the lights is deafening, as is the thump of my heart in my chest. Tears flow down my cheeks and I slump into my chair. My hands won't stop shaking and my heart won't slow down. I can't catch my breath. The wailing banshee cry that follows makes my ears ring and I hug myself.

This must be how Magellan felt at the café.

I can never tell Magellan this happened. We promised to not keep secrets from each other, but how am I supposed to tell him what's going on without causing him to relive his own trauma?

What if I do tell him and he freaks out...and hurts me?

He can't protect me from these devils and would die trying. I made this mess. I have to clean it up. I cry until it hurts. Then I clean myself up in the bathroom attached to my office. The cold water splashing against my flush skin helps to soothe my raw nerves. With a glance at the clock, it has been an hour since I got off work.

I take the time to gather up the inventory book and put it back together before I sit back down at my desk. My eyes fall on the photos of my beautiful family; the photo of us at our wedding reception, stuffing cookies in each other's mouths, Castian roaring like a lion at the playground, my sweet Helena staring wide-eyed up at me and a tiny picture of my little angel at the hospital after he was born.

Do I take the easy path and run?

Pack everything we own and get the fuck out of New York City, leaving everyone behind, tucking tail, and go home to mom and dad? They would welcome us with open arms, and we would live like kings on my royalties.

We would be safe.

Or do I take the path less traveled and fight?

Stand up against the devil himself and stake my claim in this world.

I slump in my chair and rest my chin on my hand while I debate the pros and cons of each choice. Helplessness is all I feel the longer I sit here.

What is the point of knowing people if I can't use them to protect everything I have worked for?

My instinct is to call Harold and tell him everything. He will know exactly what to do. I fear his answer is to pay the devil his due. He would save the day and stall the devil. At least until El Diablo wants more.

Do I turn to Scapelli Senior, who promised to always help? That would be trading one devil for another. Stella told me exactly what Harold had to do to get out from under Scapelli's control. To throw away all of Harold and Stella's sacrifices by hiding under Scapelli's umbrella from this storm would betray my closest friends.

I'm a God damn Wolfe and no fucking devil is going to move in on my territory.

"Awoo," I bark at myself. My resolve is ironclad, and my path is clear.

When I pick up the phone, I dial Mac's number. He made this mess for me. He's going to help clean it up.

"Hello," Sophia answers.

"Hi, Sophie. It's Hope-Marie. Can I talk to Mac?"

"Sure, sweetie. Mac. It's for you."

"Hello?" Mac's deep voice is soothing to my battered nerves.

"We need to up security. I want cameras, and all the locks changed. Only use people you absolutely trust."

"What happened?" he growls?

"The devil came knocking." I hang up the phone, grab my things, and hightail it to the pizza joint Mick loves.

You Are My Mistress

Friday Night (Three Days Later)

Devon kneels in the center of the salon, naked. He holds a piece of paper in his hands and can barely contain his excitement.

I'm furrowing my brow, trying to figure out what he's up to. Devon has been increasing his sessions until he is here every day. I'm concerned he is growing attached in a way that is not healthy for him. With everything else going on, I've let it slide. He's throwing money we desperately need for the club.

El Diablo is right. The business is hurting without the boys drawing in the crowd.

"What is zhis?" I tap the paper with my riding crop.

"It's my resumé!" His smile is jubilant as he offers it up to me.

"Why did you bring me your resumé?" I ask as I circle him.

"Because I'm your submissive." He shudders from me lazily trailing the riding crop over his bare skin.

"Oui, zhis does not require a resumé."

"Oh, I know! The resumé is a formality. I understand you have to make it appear fair on paper." He winks at me.

We're definitely performing our own "Who's on first" skit at this point. I can't shake the feeling I'm missing something and the pit of my stomach knots in foreboding dread.

"Devon, are you applying for a job here?"

"Well, I already have the job. Like I said this is a formality. I understand having to file paperwork."

"I have not hired you."

"You haven't?" The crestfallen looks on his face is exaggerated, and I have to look away to keep from laughing.

"Why do you think I'm hiring?"

"I heard Mac say he's planning on putting the ad in the paper. I thought I would save you the trouble. I can start today if it pleases you."

I can't decide if I want to laugh, cry, or scream at Devon. This situation has gone completely off the rails. I didn't authorize hiring any people, especially not subs. We can't afford more staff.

"Devon, I'm not hiring anyone."

"Mac was quite adamant on the matter," he whines, sounding more like a child.

I could shut Devon down completely and send him packing. It would crush him as he does not handle rejection well. The sense of dread is making me sick to my stomach as I'm worried Devon has done something drastic and thrown all his eggs into the Le Salon basket. "Devon, zhis is an interview. Interviews are done while dressed."

"Yes, Mistress." He lights up and springs to his feet to hurry to his suit.

While he dresses, I knock on the door.

"Yes, ma'am?," Mac asks as he pops his head into the salon.

"Could you come in here, please?" I try to keep my voice even when what I really want to do is scream at Mac for making decisions for me again.

"Everything good?" Confusion and doubt wash over Mac's face that Devon would need to be handled.

"Just come in here." I snap as I turn back into the room. I pass by Devon, step behind the screen, and pull on a robe. Unfastening the mask, I leave it on the table. If we're truly interviewing Devon, he needs to understand Giselle is an act.

"Take a seat, Devon," I motion to the chaise.

"Oh, your American accent is superb." He smiles at me.

I cut Mac a dirty look.

He shrugs his shoulders, looking as confused as I am.

I offer my hand to Devon to shake. "Devon, I'm Hope-Marie Lacienda, the owner of Le Salon."

Devon's face is a whirlwind of emotions as he processes the revelation that Mistress Giselle is only an act. His cheeks flush red with embarrassment, shoulders square, jaw tightens, and any hints of the bubbly submissive I've come to enjoy, disappears. "Oh," he says as he takes my hand, shaking it with a firm grip.

I release his hand and motion for him to sit. I'm sweating nervously and fuss with my robe more than is necessary. Fear is threatening to bubble to the surface that I might be ruining everything with our best client.

Mac's quick to understand what is happening and grabs chairs for the two of us.

While I want to dismiss this entire scenario, the idea of having another person isn't out of the realm of possibility. We can't afford Devon, especially without his generous sponsorship.

"Mac, since you posted this job offering, would you like to get us started?"

"What job offering?"

Devon cuts in, "The position of her submissive that you were discussing with Master Lewis." Devon's tone is all business and cold.

I glance at his resumé and both my eyebrows shoot up. He's the Chief Marketing Officer for a pharmaceutical company. There's no way in hell I could afford to pay him what he currently makes. I can barely afford to pay myself.

"I didn't post a position for a submissive yet." Mac confirms my suspicion.

"Well, obviously you have, or Devon would not be applying, now would he?" I try to give Mac the meanest face I can muster without airing our dirty laundry in front of Devon. This is exactly why I told Mac he needed to stop talking shop on the main floor where guests can hear.

"The conversation he's referring to was a discussion, at best. We were thinking another person in the room with the doms would be a good idea." He then adds, "For security purposes. I was going to bring it up with you on Monday when we go over all the other security measures you asked for."

"What kind of threat are you under?" Devon cuts in.

I rub my temples as I struggle to view Devon as anything other than a sub; even if I already knew he was not submissive outside of our sessions. I can't be angry with Mac for doing what I asked of him. I can be angry with Devon for eavesdropping.

This is the worst interview ever.

I decide to lay the cards on the table. Devon will see this place is too dangerous for him, and we can go back to normal. "I'm being threatened by a local gang who wants me to pay them protection money and let them sell drugs in the club."

Devon crosses his arms and leans back in the seat. The man is oozing power and confidence. "Then my decision to join you is the correct one."

"Devon. I can't... This isn't your fight. I can't guarantee your safety, or pay you what you're worth." I'm gobsmacked by the finality in his voice. I can't decide if I like the eager puppy of a submissive, or the ruthless businessman more.

He looks me square in the eyes and nods. "I know. You are my Mistress. It's my duty to protect you. I'll see you tomorrow for orientation." He stands to walk out.

"Devon, sit back down," I order. "There's more."

He complies.

I resist the urge to laugh again. The juxtaposition of his submissiveness to his business mind is fascinating, but I'm the one in charge here, and he'll need to understand that before I fully agree to hire him. "I'm only your Mistress when in the club. I'm married, with three children. Outside of this salon, I'm Hope-Marie, and your employer, not your Mistress. Are you able to handle that?"

"Hope-Marie, what you've done for me over these past few months is indescribable. If I get the chance to pay you back even a fraction of that kindness, then I'm yours. I understand you're a happily married woman."

I instinctively reach for my left hand. I don't wear my wedding rings while in session.

"It's obvious your wear rings," he chastises me, giving me his boyish grin. "What I'm trying to say is I understand you have a life outside of this club. My confusion came from discovering you're not French. You are quite convincing." He sighs. "Listen. You're in trouble and I can help. I understand I'm going to make a pittance and won't be insured."

"We offer benefits," I say with a huff.

"That's actually more than I expected." He grows quiet, his brows drawn together in thought.

I glance at Mac to see how he reacts to this weird interview.

He shakes his head with a shrug, being no help at all.

Devon's face wrinkles as if his thinking process is hurting him. "You can't hire me." He blurts.

I purse my lips, confused. "You said..."

"I did. You can't afford to lose me as a customer." He waves his hand dismissively.

The shade of red staining my cheeks rivals the red leather heart on my chastity belt, embarrassed that he put all of it together this fast.

"I would like to make a counter proposal." He reaches over and takes the resumé out of my hand. "What if I buy in as a silent partner?"

Mac snorts and quickly regains himself when I cut him a dirty glare.

Harold and I briefly talked about seeking a third partner with bigger pockets than us. Tears well in my eyes at the godsend that is Devon Wilcox. "Oh Devon," I pause to get my emotions under control. "If you're truly interested, you need to meet with my business partner first."

"Of course I'm interested. I wouldn't have left my position otherwise."

"What?!" I gasp. "Devon Wilcox, you did not?"

Mac snorts with trying to keep his laughter in check.

Devon gives me another boyish grin. "Well, Mrs. Lacienda, what's done is done. You said there's another person I need to meet?"

I blink, stunned. A tiny part of me wants to take a riding crop to his ass until he relents and gets his position back. A large part of me is counting my blessings that he wants to be my submissive in shining latex.

Mac wipes the tears from his eyes, still chuckling. "I swear to God, HM, you're the luckiest damn woman I've ever met." He shakes his head as he stands. "I need to get back to work, Ma'am."

I nod, still flabbergasted at Devon. "Well, come on then." I lead Devon from my salon through the dark corridor that leads into the Oyster.

We pass the stage with the girls dancing on it.

Devon tries to hide his ogling of the strippers but stumbles more than once.

I chuckle and rest my hand on the small of his back. "Zhis way. Zhey will be there when we finish zhis meeting."

We trudge up the stairs and down the narrow hallway like the following-the-leader montage in Peter Pan. Finally arriving at Harold's office, I open the door and motion for Devon to enter without bothering to knock. Closing it behind us, I turn to face Harold, who's raising a brow at the intrusion.

"Harold, meet Devon Wilcox. Devon, meet Harold Rittendorf, my business partner."

Trouble With A Capital T

"Gentlemen, I need to bow out. I have another client." I retreat backwards to the door.

The three of us have been talking for several minutes and I need to prepare before my next client.

"You can't leave, we're negotiating," Harold whines.

"Harold. You have always done right by me, and I trust Devon as well. You two haggle it out and I'll sign it."

Harold huffs and points at me. "You are way too trusting with your money, you know that?"

Devon chimes in, "Agreed. You should stay." He shifts his weight like I took a riding crop to his ass and the sting lingers.

I rub my hand over my face. "Well, Harold, unless you know of someone else who can do my job we will lose even more of that money you say I'm not safe enough with. This is a Pony Package client."

"Wait! You actually sold one of those?" Harold dramatically shudders and looks at me with a comically false surprised look. After Tony Scapelli, Harold dam well knows men will pay for anything.

"Yes, and this is his second session. I'm leaving." I wave over my shoulder as I'm heading out of the office. "Good evening, gentlemen."

Devon asks Harold, "Is she always like this?" Then the door clicks closed.

When I get back to my office I pour a stiff drink. I can't believe how lucky I am, even if I think Devon is making a huge mistake.

It's his mistake to make.

Dr. Lamb's voice echoes in my head.

I'm exhausted. I worked a full eight hours at Bellevue today, and didn't even have time to go home before I had to come here to entertain clients. I'm pulling on a different mask when I hear my office door open.

"What in the hell were you thinking letting that fuck book another session?" Mac's anger boomerangs off the walls as he shouts at me.

"Because he's a paying client." I finish tying the mask in place.

"HM, this is too dangerous. He could hurt you." Mac crosses his arms and puffs up to block the entire doorway. He looks as if he might body check me should I try to leave.

"No, he can't. He's wearing hooves for most of the session, Mac." I cock my hip as I brandish the riding crop at him.

"And the parts where he's not dressed up? You were afraid of him last time. I saw how you danced away when you released him. For fuck's sake, you made me watch him crawl his naked ass across the room to kiss your fucking heart!"

"Well, he didn't know then what he was paying for. The fact he paid for the package a second time means he liked it. You don't accidentally pay for the Pony Package twice."

"No, Hope-Marie. Especially not after the boss man of that prick showed up. How do you know it's not a setup to collect what they think you owe?"

"Really, Mac? Do you think this kid would drop fifty thousand dollars to get twenty-five?" I rest my hand on my hip.

Mac's chest puffs in and out as he struggles with my matter-of-fact responses. "How the fuck am I supposed to protect you when you take risks like this?"

"You can pat him down for weapons before he goes in. You'll be outside the door, like last time. I promise it will be fine. First sign of trouble and I swear I'll call for you."

Mac grunts. "I don't like this. You're playing fast and loose with the cartel. Someday, your luck will run out." He brandishes a finger at me, like a father scolding his daughter.

"Not today," I coo. I'm channeling Giselle already and I can't let Mac rattle my cage. I pat his chest as I wiggle past him.

We head downstairs.

Lou comes rushing up, "There's a problem in the kitchen."

"Then deal with it," Mac snarls.

Lou looks from Mac, to me, sucks in his lower lip and looks back to Mac. "Pauly said if I didn't come back with you, he'd knock my teeth out."

"Go already," I wave him off.

Mac inhales sharply and narrows his eyes at me. "Don't you dare start that fucking session until I get back." He relents and follows Lou.

My salon is quiet when I enter. I don't see Junior anywhere. If he were waiting, I would have stepped back out and waited for Mac. Since I have a few minutes to myself, I untie my robe and head for my screened off area.

A hand covers my mouth and something hard jams into my side.

My scream is muffled by the hand over my mouth. I jerk my body to free myself and the hand tightens its grip on me. Panic rushes through me like a tidal wave as the conversation Mac and I had a few minutes ago plays over in my mind.

"You're mine now, puta." Junior hisses in my ear. "Be a good girl and I'll go easy on you."

I open my mouth to bite his hand.

He pulls the hammer back, the click sounding like a clap of thunder in my quiet salon.

All struggling ceases.

"Good puta. Put on the gag," he slowly pulls his hand from my mouth to motion to the ball gag on the table.

With my luck, I will end up scarred for life if I scream, which would be far worse than being killed in my mind. My hands tremble as I pick up the gag. As afraid as I am, I believe he can't rape me because of the chastity belt built into my costume.

Magellan insisted it be part of my costume, permanently. He doesn't care if I only flaunt the goods. To him, it's a weird power trip of showing off something he "owns" and they can't have.

I obediently put the gag in my mouth and fasten it around my head.

As soon as I finish, he slaps a handcuff on my left wrist and twists my arm around behind me hard enough force me to arch my back.

I whimper in pain; afraid he's going to break my arm. The gun leaves my side and I reach up and claw with my free hand only to have it caught in his.

"Tsk. Tsk. Oh, Señora, you are being naughty," as he jerks my other hand around to handcuff my hands together. He shoves me and smirks as he commands, "To the center of the room."

When I don't crash to the floor from stumbling, I contemplate bolting for the door.

He flashes his gun again.

I stop in the center of my salon, trembling. My heart hammers in my chest, and tears well in my eyes. It's hard to breathe with the ball gag stuffing my mouth.

The rigging hisses along its oiled track, like a basilisk slithering towards its prey.

He jerks my cuffed hands back to hook them.

I'm forced onto my toes, bent over like I did to him during our first session when he presses the crank button.

He walks around to face me, grinning down at my prone position. "Are you ready to pay your taxes?"

As afraid as I am, I shake my head no. My father would say I'm being a hard-headed Deutsch and should have never gotten myself into this position to begin with.

"Oh, brave, Señora. My father expected no less, and he told me that if you're not willing to pay in cash, I'm to take alternative payments." He reaches into his pocket and pulls out a switchblade. He rests his hand on my shoulder after he moves behind me.

The sting of the tip of the blade makes me wince he cuts my corset ties one by one.

With the last tie cut, he shoves his hands out from my spine, sending the corset fluttering to the floor. His body presses against my ass, and his raging hard-on makes me sick to my stomach. The scent of his cologne burns my nostrils as he leans his weight on me to reach around and squeeze my breasts. "Awe, Señora Lacienda, you're so soft. I can't wait to feel that tight pussy around my cock."

I close my eyes and bite against the gag to keep from reacting to anything he does to me. From my education, rapists get off on causing their victims turmoil, as much as the sexual act itself. If ever there was a time I believed in telepathy, it was this moment, as I try to summon Mac to come rescue me. Tears stream down my cheeks, uncontrolled. Junior's going to penetrate me and Magellan will leave me because I broke his one rule. I'll be a whore for these monsters to play with. Try as I might, the thought of losing Magellan causes me to sob.

"Don't cry, puta. You'll like it." Junior coos as he tugs at my chastity belt. "What the fuck is this shit?"

I yelp when the knife bites into my ass to cut the belt loose. Eventually, the leather gives way, fully exposing me to him. I'm trembling as I hang from my wrists. My arms burn from the angle and weight. Vulnerable and exposed, my skin crawls with goose flesh. My fear grows when he stops touching me and moves out of my line of sight.

His fingers touch against the cut he created on my ass

I yelp against the gag and close my legs as tight as possible.

His fingers slide down my cheek until he traces them around my asshole.

I clench and squirm away, despite not wanting to give him a response.

He whispers in my ear, "I have heard stories, my puta. That this little toy has a very special meaning to you." He brandishes the riding crop before he cracks it against a breast.

I scream against the gag.

Quickly, he follows the first strike with another.

I jerk and twitch, trying to escape his stinging slaps with the riding crop until I'm panting, hanging from the hook, and he's behind me.

He happily slaps my ass cheeks until they burn. Then, to my horror, he's spreading my cheeks and kicking my feet apart. "I hear, my puta, karma's a bitch. Scream pretty for me."

"Giselle, did that boy ever—."

Mac's voice has never sounded sweeter to me.

"What the fuck?" He roars.

Time slows as both men jump into action.

Junior goes for the gun.

Mac snatches the cat-o-nine-tails off the table and cracks it against Junior.

Junior hits the floor, rolls, and bounces to his feet.

Mac lunges for him, trying to get him in a bear hug.

Junior bolts for the door like a third-base runner stealing home plate.

"Fuck!" Mac chases after Junior.

I'm left hanging in the center of my salon. Relief at being rescued is enough to help calm my nerves. Without the constant threat of Junior assaulting me, I manage to get my toes barely touching the ground to ease the numbness forming in my hands.

"Easy, HM. It's me," Mac's voice is reverent and soft as he approaches me and rests a hand on my back. "I got you. You're safe." He lowers the hook and puts an arm around me to hold me up while he unhooks me. Then he releases the ball gag and fishes out his keys to uncuff me. These aren't cuffs from my collection, all of mine have safety releases. Mac scoops me up and carries me behind the screen.

I tense and whimper. My brain and body aren't firing on the same cylinders and the unknown is causing fear to win over rational thought, and me to struggle against his hold.

"Easy. We need to get you cleaned up. I got you." He repeats as he sweeps my personal table, scattering my things to the floor. He gently lays me on the table. "Get me a first aid kit," he barks over his shoulder.

I close my eyes and bury my face into my arms, embarrassed and ashamed. I can't stop shaking and I'm crying hard enough it's shaking my whole body.

Mac's hand gently pets me as he keeps repeating, "We got you. You're safe."

All For One

Mac carries me to my office and leaves me with a glass of whiskey.

I sit in the dim light and sip the alcohol. The further away from the incident the less afraid I am and the angrier I get. To them I'm some whore they can fuck with. I'll be damned if I let them turn me into the damsel in distress.

This is the last straw. Fuck these assholes. This is MY club.

When Mac doesn't immediately return, I worry that further incidents are taking place in my club. My mind conjures shootouts in the cabaret, followed by screaming strippers and dancers running like a stampede of wild animals.

That fear is dashed when Harold, Devon, and Mac come storming in like the three musketeers.

Mac's jaw twitches like a bird on a wire.

Harold's eyes are shifty, and he keeps fidgeting with his tie, the same anxious expression he had the night Mistress Giselle was born.

Devon is the most composed of the three. He can't take his eyes off me, and his handsome face is drawn into a small frown.

I changed into my street clothes once Mac got me back to my office. They're a far cry from the corset and chastity belt Devon is used to seeing.

Mac closes the door behind him and the men shuffle to make room for each other in my tiny office.

I cling to my glass for dear life, not wanting to show my hands are still shaking.

"Why can't we call the cops?" Devon asks.

"Because cops only make shit worse," Mac replies.

"We should call them," Harold says with a frown as he stares at me.

"And tell them what? A guy came to a sex club and got handsy with a girl?" I retort.

"BDSM club," Harold says in defense of Le Salon.

I snort at him correcting me on the type of club I own. "There's no proof it wasn't consensual. It's my word against his. Who knows, maybe I like getting cut up while having sex?"

"Do you?" Devon's eyes grow wide.

The man has no limits when it comes to him being dominated, but the idea of me liking it rough surprises him?

The room goes silent and the other two stare at him like he grew a second head.

"I was being sarcastic, Devon." I take another sip.

"Whew. I was worried." He plops down on my couch. "Still. We should report it in case they come back."

"They're definitely coming back," I mutter.

"Why would you say that?" Harold asks.

"They want twenty-five thousand," I reply.

"For what?" Harold runs his fingers through his hair, causing his hair to stick out like a mad scientist.

"She flushed their drugs." Mac rats me out.

Harold dramatically flops down next to Devon and groans. "Fuck. Pay them and be done with this shit."

"No!" I slap my hand on the desk for emphasis. "It's twenty-five today. Another ten next week. Then it's let us sell in your club. Oh, and your girls will entertain guests. Then we're a fucking brothel."

"You're not wrong," Harold confesses.

"I guess this is the threat." Devon pipes up.

"One and the same," Mac confirms.

"Devon. If you want to walk away, now is the time to do it." I level my gaze on him and hold my breath.

Please don't abandon us. Please don't abandon us.

"What? And leave you to the wolves?" Devon's face blanches, and he huffs, puffing out his chest.

I laugh hard enough tears come to my eyes.

Devon frowns.

Harold joins in with the laughter, and even Mac has a smile on his face.

"Is somebody going to tell me what's funny?" Devon asks.

"Awoo!" All three of us crow.

"Wait! When did I become D'Artagnan? I always thought of myself as Aramis," Devon mumbles as she sulks.

I wipe the tears from my eyes. "My maiden name is Wolfe, Devon."

His pouty lips give him a much younger look than he is. "You know I don't like being left out. What's the Awoo thing?"

Mac, who is still chuckling. "Try it."

"Awoo?" Devon asks, his voice timid, like a child testing out a curse word.

"Awoo!" I call back firmly. I breathe deeply and close my eyes briefly, enjoying the flooding warmth the whiskey is giving me. "I needed that," I down the rest of my drink and lean forward.

"The cops won't help and calling them only puts a bigger target on my back," I say, much calmer.

"Then pay the man, and be done with it," Harold suggests.

"We're past that. We're at pay for the product, pay for wasting his time, then pay to keep him off our backs. You got that kind of cash lying around, Harold?"

"No. D'Artagnan here does, though." Harold flashes a grin.

"I'm not D'Artagnan! She can't even be a Musketeer, she's a girl!" Devon protests.

I laugh again. Devon is the most adorable man when he pouts like this. I must be in shock as everything is inappropriately funny to me. Getting myself under control, I finally say, "I'm not going to cave to these men. We've worked too hard for too long to roll over and be their bitch. I didn't cave to Tony. I'm not caving to an arrogant prick who calls himself the Devil."

"Wait. You're in shit with Los Diablos?" Harold asks. He cuts Mac an angry, accusatory look. His posture shifts from concerned friend to mafioso instantly as he rights his suit, sits up straight and rights his frazzled looking hair. He claims he's out of the life. The way he reacts to this news says otherwise. "Why the fuck didn't you tell me?"

"I don't work for you, Harold. She's the boss." Mac crosses his arms and nods towards me.

I drum my fingers lightly on the desk. While this conversation has some brevity to it, the problem of Los Diablos still looms over us. I can't ask these three men to put their necks on the line for me. I may have to ask Magellan for the money and that makes me sick to my stomach. I'm getting tired of being pushed around by all these men.

"This is my fucking club and my fucking territory." I don't realize I said it aloud until the three men turn to face me.

"That's how you want to play it?" Harold breaks the silence.

"It's the only way we stay free of someone else's control."

"Well, not the only way? We could close up shop, and scatter to the wind." He offers a lopsided grin.

"Yeah, right. Harold Rittendorf isn't going to protect his girls?" I lean forward in my chair and rest my arms on my desk, staring at him.

"You always knew you were his favorite," Stella chimes in as she comes into the office.

"No. That's fucking bullshit. Too many people depend on these jobs. We're fucking helping people. Prime example," I say as I motion to Devon.

"Wait. I was perfectly good before I came here." He holds his hands up, trying to appear innocent.

"Were you, really? From what you said, you couldn't get what you needed anywhere. That's not the point, anyway. The point is. If we don't make a stand, they're going to bulldoze their way in and ruin everything. You want to be like every other fucking strip joint, Harold? Going to give up your modeling gigs? The cabaret? How do you plan to put your kids through college with no income? Are you going back to work for Scapelli?"

"She has a point," Stella frowns as she stands alongside Harold. Her hand rests on his shoulder in a small gesture that visibly relaxes Harold.

"Fine. Let me make a few calls. We need more people if we're doing this." Harold grouses.

"No. I'm head of security," Mac says and puts a hand on Harold's chest to stop him.

"Yeah. And you did such a bang-up job today." Harold snipes.

Both of my brows raise in surprise as Harold and Mac have been friends a long time. To see them standing toe to toe, throwing jabs at each other worries me.

"I know a guy. Owes me a favor. Head of a security firm. I can get you the guys you need. Let me make the call." Harold shoves Mac's hand off his chest.

Mac's shoulders hunch as he tenses and his ears burn red. He breathes hard through his nose, and his free hand curls into a fist.

"Make the call, Harold." I say.

Harold nods and bolts from the office before I change my mind.

I avoid Mac's hurt look as I point at Devon. "Go home."

"I..." He opens his mouth to offer what he can do, deflates, then perks up again, revealing the eagerness to be a part of the club.

"You're a silent partner, there's nothing else you can do tonight to help me, and you have to be here in the afternoon for orientation. Go home." I use my Mistress voice to command him.

Devon shifts his weight. The glint in his eyes and the faint smile ghosting his lips reveals he weighs disobedience versus compliance. In our sessions, disobedience usually wins so he can get further punishment.

To my surprise, he nods without a fight and leaves.

My shoulders visibly relax at not having to fight with him further.

Stella hesitates, looking between Mac and me before she moves. "I'll give you two a minute." She ducks out of my office, following the other two men and pulling the door closed behind her.

"HM... I'm—." Mac's voice is thick with guilt. His shoulders sag and he looks to the floor, avoiding my gaze as he rubs the back of his neck.

"Save it. It's not your fault. You told me not to let him in. Find out how he got into the club with no one knowing. He never should have been allowed in the salon without one of us being notified. Either someone is incompetent or can't be trusted." My voice waivers in confidence. To think someone here would let someone in to hurt me leaves me mixed with a sense of vulnerability and fear.

"Yes, Ma'am."

"Bring them to me when you find out what happened."

"Ma'am?"

"I didn't stutter." I lock eyes with him. "The girl you know is gone, Mac. Do what I told you to do." I hold his gaze from where I sit. Any kind of plucky, fun-loving girl I had been is currently locked in a closet somewhere, crying her way through a pint of ice cream.

"Yes, Ma'am," he says before he leaves.

The Lion Roars

Stella comes back in, a bottle in hand. She sets a glass next to mine and pours both.

"I've had plenty."

"Sure you haven't." She caps the bottle, sets it aside, then takes a hefty sip of her glass. "I called Mick."

"What?!" I whine.

"Shut it. He's your fucking husband and deserves to be a part of this."

"He can't fucking handle it." My body tenses and the knot between my shoulders grows tighter. The sensation to vomit all the alcohol I've consumed grows.

"He's stronger than you think. Trust him." She points at me with the glass in hand, admonishing me with her fucked up wisdom. Stella was a Scapelli too.

"So he can strangle me again?" I instantly regret spewing those words.

He has worked damn hard to make things better. Between the therapy sessions with a licensed doctor, the AA meetings, and the support groups with the Vets, he has turned a corner. Setting his own schedule as my financier and having complete control over our home life helps as well. Magellan needs control and order.

Stella's crow's feet deepen as she narrows her eyes. She loses the big-sister vibe and turns back into Madame, taking control of this conversation. "Hope-Marie. That was out of line and you fucking know it."

I pick up the glass and down the whiskey to calm my frazzled nerves. I savor the burn down my throat and try to ignore the throbbing pain in my ass from Junior's handiwork. "I don't want to drag him back into the trauma he has lived. I can handle it."

"No, you fucking can't. You're planning on getting into a turf war with a drug cartel. Your husband has the right to know the danger you're bringing to your family. You don't get to make these decisions in a vacuum anymore. The moment you said I do you gave up the flying solo bullshit."

I shoot out of my seat.

We become angry mirrored images. Our nostrils flare, fists clench, and neither will back down.

Breathing hard, and light headed from the alcohol, I hate that Stella has called me on my bullshit once more. How am I supposed to trust Magellan with this? He doesn't have a great track record of handling our problems. I'm scared and angry at being this mistreated and having no recourse. I retreat first, hugging myself and turning from Stella.

"He's waiting downstairs for you. Talk to him." She commands like an army general. She takes the bottle with her when she leaves me alone in my office.

I drag my feet going down to him. I have no idea how to tell him everything.

He's pacing, and he runs his fingers through his hair when I finally come downstairs. He looks as frazzled as he did the day I gave birth to Angelo. He lights up seeing me and rushes to me. Whatever Stella told him was enough to scare him. "You okay? They said you were hurt." He pulls me into an embrace.

I gasp as he touches one of my wounds. "I'm fine," I whimper.

"You don't sound fine," he says as he keeps holding me.

"Let's go home." I nestle into him, barely holding myself together.

"Okay," he guides me to the car and helps me into the passenger seat.

"Where are we going?" I ask because he pulls out of the

Oyster's parking lot in the opposite direction of our home.

"I think we need to have a talk, uninterrupted."

I dreaded this. My hands tremble and I cross my arms to hide it, tucking them in as tight as possible. As afraid of Junior as I was, I'm more afraid of triggering Magellan's temper.

He pulls into a spot next to the park where he proposed. We stop at a street vendor and he orders us two hot chocolates.

My cheeks flush as we head to the bench where we traumatized that poor jogger with our sexcapades.

We sit in heavy silence for several minutes, enjoying the sunrise.

"Hope-Marie, I love you, and I'm here for you. Please, don't shut me out." His voice cracks with desperation.

I stare down at my cup of hot chocolate, white knuckling it. My jaw clenches and tears form in my eyes again. My brain keeps circling back to how close Junior came to penetrating me. How he's going to fly off the handle and all the good we've had for the past few months will be gone. "I'm not shutting you out. I'm protecting you." I whisper.

"Is that really what you're doing? Feels the same to me."

"Did you feel this hopeless when they shook you down?" I can't keep the bitterness out of my tone. I tense as he eases closer.

"Is that what's happening? You're being shook down by gangsters?" Magellan's shoulders sag and his lips form a tight line.

My body feels like it's suddenly made of lead and grows heavy. Guilt weighs on me as my confession will reveal I have kept all this bullshit from him for months. "They were selling drugs in the club, and I flushed them."

"Have you called the cops?"

I give a bitter chuckle at being asked this perfectly reasonable question for a third time tonight. "No. Mac said it wouldn't do any good when I took the drugs. Then he said we had no proof of wrong-doing when they came back for the drugs. And tonight it's a game of he said she said on whether Junior assaulted me."

He grinds his teeth loud enough to be heard, and hisses, "Assaulted?"

I drop my cup as I shake uncontrollably. I expect him to take out his sudden anger on me physically and I shrink from him. I bring my arms up to prevent him from hitting my face before I can stop myself.

"I'll kill every last one of those fuckers." He throws his cup and roars.

I yelp and brace for impact. When nothing happens, I peek through my arms tentatively.

Magellan stares off in the distance, not looking at me at all. His chest rises and falls rapidly. His fists are clenched tight, but are firmly planted on the tops of his legs. The hot puffs of air cause him to look like a dragon ready to breathe fire. He slowly turns his head to level his gaze on me.

I shy again, afraid he will hit me. Again, nothing happens and I sit up again, facing him.

Tears cling to his lashes and his breathing is even more labored as he looks absolutely devastated.

I lower my arms entirely, still trembling.

He slowly brings his hand up, like he would to a skittish animal, then pulls me into his chest, holding me tight. "Tell me who did this to you. I'll make every last one of those sons-of-bitches pay." He whispers against me.

I cry against him and cling to him. His strong arms around me instead of his fists pounding allows me to submit to his embrace. "Oh Mick," I blubber. "I did something awful. You're going to hate me. It's a drug cartel and I'm going to fight them and it puts us all in danger and you're going to leave. Oh God. I can't do this without you. Please don't go. I'm sorry. I love you."

"I will never abandon you. I love you more than anything in the world, Hope-Marie." He pulls me tighter against him.

"Even if I have to become a mobster and keep secrets from you?" I cry harder. "I can't lose you."

"Hope-Marie, if you're in this, I'm in this. Awoo?"

"Awoo." I sniffle against him.

Kiss The Flame

"I'm ready! You're the one that's dragging your feet." Junior growls at his father, pacing in his office.

"You wouldn't know what ready looks like if it bit you in the face." El Diablo replies as he leans back in his chair.

"You're pissed you can't have that whore!" Junior shouts.

"You mean the woman you said you would take care of and got bested by?" Mirth dances in El Diablo's eyes.

"She didn't fucking best me!" Junior throws his hands in the air.

"Then why do we not have the club under our control?"

"It's those fucking Scapellis she has working for her."

"Are you telling me the Scapellis control that club?" El Diablo leans forward.

"No!" Junior huffs.

"Decide, boy. Is it the Scapellis or the woman that's the reason you still don't have that club?"

"Fuck. It's a sex club. What the fuck is the big deal?" Junior crosses his arms and looks more like a child throwing a tantrum than a lieutenant in a drug cartel.

"The big deal is your failure, not the club. You have ruined our reputation by letting that whore get away with stealing your product and humiliating you." He points a tattooed finger at his son as he continues to berate him.

"I don't see you making her comply." He gives his father a smug look, as if his words are a worthy punch at his father's ego.

El Diablo narrows his eyes at his son. "Because I was not the one who caused problems to begin with. You are the one who decided to move on that club and failed, forcing me to clean up your mess."

"Is that why you've given all my work to that prick, Carlos?"

"He gets results. You get results, you get work. Simple as that," El Diablo leans back and shrugs.

Junior punches the wall and storms out of his father's office, blowing by his younger brother without a thought.

Esteban leans against the wall with his arms crossed, watching his brother storm off. He heard the entire conversation. Their life has been one long game of impressing their father to one day take over from him. He idolized his older brother until he learned of Junior's little escapade with that whore. This entire business with that club makes Esteban want to smack his brother.

That whore is putting a wedge between his brother and father. She needs a reminder of what protection brings. He could impress his father, help his brother, and get some payback in one fell swoop.

He pushes off the wall to get his supplies, feeling smug his plan will succeed. The drive to Le Salon takes a good thirty minutes in the winter weather. He parks his car well away from the club and carries what he needs in a backpack.

With the cold, the kitchen door takes several minutes to jimmy open. He slides in and holds it closed. There's no music, no voices, and no ringing of alarms.

A triumphant smile crosses his lips, and he gets to work rigging the kitchen to burn. He doesn't want to burn the whole place down. He wants to make enough of a mess that the sprinkler system will ruin the rest of it. He hums to himself while he thinks up the spiel he will give her after her club's ruined. His father will be impressed and Esteban will finally be better than Junior in his eyes.

Once the flames are dancing happily across the counter, he grabs his bag and exits from the same door he entered. Still humming to himself, he hurries across the street to watch the show from the stoop of the building. He lights a cigarette while he waits.

The fire alarms don't go off.

A quick glance at his watch and they should have gone off by now. If the alarm doesn't go off, the sprinklers don't activate. No sprinklers means that fire will rage through the entire building, maybe even the strip joint next door.

"Fuck," he mutters as he tosses his cigarette away and pushes off the stoop to rush back across the street. He's two-thirds of the way there when the large blacked-out windows explode into midnight shards of glass from the flames raging through the entire club.

"Shit," he whines as he peeks out from under his crouched position.

He takes off at a dead run for his car. If his old man finds out he burned the whole club down, he'll kill him.

Esteban knows the real reason Junior failed here, and it has nothing to do with ability. Junior's got a thing for that hot little club owner. He'll be pissed to if he finds out it was Esteban.

Panting by the time he reaches the car, there are still no sirens to indicate someone is coming to rescue the building. "Are you fucking kidding me?" Frozen in place he contemplates letting it burn to the ground and lying low for a few days. He kicks one of his tires, realizing he can't do that. He trudges to a payphone and dials 911.

"911 what's your emergency."

"There's a fire at that strip joint, The Blue Oyster." He hangs up and hurries back to his car before anyone else shows up. His palms are sweaty and he can't catch his breath. The amount of shit he's started if she really is with the Italians means he's a dead man. The last place Esteban wants to be is here.

My doctor put me on the pill immediately after giving birth to Angelo. Everything had been fine until I missed a period last month. No big deal. I've been under a ton of stress and the pill can cause irregularity. I didn't even think to take a pregnancy test last month.

Eggs made me vomit three days ago.

Still, I didn't connect the dots, as it could have been a bad batch of eggs. Magellan and the kids didn't get sick, causing the niggling doubt to rear its ugly head.

Dread filled my heart as the scent of eggs made me nauseous yesterday. Lunch brought whole new meaning to hell as everything in the cafeteria made my stomach churn.

So here I am at the phlebotomy cart, nicking a blood draw kit. Five minutes later, I'm standing in front of the lab window with my specimen.

"Hey, Mark, can you put a rush on this?" I hand him the vial labeled in my nice, neat handwriting.

"Hey, Hope-Marie. Sure can. You don't usually work this late, do you?" He looks over the vial.

"Nah. Got roped into a double today," I say as I shrug, trying to play it cool and not like I'm abusing hospital resources for my own personal needs.

"Sucks to be you. Didn't think you residents had to work doubles." He fills out the paperwork for the vial.

Me and my smart-ass mouth are why I'm working a double.

I smile at Mark. "As long as Lamb's here, I'm here."

"Well, that sounds shitty." He shakes his head.

"Yeah. Send me the results on that one, 'kay?" I point to the vial.

"Uh-huh. Should be ready in a few hours."

I walk away, feeling smug in my covert operation, and resume my duties.

Lamb finally sends me home at seven in the morning.

I hot-foot it to the club to pick up the schedules, hoping to get home before everyone else is up.

When I get to Le Salon, the whole area is blocked off and I'm forced to park my car in front of the diner on the corner. As I walk towards the club, the crowd of onlookers grows. My brow furrows as the line of fire trucks light up the area in creepy waves of red lights. I stuff my hands into my coat the cold affecting my feet and legs. Having gotten frostbite, the cold affects me more than normal people.

I come around the fire trucks and I stop in my tracks.

If I thought the eggs made my stomach do flips, what I see before me is fucking cartwheels of bile-causing anguish. Where Le Salon once stood is a burning pile of rubble. Smoke pillars waft into the air like fucking pole dancers luring in their wares.

I blink trying to will away this nightmare. "No," I mutter. "This can't be happening."

"Hope-Marie?" Harold comes alongside me.

I'm frozen in place, staring at the rubble. "Where is Le Salon?" I whimper.

"I know. I know, kid. It'll be okay," he stammers as he pulls me into a hug. "I promise we'll get through this. I'm glad no one was hurt."

"How... how am I supposed to make the schedules?" I mewl.

Harold's chest shakes with the dry laugh he gives. "It will be okay. I'll handle everything. Go home."

How can he be this fucking calm? Le Salon is GONE!

"The schedules..." I repeat. I can't process what I see before me. The ringing in my ears grows louder, making everything tilt and forcing me to swallow hard to keep from puking.

"I'll send someone with the paperwork later. Go home, kid. There's nothing you can do here."

I wilt in defeat.

Harold walks me back to my car before returning to the burning pile rubble of my club.

I don't remember driving home or getting into the elevator to ride to our floor. When I walk in, I drop my keys in the bowl and stand in the foyer, staring blankly ahead.

Magellan's making breakfast.

Our kids are happily watching cartoons in the living room.

I want to say something to get Magellan's attention, but I can't function. I need him to hold me and say it's going to be alright. I'm not supposed to be home for another hour. I was supposed to be working on the schedules.

"Hope-Marie? What happened?" Magellan leaves the cooking and rushes to me when he finally notices me. He rests his hands on my forearms, quickly inspecting me for injury.

I stare up at his beautiful brown eyes and my lip quivers as I threaten to cry again. "I wanted to make the schedules."

"Okay. Why couldn't you make them?" He keeps rubbing my arms and eases closer.

"They're gone," I say.

"How are they gone?"

"Fire." The word slips from my mouth in a disbelieving whisper. I want to say more, but I can't function. I want to curl up and cry myself to sleep.

"Fire? What happened? Are you okay? Talk to me," he shakes me.

I blink, whimpering. "Le Salon burned down," I sob as I fling myself against him.

"Oh, honey." He wraps his arms around me and holds me tight. His steady heartbeat calms my nerves as I blubber against him. He kisses my temple and murmurs, "It'll be okay."

From The Ashes

Thursday (Two Days Later)

I vaguely remember showering before going to bed on Wednesday. Then everything went black. Magellan must have performed some sort of Spanish voodoo to let me sleep. Not even a peep from the kids managed to rouse me. My alarm needing to be destroyed due to angrily blaring at me Thursday morning is the first conscious thought that crosses my mind since Harold sent me home.

Trudging into the bathroom I put myself together for the day and spend most of the shower in a mix of wanting to vomit and rage-filled tears.

How could this be happening?

We worked too damn hard, and now it's a pile of ash.

I get dressed in the dark to not wake Magellan. "I love you," I whisper to him before disappearing out the door to head to Bellevue.

In the car, I give myself the pep talk I need to focus. "It's out of your control. Harold's taking care of it. It will be alright. Focus on school. You can't fix the club." My mantra still bounces in my head like one of those damnable children's songs when I walk into Dr. Lamb's office.

"Take a seat," he commands. His normal gruff tone holding more bite than usual.

I obey.

He pulls a single file from the stack, opens it carefully and begins, "Patient is a Caucasian female, aged twenty-seven, no mental medical history, blood work reveals positive results."

He makes a show of closing the file and leans on his arms on the desk before he addresses me.

"Care to tell me why you decided to use hospital resources when you could've bought a test over the counter?"

My lip quivers and the floodgates open. "I'm pregnant?" I ask as I sob.

His brow raises. "That's not the reaction I was expecting from such joyous news."

"I can't be pregnant. Fuck! This isn't happening. He said not to get pregnant. I'm on the pill. This has to be wrong. Mick's going to be pissed." Sheer panic controls my mental faculties as I hyperventilate between sobs.

"Hope-Marie!" He barks at me like a drill sergeant. "Breathe, otherwise you're going to pass out. Then I want you to calmly explain to me why you're this upset."

The several minutes I take to get my emotions under control are embarrassing. My voice quivers as I begin with what happened during Angelo's labor, and how rough that pregnancy was. "...and that's why the doctor said I shouldn't get pregnant anymore." I leave the club burning down, or anything related to being a dominatrix out of the already long list of reasons having a baby isn't positive.

"I see. Hope-Marie, I suggest you go home and give your husband the good news. Then call your doctor to make an appointment."

"I can't go home," I wail.

Dr. Lamb pauses, then asks, "Do you not feel safe enough to go home?"

"No. I mean, Yes. It's safe. Well, I think. No. My club burned down." I reply. I'm too emotionally spent to provide a coherent answer.

The wrinkles on Dr. Lamb's forehead make him look like a caricature, and I snort the snot bubble from crying, which causes me to steal a tissue from the box on his desk. He stood to show me to the door. With my blundering answer, he sits back down, re-opening my file at the mention of Le Salon.

"Club? I said to go home. Not to a club."

"I know," I hiccup. "If I go home, Mick'll be upset that I lost my residency. This is all I have left. Please don't take it away. My club is gone!"

"Why don't we start at the beginning?" his words soften, even with confusion still dancing across his face. He motions for me to explain.

I blow my nose before I begin, imagining I sound like a honking goose. "I own Le Salon, in Brooklyn."

"You own a salon? I thought you said it was a club."

"Uh, huh. Le Salon is my club."

"Then what are you doing here?" He makes a circular motion with his finger.

"Helping people," I hiccup and the waterworks start again.

"And this club burned down?"

"Uh-huh. On Tuesday," I sob.

"Then why didn't you call in?"

"If you're here, I'm here." I say for the millionth time.

He rubs his hand over his face and growls at me. Frustration and irritation are clear when he speaks again. "Hope-Marie, you've racked up enough hours, you don't need to come back until January."

"What?" I ask as I don't understand what he means. I tighten my grip on the tissue and inhale a jagged breath.

Oh God! He's going to kick me out of the program!

"Your advisor very clearly stated as a resident you're not to work more than eight hours in a single day. He threatened to report me to some board." He rolls his eyes.

"Oh," I utter. "How do I learn what it's like if I don't shadow you correctly?"

"You know, there are moments I ask myself if you're truly this naive. You are learning what you need to learn. You have an excellent work ethic, and you're probably the most compassionate New Yorker I've ever met."

"That's cause I'm from Missouri," I say as I sniffle.

"What the fuck brought you to New York?" He laughs and

waves his hand around the room as if this room represents all of New York.

"Vogue."

"Since you're here, I can assume that didn't work out."

"Sort of," I smile and half shrug. Telling him my story is causing me to breathe easier, and I lean back in my seat.

"Okay," he rubs his temples. "Out with it."

"I got a letter for a job interview I thought was the actual job offer. Guy tried to make me suck his dick, and I ran away. Still had to pay rent, and the diner I got a job at didn't cut it. So I did what every down-on-your-luck girl does, I became a stripper."

"This is a pull-yourself-up bootstraps effort, then?" He looks at me skeptically as he laces his fingers together, leaning on his arms on the desk.

"No. My royalties cover most of our expenses." I leave out the part where my royalties are from porno movies.

The way Dr. Lamb's face wrinkles when he doesn't understand something, or when he's frustrated and doesn't want to unleash on the cause of the frustration makes him look like one of those bulldogs with all the wrinkles; adorable and hideous all at once.

"I was not aware strippers made royalties."

"Well, depends on the contract. You see. Mine's an exclusive all-in-one contract with Rittendorf Modeling. I got paid to strip, model, perform, and whatever else produced profits that's not illegal."

"All this led to owning a salon or a club?"

"The club is named Le Salon." I huff, frustrated that his questions make him sound like the doesn't understand a word I'm saying.

"And I assume it is a strip club?"

I turn as red as a cherry. I hate that people assume it's a strip club. "Well, no. That's the Oyster."

His expression goes from confusion to dawning realization. "Wait. You were a stripper at The *Blue* Oyster?"

Panic washes over my face as I desperately try to recall if I ever saw him there. "Oui," I squeak. "Je suis Giselle."

His lack of reaction or realization can mean he's better at hiding his emotions than I thought, or he doesn't recognize me for Giselle.

"Whew, glad you weren't a customer." I relax in my seat.

His cheeks flush, and he blinks at me for several seconds, still not confirming if he knows me from the club.

I can't read what is going on, other than he shifts like he's uncomfortable with my revelations. "None of the girls use their real names on stage and my persona while on the floor was French. Her name is Giselle Chastane. I became Mistress Giselle in the VIP rooms, and it evolved into a BDSM show. Which then evolved into owning my salon for BDSM clients. I'm a dominatrix." Choosing to come clean has taken a huge weight off my chest. "And on Tuesday, my newly opened club burned to the ground."

"Okay, I'm going to rewind this conversation back to my original question. Why in the hell didn't you call in? With that much shit going on in your life, it would've been perfectly acceptable."

"Well, Sir, two reasons. One, I wanted those results before you got the file," I motion to the folder, and hold up my fingers to count on as I talk. "And two, all I'm going to do at home is sit around and worry about all the things I can't do for the club, and how I'll support my family if the club doesn't re-open. Or worse, forcing my husband to have to find new employment. This place is a cakewalk compared to home. I just want to do a good job, and to help someone get through their shit today. Because I don't want to end up here on my own."

"Unfortunately, your hours this month are already used. I was not exaggerating when I said you have enough hours for the next two weeks. Go home, enjoy Christmas. I'll see you next year. I have patients waiting."

My mouth falls open and I stare at him, dumbfounded.

He stands, takes his files, and leaves.

I have half a mind to chase after him and make him let me work. Slowly, I get up and I head back to my car. It's not even seven in the morning. To lighten the burden of bad news I have, I stop at the bakery near our building and pick up everyone's favorite pastries.

God, please let Mick be want another baby.

Bear Claws of Bribery

I manage to fish my keys out without dropping any pastries to open the door. Once through the door, I kick it closed. I drop my keys in the bowl, and step on the heels of my pink Adidas to leave them in the shoe pile next to the door.

"Hope-Marie?" Magellan pops his head around the corner. "What are you doing home?" Then his eyes fall on the Rosalyn's box and his tone lowers, full of mirth mixed with anxiety. "You brought bribes."

"Mhm Hmm. Got your favorite," I smile at him as I offer the box, not answering the other question.

"At least you're good at bribery," he takes the box and fishes out a bear claw. He happily holds it in his mouth as he struts back into the kitchen with my bribes.

The lack of cartoons, toys, or squealing children means Castian, Helena, and Angelo are still asleep.

"You did not answer my first question," He reminds me between bites.

"Well, I think we should sit down first," I bite my lip and smile at him. My voice raises in pitch, causing me to sound like a squeak toy.

He stops and stares at me long and hard while he munches his bear claw. "Bribery and sitting down. This must be important."

I snake my fingers into the belt loops of his jeans and gently tug him with me toward the couch. "Well, you know, we can be a lot closer on the couch for the news." I wriggle my eyebrows.

"Hmm. Let's see. The only time you ever butter me up is if you're making another movie. Or... you're pregnant."

I smile at him, nervous he's going to take this conversation somewhere dark.

Magellan's eyes light up and he snatches me up, spinning me around in excitement. He squeals, "You're pregnant!"

Thank God I didn't eat anything this morning, or Magellan would be covered in it. "Put me down!" I laugh and nudge him to the couch, snuggling into his lap. "Yes." It's hard for me to keep smiling, as I'm afraid of what he'll say next.

"Looks like we'll need to actually buy that house!"

"That's not what I thought you'd say," I chuckle.

He pauses and looks me square in the eyes. The silence falls between us as the memories of Angelo's pregnancy rear their ugly heads.

"It won't be like that. I promise," he murmurs. "We'll get you all the bed rest you need. I can take care of the kids. We'll have to get them to let you have light duty for the residency. Fuck, we'll have to get rid of the car."

"Oh, Hell no! That car is mine. You can go buy yourself a van. I get the Roadrunner."

His face screws up in a mix of disbelief and pouting at my demand. "The Roadrunner's my baby."

"Who you were going to throw away like trash. Dibs!"

He erupts into laughter. "Fine. You can have her." He pulls me to him and roughly kisses me.

His excitement is contagious, and I get lost in kissing him. If the kids weren't able to walk out here on their own, I'd be stripping down to celebrate.

"This is great. You'll get to share the news with Harold and Stella over dinner."

"Over dinner?" I wasn't aware of any plans with the Rittendorfs as I've been avoiding them with how Magellan reacts to anything Harold related lately.

"Yeah. Stella called after you headed to work. They want to

talk shop."

"Oh," I relax. "I told Dr. Lamb what happened. That's part of why he sent me home. That and he was pissed I used the hospital's resources for the pregnancy test."

"Wait. Did he fire you?" Magellan's nostrils flare and his hands grip tighter on my waist. He reminds me of the morning he went off on his brother for accosting me.

"No. No. Turns out, I'm only supposed to work eight hours a day there." I rush the words out as I pet his forearms, hoping to sooth him.

"I told you it was weird for you to be working half days."

"Yes, you did." I kiss his nose. "And, as such, I have worked enough hours. I'm off until January." I keep peppering him with kisses until I feel him relax against me.

"Does that mean we're going to Missouri for Christmas?"

"What? No. You *want* to go to Missouri?" I crinkle my nose like I got a whiff of one of Angelo's diapers.

"Oh hell yeah! Your family Christmases are the best. Especially when Rachel's there. The way you get to rub all your success in her face is epic." He flashes me a devilish grin.

Thankfully, he saved himself by saying why he likes Rachel being there. She and I are hyper competitive to show Pop how successful we are. That mischievous twinkle in his eyes makes me wonder if he's trying to get a rise out of me. "Okay. Fine. We'll go to Missouri." I roll my eyes.

"Then we'll fly to Spain and spend a week on the vineyard."

"What happened to bed rest?"

"There are plenty of beds at our parents' places." He wriggles his brows.

"Uh-huh," I reply, swatting him.

He then rolls me off his lap and plants a heated kiss on my lips. "I'll call Stella to bump it to lunch." Then he pushes off the couch.

I manage to sneak in a quick nap before lunch. Emerging from our room dressed in a fuzzy sweater and a pair of jeans, it warms my heart to see all the kids playing together. I've missed hanging out with Harold and Stella.

Magellan's in the kitchen, an easy smile on his face while he cooks lunch.

Harold and Stella sit at the table facing him, having an intense, hushed conversation.

Stella sees me first and launches from her chair to wrap me in a big hug. "How are you holding up?"

"Uh," I hesitate, and she narrows her gaze at me. I swear the woman is looking into the depth of my soul to unravel all my secrets.

"You're pregnant," she blurts.

My ears turn pink along with my cheeks.

"You're pregnant?" Harold asks with enthusiasm.

"Yup!" I confirm. Hiding anything from Stella is like screaming in a hurricane.

"Wait. How did she figure it out?" Magellan grumbles.

"She pukes her brains out any time she smells eggs, and she's glowing like the Rockefeller Center at Christmas. How did you not see it?" Stella's grinning as she teases Magellan.

Harold's quiet voice cuts through the joyous banter. "What did the doc say?"

The room grows heavy with the pendulum swing of emotions.

"I haven't told him yet." I confess as I fidget with the end of my sweater.

"Hope-Marie," Harold growls in a far-too-fatherly tone.

I jump in surprise, and I give him a dirty look. "I only found out this morning, thank you. I haven't had a chance to call the doctor."

"Oh," Harold deflates and his cheeks flush red.

Walking with Stella, I kiss Harold on the cheek before I take a seat across from them.

Magellan sets the kids up at the coffee table with their lunch before he brings ours to the table.

After we finish eating, Harold starts into his business. "Considering your good news, my original plans for today's meeting no longer apply. Hope-Marie, you're fired." He gives me a proud smile. "You and Mick should hop on the next plane back to Missouri. Buy yourself a house with a white picket fence, and continue to make lots of fat, healthy babies.”

I choke on my food, frowning. Harold can’t fire me. I’m part owner of the club.

“Harold,” Stella rolls her eyes.

Magellan remains silent, watching this interchange with his arms crossed. His poker face is far better than mine when it comes to Harold and Stella. He’s staring at Harold and his jaw muscle is tense.

“You can’t fire me and I’m not quitting,” I say when I finally stop coughing.

“Why the fuck not?” Harold’s voice rises in pitch as he doesn’t cover up his frustration.

“I mean, it’s my fucking club and there are too many people who rely on me to walk away. I can help people there. Besides, I’m not going back to live in Missouri… *ever*. There’s *nothing* there.”

“Exactly, there’s nothing there! No people trying to hurt you. No people trying to kill you. No people trying to burn your shit to the ground.”

“Then you sell me the Oyster and you move to fucking Missouri yourself!”

“Why would I move?” Harold dramatically raises his hands for emphasis.

“Exactly. I already said I was keeping my club. I’m not letting some fucking prick who calls himself the Devil destroy my dreams. I can make a real difference in the world there. The more I learn about behavioral therapy, the more I’m convinced this is the correct path.”

“You’re being bull-headed, and ignorant. There’s no fucking sainthood for strippers. I’ll give you that you know how to make those men do things. We all know the only help you give them is to get their rocks off, and they pay you a shit-ton of money to do it. You’re going to get *killed*. Walk away.” Stella shouts at me.

“That is uncalled for. Hope-Marie has made her decision. If she chooses to pursue her dreams, who are you to say it’s wrong.” Magellan says with an air of command.

The table erupts into the three of them talking over each other in broken shouting words.

I sit back, watching in silence. The sting of Stella’s hurtful words burns throughout my chest. She's one of my closest friends and she called me a glorified whore. Letting them verbally duke it out, I fight to keep from bursting into tears.

Harold and Stella are a unified front for once against Magellan. The three of them are getting louder and louder as they talk over each other.

There must be something Harold and Stella aren't telling me.

Magellan's body language is oddly calm for how angry he sounds. He keeps his arms crossed and not once does he waiver from supporting my decision.

Watching them fight makes me want to flee into the other room. Instead, I need to get control of this conversation before someone does something rash.

"Enough," I slap my hand on the table to get their attention. "This isn't up for negotiation. Le Salon is more than a sex club, Stella. The relationship I form with my clients helps them in their day-to-day lives. Even if that help is release. El Diablo and his little devils can't win. If I don't rebuild, who do you think they're going to go after next?" I pointedly look at Harold. "Do you really want to get in bed with Scapelli again to keep your club devil free?"

"No," he grumbles, and his shoulders slump as he leans back in his chair.

"This is madness," Stella groans.

"Even so, she's not wrong," Harold speaks up and rests a hand on Stella's shoulder. "We both know the only reason Los Diablos aren't messing with us is because of Scapelli. If we don't stand up for ourselves, we're back to where we started." Harold stares at Stella.

She relents and leans into him when he wraps his arm around her.

"I understand this isn't your fight. Tell me now and I'll buy you out of Le Salon. But I'm doing this, with or without your support."

The Devil's Due

"You are not going to that fucking party, and that is final." El Diablo snarls at his son as he smacks him upside the head. "Go help your mother."

Esteban stares daggers at his father. The sweet little thing he promised to meet tonight will be heartbroken, and some other jerk will move in on his girl. He clenches his fists and grinds his teeth as his father stares back at him, uncaring.

El Diablo half expects Esteban to lose his temper. The only thing that boy will find at that party tonight is trouble. Once he got wind of who Esteban was sneaking off to see, he decided to put an end to that Romeo and Juliet affair. With the shit storm burning that whore house caused, Los Diablos don't need any further complications.

"You know he's going to sneak out," Junior chimes in once his brother is gone.

"Your job this evening is to keep him from fucking up shit more than he already has. Comprendes?" El Diablo jabs his finger into Junior's chest.

"Si, Señor." Junior rubs his chest where his father jabbed him. Once again, anything Junior had planned is tossed aside because his brother is chasing tail. He heads out of the office, following his brother until the hallway diverges to the back entrance. Junior knows all of Esteban's tricks. All he has to do is set up and wait.

When Esteban comes skulking around the corner of the back of the house, Junior grabs him and slams him against the wall. "Where in the fuck do you think you're going?"

"Out. Why the fuck do you care?" Esteban growls as he shoves out of his brother's grasp.

"You know *he* won't be happy." Junior says.

"I'm supposed to suffer because he's a paranoid little bitch?" Esteban's head whips back as Junior's fist connects with his jaw, causing the younger brother to slam into the wall again.

"You know better than to talk about El Diablo like that." Junior closes the distance between them and pins Esteban to the wall. "You have one chance to tell me why the hell I shouldn't drag your ass back into the house and lock you in the cellar."

"I promised her I'd be there." Esteban whines. "Besides. You're the one always whining how a man always keeps his word." He shoves his brother. "Which is it? Be a man and keep my word? Or pussy out because there *might* be trouble."

Junior sighs heavily and rubs his hand over his face as he glances back at the house. "She mean that much to you?" For all his bravado, he's excited his brother has found someone. Their lifestyle doesn't leave a lot of room for real relationships.

Esteban's face lights up with a wolfish grin as his brother comes to his way of thinking. He slaps him on the shoulder and motions. "C'mon. I parked out back."

"This is a bad idea. We should at least tell someone where we're going. What if the Jefes show up?" Junior follows his brother, checking his pistol's still holstered in his shoulder strap.

"Then we beat their pussy asses. Lighten up. It's a party. Besides, the place will be packed. No one is going to know we're there."

"Then how will your girl find you?" Junior teases as he slips into the passenger seat of Esteban's car.

"Funny, asshole." Esteban slips in and eases out of the parking spot.

The club is well out of Los Diablos territory, which makes Junior wonder how Esteban met this girl in the first place. The place is teeming with people by the time they get there.

Esteban parks, and the two men check themselves out before approaching the door.

Junior primps and straightens his suit, using the rearview mirror for a final check.

They pay the cover and saunter in like they own the place. There are more people than the Fire Marshall would ever allow inside, assuming anyone in here cared for what the Fire Marshall had to say. The DJ blares Latin dance music.

Esteban ducks through the crowd toward the bar.

Junior lingers a few steps behind his brother, scanning the crowd for any threats.

A couple of guys push off the wall to follow Esteban.

"That can't be good," Junior mutters and follows.

The cute little brunette leaps into Esteban's arms and plants a sloppy kiss on his lips.

Esteban returns the favor, excited to see his girl.

The two guys grab hold of him, ripping him from his blissful greeting.

Her screams are lost in the music as she falls to the floor.

Esteban struggles and kicks against the two men dragging him to a side door.

Junior fights his way through the over-packed crowd to follow his brother. He'll get the drop on at least one of them and give his brother a fighting chance to get out of here. His father knew there would be trouble if Esteban came here tonight. Seeing the scene unfold makes Junior regret not doing as his father asked. He slams open the door in time to see his brother drop to his knees from a bat to his stomach.

Both men turn to see who is interrupting their fun and their eyes widen in surprise at Junior's frame blocking the door.

He doesn't think twice and leaps into the fray, throwing a solid right hook to the closest guy.

The four men turn into a tangled mess of limbs, baseball bats, and blood.

Minutes later, two men turn into four against Esteban and Junior.

Neither brother is willing to give up and fight harder to get away from the Jefes circling around them.

A lone gunshot bangs in the night, and all the assailants scatter like quail.

Esteban freezes as he looks at Junior. "Oh, fuck," he cries and rushes to his brother. Panic causes him to shake as he reaches to cover the wound. Blood stains Junior's white cotton suit bright red.

"Get me home," Junior croaks as he brings his hand up to hold his stomach.

"Fuck home. You need a hospital." Esteban wails.

"And what? Tell them we got caught in a gang fight? We'll go to jail. If you thought Papa was mad before, imagine his temper if cops show up to arrest us." Junior's gritting his teeth as the pair move to the car.

Esteban helps his brother into the car. He has half a mind to ignore his request and rush him to the ER. The hospital is only a mile away, versus home all the way back to Brooklyn.

"I'll be fine. Get me home so I can get patched up." Junior's strained voice is as calm as he can force it to be. He doesn't want to show weakness to his brother.

"I got you, man. I got you. Hang in there." Esteban gasps and tears well in his eyes as flies around the car. Not caring if they get pulled over, he drives like Batman to get his brother home.

"That girl of yours," Junior grunts, "pretty... damn... hot." He pauses and shifts his weight. "See... why... you liked her."

"Fuck! I should have listened to you," Esteban cries as he presses down on the pedal more.

"Too late for that, Hermano. Just...get me home. Whatever happens... be there... for mama." Junior's voice fades as he talks.

"You'll be there for mama too. C'mon man, hang in there." Esteban reaches over and gives his brother a shake.

He peels into the driveway and up the lawn, getting as close to the house as he can several minutes later. He screams for help as he drags his brother out of the car.

Junior is heavy in his arms, not moving on his own.

"Please! He needs a doctor!" Esteban screams again.

"We're almost there. Come on, wake up, Junior." He groans as he drags him toward the door.

The security guards move toward the boys, one calling for El Diablo via his walkie-talkie.

El Diablo and his personal physician barrel out of the front door.

One security guard gathers Junior from Esteban, following El Diablo and the physician into the house.

The other clamps a hand on Esteban's shoulder and forcibly guides him after his brother.

The entire entourage takes care to avoid the partygoers as they slip into a guest room. Once secure, the guards step out to prevent accidental interruptions.

The physician checks the boy's pulse while he also gives a cursory glance at the wound. He steps back and grimaces as he shakes his head no. He rests a hand on El Diablo's shoulder in comfort before he leaves the room.

Esteban stares blankly at his brother. Guilt freezes him in place and weighs on his chest like a lead balloon. How could his brother be dead? He said he would be fine. He promised.

El Diablo stands as still as a statue, staring at his dead son, his firstborn. Junior had been everything he wanted in a son. He was smart, funny, had compassion, and knew how to get things done. He wants to beat Esteban to death, which would solve nothing. His wife will be inconsolable as it is, blaming him for his son's death. All the muscles in his body ache with the restraint he shows in not murdering his second son.

The room is like a tomb.

The guests counting down from ten to ring in the new year is like a timer on a bomb to El Diablo's temper.

Without looking at Esteban, he hisses, "What did you do?"

Working Nine To Five

March 1988

"Your break starts now. If I see you on your feet for the next fifteen minutes, you're fired." Lamb informs me while looking at his watch.

"Wait. What? Break? We still have fourteen clients to see." I motion anxiously at the stack of files in my arms.

"Yes, I do. You are on your break." He plucks said files from my grasp. "Sit." He motions to the bench behind me.

"But…"

"The only butt I should hear is yours hitting that seat, Mrs. Lacienda." He tilts his head down to watching me over his glasses at me.

I gingerly sit on the bench, looking to see if I'm being pranked.

"Good. I'll be back when I finish up with this patient. If I get one word that you were standing, you're fired." He enters the room across the hall from the bench.

"Am I being punished?" I ask the empty hallway. I glance at my watch after only two minutes. No one else is in the hallway. I could get up.

Who would know?

I could pop off my shoes and give my aching feet a few minutes of respite. I end up doing neither because it is unprofessional to take off one's shoes during work. As much as I don't like being told to sit and stay, getting off my feet feels wonderful.

The baby is starting to show. After all the office visits and math to figure out how far along I'm, we're at five months. I swear, I'm never letting Magellan touch me with his dick again. Well, at least not there. I close my eyes and gently rub my stomach.

"Good. Your break's over."

Dr. Lamb's voice startles me awake. Fifteen minutes went by too fast. Hopping to my feet I reach for the pile of paperwork.

Dr. Lamb shifts it to his other arm as he reads the next patient's information.

We work steadily for the next two hours when he stops me in front of his office. "You have thirty minutes to enjoy lunch. If you come back early, you're fired."

"What?" I huff in frustration.

"I did not stutter. Go to lunch. Tick Tock." He motions to the clock on the wall.

"You're not taking a break to eat." I say as I cross my arms, being petulant.

"I'll make do. Go." He waves me off as he steps into his office and shuts the door in my face.

"What the fuck is going on today?" I mutter. I take the opportunity to grab lunch in the cafeteria. Whatever they're cooking today smells divine. When I get in line, the sign shows a picture of Salisbury steak, green beans, mashed potatoes, and a lake of brown gravy.

I reach for a soda, and the cafeteria worker smacks my hand. "Dr. Lamb said you could have water, milk, hot tea with honey, or juice."

"I'm not a... He can't... Fine! Give me a milk," I sulk, like the child Dr. Lamb is treating me like.

I decide if he's going to force this regiment on me, I'll savor it. I take every last minute of my lunch, enjoying the Salisbury steak meal. I have thirty seconds to spare when I'm standing in front of his door, eyeing the clock on the wall. My hand hovers over the door as the second hand slowly winds around.

"Enjoy your lunch?" He smiles as he answers the door.

"I did," I pull my hand back and preen, trying to make him sorry for pampering me.

"Good. Next patient on the docket," he steps by me, walking down the hall.

I narrow my eyes as I stalk after him. The next two hours are perfectly normal. We see patients. He asks me questions. I take notes. When we step out it's two in the afternoon.

"Sit. If you get up in the next fifteen minutes—."

"Why are you fucking treating me like I'm in fucking kindergarten?" I clench my fists and stomp my foot.

He gives a heavy paternal-like sigh and motions toward his office.

I crinkle my nose, wanting to demand an answer here in the hall. I follow, even though going back to Dr. Lamb's office usually means he wants to yell at me.

He holds the door open for me and closes it quietly before he takes his seat behind his desk. "Why are you still standing? Sit already."

I take a seat and chew against my lower lip nervously.

He takes his time setting his files down, removing his glasses, cleaning them, and returning them to his face before he decides to address me. "There's no delicate way to put this, so I'm going to be blunt."

"You weren't being blunt before?" I raise a brow.

Lamb's lips twitch with the hint of a smile. "I talked with your gynecologist. Got the full run-down of your last pregnancy. You were not quite descriptive enough in calling it *rough*." He air quotes the word rough.

My ears turn pink, and I fidget with the edge of my shirt.

"Therefore, I'm taking it upon myself as your employer to guarantee you get your federally mandated breaks. You are damn lucky I don't put you on bed rest."

"You can't do that." I huff, suddenly anxious he could.

"Actually, as a consulting physician for your pregnancy, I can. The moment you put my name on the blood work, you gave me the keys to the kingdom." He smiles at me, like a damn wolf.

"I can't see patients on bed rest," I mutter and cross my

arms. "I'm fine."

"No, you cannot, and…" He points at me. "You are not fine. Between an already stressful job, and everything else going on in your life, there's no way in hell you are fine. This job alone is enough to win you bed rest."

I swallow hard, fearful he's about to kick me out of the program. "Please don't," I beg.

"Please don't what?" His face scrunches into the confused bulldog.

"I need this. If you kick me out, that asshole at Columbia will never get me another residency, and I'll be done. This will all have been a waste."

"Why in the hell would I kick you out? You're the best damn resident I've had. All I'm saying is you need to take care of you as well."

I slump in my chair, relieved. "How am I supposed to complete everything if you're making me sit and do nothing all the time?"

"Hope-Marie, fifteen minutes won't ruin your track record." He stops and tilts his head in thought, eyeing me.

Dread fills me.

"You know what? I think it's time you learned the other part of your job." His wolfish grin turns feral.

"What other part?" I shift in my seat, knowing I'm not going to like this.

He leans forward, resting his elbows on the desk, and steeples his fingers like a madman. "Yes. I think this will work out perfectly." He gets up and motions for me to come around the desk. "Take a seat."

When I sit in his chair, he turns me to face a box in the corner with his name on it. "Your job is to figure out that." He motions to the box vaguely, grabs his files, and bolts for the door.

"Figure out what?" I furrow my brow. The box is covered in dust, with files piled haphazardly on top of it. Taped to the side of the box is a note with Dr. Lamb's name on it. I roll forward in the chair and pull it off the box.

Here is your new computer. Please start entering your notes via the system. An orderly will be around at six every night to collect the floppies. Please label them with all relevant patient identification, including the patient file number. If you need assistance, please call extension 503 where William can assist you.

"Great. What the hell is this?"

I study at the box with surrounding files and realize I can't even get to it with how things are.

"First, we organize."

I spend the next hour and a half shuffling files to get them in chronological order, by patient, even combining repeat visitors, and take them to the file cabinets on the other side of his office. I set my stack on the first file cabinet and pull open the first drawer. Low and behold, a treasure trove of unsorted files consumes the drawer.

"Really?" I sigh in frustration.

Why do men never organize anything?

I close the drawer and peer in the others, one by one. None of them are sorted. "How does he find anything?"

"I find things, because I know where *I* put them."

I scream and slam the file cabinet door closed, instinctively covering my stomach. I swear my heart just leaped into my throat.

"Don't sneak up on me!"

"It's my office. I thought you heard the door open. What are you doing?"

He motions to the cabinets.

"What you asked."

"I didn't ask you to organize my files. I asked you to figure out that contraption."

He flicks his head towards the box as he moves to his desk.

"That contraption, turns out to be a computer, and someone named William knows how to make it work. If you want me to access it, I have to rescue it from your mounds of files. To put away your files, I have to organize them. Why? Because, Dr. Lamb, if I'm going to *figure out that contraption* and follow the instructions in the letter that was taped to it, the files have to be in order. An order the rest of us can follow."

I rest my hands on my hips, feeling quite smug.

"Good. Then that's your task the rest of this week. Go home, it's five o'clock."

The Life We Live

May 1988

Esteban did not lie to his father when he confessed his sin. He told him they snuck out to see the girl he promised to see, and that he convinced his brother to go with him. He bowed his head to his father and accepted whatever fate El Diablo had planned for him.

El Diablo beat his son to within an inch of his life. He took all his sorrow and pain and pounded it into Esteban's body. He broke bones, tore flesh, and left his son to pick himself up off the floor next to his dead brother. He waited until after the party ended to tell his wife she lost one of her babies.

Esteban threw himself into work. He tossed aside his trouble-making friends and followed the rules. He took whatever job his father demanded of him and expected nothing in return. Months of doing shit jobs in horrible places, work no one else would take, has earned him acknowledgment at the dinner table again. He even has protected his younger brother from being brought into the fold.

El Diablo has spent the past few months avenging his son's death. Be it ratting out drug deals of the Jefes to stealing their protection rackets and growing his territory.

Los Diablos won't let Jefes pass.

Car crashes end in bloody, twisted wreckage. Heroine is laced with rat poison in their supply. Clubs are shot up until the walls resemble Swiss cheese. Death and destruction have plagued the streets of New York City with the violence between the Jefes and Los Diablos.

As angry and vengeful as El Diablo has become, his wife insisted he give his daughter the party she deserves. He pulled out all the stops for today's festivities. His wife ordered three bouncy castles, a pony they can ride on, some gringo in a clown suit making balloon animals, and the biggest birthday cake he has ever seen.

Balloons and streamers are strewn across the pavilion and tree surrounding. His precious baby girl is dressed in a frilly, lacy blue gown she fell in love with at the store. Her little pigtails flutter happily as she giggle-shrieks in the air with each bounce. Live music comes from the band he hired.

The parents mingle and enjoy an open bar.

Every time his wife looks at him, she smiles. While he's filled with fury and sadness on the inside, he puts on the happy face for the party. He even acquiesced to his wife's demand to allow Esteban to attend. He had already forgiven the boy. The harsher he treats him, the better Esteban becomes. It has the extra benefit of sending the message to his lieutenants that not even his sons escape his wrath.

The afternoon is the epitome of domesticity. Children are happy. Parents are pleasantly drunk, and no one is talking business. El Diablo's wife comes alongside him and hands him a beer. "You made her day perfect," she coos before kissing him on the cheek. "I might have to celebrate some more when we get home."

"Mhmm. Ready for número cuatro?" He wriggles his brows at her.

She laughs and calls him a pig as she swats him.

He smiles and notes she doesn't say no.

The perfect moment shatters when the rat-a-tat-tat of automatic weapon fire rings over the park. The gunfire and squealing tires last only a few seconds. Screaming erupts. People crumple to the ground as chaos floods the area.

Blood splatters across El Diablo's face and his entire world comes to a halt as the surprised, marred expression of his wife sinks to the ground next to him. The bullet has ripped through her skull and covered him in a mix of blood and brain matter. Frozen in place, he stares at his murdered wife.

Esteban snatches his sister and hits the ground, covering her head for protection. "Close your eyes Hermana and hold on to me. I got you." Her heart-wrenching sobs against him sets a fire in his core. He will kill every last one of the bastards who did this.

Sirens blare in the distance.

The cars are long gone, and men who can't be present when the police arrive scatter to the wind. All that's left are women, children, and the dead. The second in command of Los Diablos hoists El Diablo to his feet. "You can't be here, Señor."

El Diablo comes up swinging at his friend. "This is my fucking wife!"

"I know," the man's voice softens. "You cannot be here when the police arrive."

El Diablo huffs and puffs before he lets out an anguished cry, not wanting to leave his beautiful wife alone on the ground. Finally, he succumbs to his friend's insistence and retreats. "Where's my daughter? Who the fuck has her?"

"I do," Esteban gasps as he comes running up with his sister clinging to him. He's quickly followed by his younger brother. All of them are ushered into a suburban and raced away.

Esteban keeps his sister turned away from El Diablo to prevent her from seeing the gore on their father. Despite her protests to be held by Papa, he keeps her in the third row with him.

"What the fuck happened? I thought we had that place secure." For a man who witnessed his wife's brains being blown out, his tone is ice cold. His eyes bore into his friend, who is driving the Suburban.

Carlos looks back in the mirror. "I think this conversation should wait until we get home." He flicks his eyes to where his daughter is being held.

El Diablo narrows his eyes and merely nods in response.

The rest of the trip home is uneventful.

Esteban gets his sister settled in her room, surrounded by her toys and their younger brother. "You don't fucking leave this room for any reason," he growls at his brother.

"I want Mama!" their sister whimpers.

"I know, baby girl. I know." Felix, the third son, murmurs to her as he pulls her into his lap.

Once satisfied his brother will take care of her, Esteban leaves them to join the business meeting forming downstairs. The men gathered in his father's office range from pristine, as they were not invited to the party, to gore covered, as they were at ground zero.

"Where is Julio?" El Diablo asks. His expression is blank and his tone is devoid of any emotion. On the inside his heart rages for the loss of his wife. He was sloppy, and it cost him. He will bring all the fury of Hell down upon those responsible.

"At the ER with his wife," one of the lieutenants confirms.

"Aron and Mel?"

"Both dead." Carlos responds. "From what we can tell, they were not aiming for anyone specific. It appears to be an act of opportunity."

"And José?" El Diablo motions around the room.

Each man looks at another. No one speaks.

El Diablo looks at Esteban, who shrugs. He has no idea where the man is. He has been too busy trying to pull himself out of the dog house.

José had been complaining about his percentage and his territory being too hard to work in at their last meeting. He has been with Los Diablos since he was a teenager. Married, and with two children, he has made a decent life for himself as a lieutenant. The idea he would betray the family that lifted him up, is unthinkable.

"No one's seen him since dinner last night." Carlos admits.

El Diablo rests his knuckles against his desk. "Bring him, his wife, and their two children to me."

No one argues, and the room cleans out, leaving Esteban with his father.

"You need a shower."

El Diablo's eyes bore into his son as if he could murder him by staring at him.

"You can't comfort my sister covered in my mother's blood. She needs you." Esteban lowers his head in submission, half expecting his father to attack him.

El Diablo does not move or say a word.

"I'll keep our *guests* comfortable until you can return. It will only show weakness if you are still covered in her blood when you confront them," Esteban says.

El Diablo moves around the desk and approaches Esteban. He studies his son with a stone-cold gaze.

Esteban struggles to not break down at the loss of his mother.

Not a single word is passed between the two men.

As El Diablo passes Esteban he dares to pull him into an embrace. As much as he would like to be as strong as his father, he needs some sign of comfort. His brother is gone, and they lost the heart of their family today.

El Diablo stiffens for several heartbeats before he relaxes and snakes a single arm around his son, giving him a squeeze before breaking free to go make himself presentable for his daughter.

The Devil's Tears

Saturday Evening (A Week Later)

The steady beat of the Oyster's music thumps against the walls of the closet I commandeered as an office. Harold's renovations of the Oyster finished in time to open for Memorial Day. With the club being open, we couldn't leave all our construction paperwork in a booth. So, here I am, in a four by six-foot supply closet with two TV trays and a folding chair as an excuse for a desk.

Sadly, my belly doesn't let me lean forward, which makes working on anything here even more miserable. In two weeks, I'm officially put on bed rest awaiting my bundle of joy.

The door swings open as it has all day.

"I swear, Mike. You need more attention than my toddler. What is it now?" I huff as I look up. My eyes widen and my heart leaps into my throat, pounding faster than a horse at the Kentucky Derby, turning my scream into a whimper.

The door clicks closed, and he turns the lock. "Don't worry, Mrs. Lacienda, I won't be taking up much of your time," he rasps as if he has been shouting or crying. His dark hair has grown out and is stringy from being unwashed. His eyes are black and sullen, with dark bags under them. The suit that hangs on his frame is crumpled. The stench of Tequilla clings to him like cologne, mixed with his body odor.

I bring my hand to my nose to keep from vomiting on him. Adrenaline pumping through my veins like blood has my muscles tensing and I try to shoot up out of my chair, not wanting to be pinned down by him. My legs betray me and turn into Jell-O, causing me to abruptly land on my tailbone in the metal chair. The pain from my tailbone brings tears to my eyes.

"Your club is mine. You tell those Italians to get the fuck out because we're moving in."

"Are you fucking kidding me?" I croak. My throat constricts, ruining my chance to sound irritated and not terrified. The last time this man appeared in my office he said the next time would be the end of my life.

"I am not," he emphasizes the T as he leans over me to further intimidate me. "My son did have one thing right. This location is perfect, which is why you're going to tell the Italians to leave and give it to me."

I don't inhale as the closer he gets the worse he smells. I rise slowly, putting my back against the wall for support. "I don't know what you think goes on here. This is *my* club and mine alone!"

"Yes. It is. You get a choice." He presses forward, slamming one hand against the wall to cage me in while tossing the chair aside with the other. The entire delicate desk system I have crumples and paperwork goes everywhere.

I yelp and shrink from him, turning my cheek. Instinctively, putting my hands over my stomach to protect the baby.

"You can either join me in this endeavor..." He reaches up and takes my chin between his thumb and forefinger, forcing me to face him. His black eyes burn into my soul. "Or you can join me alone."

I don't understand his threat, as I'm already alone in this endeavor. When his fingers greedily trail down my neck and chest to caress my bulging belly I connect that he means to hurt my family. I flinch and swat his hands away from me.

He staggers back to the door, fumbling in unlocking it. "You have twenty-four hours to sever your ties with the Italians. I'll collect my keys tomorrow."

He leaves me a trembling mess in my ruined office closet.

The entire conversation perplexes me. "What ties to the Italians?" I whisper to the empty closet. I'm still shaking when I emerge from the closet and run into Mac in the green room.

"HM, you okay?" He frowns down at me then looks past me to see if someone else emerges from the closet.

"Can you help me get to Harold's office?" I whimper.

He doesn't hesitate and scoops me up bridal style to carry me.

I curl into him and listen to his steady heartbeat the entire way to soothe my nerves. I also believe that El Diablo would kill Mac outright if Mac went after him. Whatever has happened to that man has left him in a desperate and dangerous state. Mac has a wife and a baby on the way.

"Thanks," I smile. "Could you get me some water?"

"Sure thing. Then you're going home." He leaves me in Harold's office, which is thankfully empty as Harold is downstairs networking.

I drum my fingers on his desk trying to make sense of why El Diablo thinks the Italians have anything to do with Le Salon. My first instinct is Devon is working with the Italians somehow. Anger wells and I pick up the phone to call him.

"Hello?" his voice comes over the receiver.

"Are you working with the Italians behind my back?" I growl at him.

"Uh... The only contact I've had with Italy is to import the marble for your bar top. You signed the check I sent them..." Devon's timid tone suggests he's not guilty of my imagined crime of him also being a member of the Scapelli family.

"Good. Cause if you were. I would be fucking pissed. You are not allowed to work with the Italians." I bark irrationally.

"Do you want me to cancel the marble order?"

I can imagine the confusion dancing across his face. "No," I sigh. "When you're here, I'm the boss. No one else. Got it?"

"Yes, Mistress," he knee-jerks in response, then chuckles. "I mean, Ma'am."

"Good. Bye." I hang up, not waiting for a response. "If Devon isn't the culprit..." I drum my fingers again, and it dawns on me who the Italians are. My otherwise joyful expression darkens as

I narrow my eyes and grit my teeth. "That motherfucker."

I pick up the phone again and dial Scapelli Senior's number.

"Hello?" the older man's voice rumbles.

"Hello!" I shout, the fear gone and replaced with righteous fury at being played like this.

"Can I help you?" His tone holds a mix of irritation and confusion.

"Yeah, you can help me! You can fucking show up tomorrow night!" I scream at him.

"Hope-Marie? To what do I owe the pleasure of this lovely phone call?"

I hate that men like him never lose their cool. "What the fuck have you been doing with *my* business?"

"I guaranteed your business could continue."

"What the fuck does that mean?" I shove my fist in the air, shaking it as if he could see me throwing my tantrum.

"I insured you had the best crews working on your construction project, fast tracked your permits, and solidified your security while you rebuild."

I bang the receiver against my forehead. He literally painted me into a corner with El Diablo. No wonder that man thinks I'm in bed with the Scapelli Family. "That's fucking great. You're going to bring your ass here tomorrow night to fix this! Is that understood?"

"And if I do not show up?" He chuckles.

"Then you won't like the fucking consequences!" I scream at the phone before I slam the receiver down.

"Who won't like the consequences?" Harold peeks around the corner of his own office door before he enters with the glass of water I asked for from Mac.

I'm too angry to enjoy Harold's antics tonight. If Scapelli is involved, he had to know. The man's still practically one of them. I stand, my legs no longer feeling like Jell-O as my body tenses from the unspent rage at being played for a fool. "I need to talk to the foreman," I grumble as I storm by him, snatching the water from his hand.

"Okay," Harold holds his hands up in surrender, letting me leave.

I finish the water before I try to take the stairs as they're awkward when this pregnant. As soon as I reach the ground floor, I storm my way through the club, then the green room, and into the construction zone that is Le Salon. It's quitting time for the crew and I catch the foreman as they are packing up.

"You're fired!" I shout at him like a dolled-up chihuahua.

"Ma'am?" He stops moving and faces me.

"I didn't fucking stutter. Get your shit. Get your guys. And don't come back!" I cross my arms and stand tall, trying to look intimidating.

"Did one of my guys do something, ma'am?" He glances in the direction of his crew, frowning.

"GET THE FUCK OUT!" I shriek at the top of my lungs.

"Yes, ma'am." He shakes his head and takes a step back. "Fellas, grab all the tools and gear. You heard the lady."

I stand there, with my arms crossed and my eyes narrowed as they gather up all the tools and gear. My cheeks are red and my ears burn with how angry I am. I'll be damned if I let any fucking mobster prick take what is mine, Italian or otherwise.

Ignoring the mild cramping in my stomach I stomp back to the Oyster's bar. "I need a phone book."

"Yes, ma'am." Sam smiles at me and hands me the phone book, along with the phone. He then chortles at my struggle to get onto a barstool. When I succeed, he rewards me with a Ginger Ale, cherry grenadine included. "On the house, ma'am."

"Thanks," I mutter, then sip it through a straw as I flip the book open. "Sam! I need the Yellow Pages! Not the White Pages!"

He swaps the books out quickly and ducks away to handle real customers.

"No fucking Italians are going to build my club. C. Ce. Co. Con. Construction. Great. Brooklyn. Brooklyn. Brooklyn. I don't want any fucking Brooklyn, Italian friendly, stupid company. Harlem! Perfect! No Italians in Harlem. Oh! Emergency service. Iron T Construction." I dial the number and sip the sweet, cherry-flavored drink.

"Iron T Construction, emergency line. How can I fix your day up?" The deep rumbling bass on the other end of the line sounds strangely familiar.

I'm too fixated on the voice not being Italian to care very much. "I have a big job for you. And I fired my previous crew. Be at The Blue Oyster at 8 am sharp, or you lose the job." I rattle off at breakneck speed.

"What kind of job is it, ma'am?" he asks as he laughs.

It nags me that I feel like I know this guy. I must sound like a crazy person. Especially with the music blasting in the background and the DJ encouraging each man to throw more money at the girl on stage.

"A big one," I retort.

"Eight sharp, you said?"

"Yes!"

"See you then, ma'am."

"Thank you!" I hang up and pick up the receiver to call Magellan.

"Lacienda residence."

"I need you to come get me. I'm cramping."

"Yes, ma'am. One Lacienda taxi service inbound. I'll see to it our most professional driver is at the wheel, one Castian Lacienda."

He always knows how to make me smile. "You should bring the go bag."

"Do we need church clothes in said go bag?"

"No. Just want to be prepared in case."

"Okay, one break glass bag included."

I giggle despite how angry I am. "Awoo."

"Awoo."

The House Giselle Built

Sunday Morning (Five Minutes to Eight)

"You sure you don't need me to come with you?" Magellan asks for the millionth time since I filled him in.

"I'll be fine, Mick. This is a meeting with the new foreman. Not with any mobsters."

He sighs and brandishes a finger at me. "If the whole thing with the mobsters goes sideways, I get to choose the new location." He's putting the brave front up. His defense mechanisms are stupid jokes and physical contact. Both are in abundance today.

"As long as it is in the U.S."

"Awe. Come on. I happen to have a line on a nice little villa in Spain. Are you sure those terms are non-negotiable?" He grins.

"Okay, fine. After the baby's born."

"Deal!" He leans over and kisses me. "And if it does all go to shit, this one will have a Kansas City birth certificate." He wriggles his brows. "Now, go fix your club."

I huff as I unbuckle my seatbelt and open the door. "If I can't fly to Spain, I can't fly to Missouri." I point to my stomach.

"Well, there are hospitals between here and there. Besides, I could catch whatever you pop out if we have to pull to the side of the road." He flashes me a cheesy smile.

"Magellan Lacienda, I'm not giving birth to your son on the side of the road." I growl at him.

"Which is why we would go to a hospital in Indiana, or something."

I roll my eyes and waddle out of the van.

His tone changes from playful to serious. "I love you, Hope-Marie."

"I love you too, Mick." I close the door, then blow him a kiss as I head to the Oyster's entrance. He pulls out and heads for McDonald's to feed the hungry toddlers we dragged out of bed for this road trip.

The pickup truck that comes racing into the parking lot has a magnet slapped on the door that says, "Iron T Construction".

A quick glance at my watch and it's only seven fifty-nine.

The man parks his truck on the other side of Harold's car and grabs a clipboard before peeling out to race to the door. He's tall and muscular. His ebony skin is tucked beneath a white tank top and flannel shirt, giving way to blue jeans and construction boots. To any other woman in the world, he's a tall drink of mouth-watering muscles.

To me, he's a drug-dealing gangbanger that accosted me on the doorsteps of my second apartment in New York. "T-Bone?" I ask and blink in disbelief.

The man stops in his tracks and stares at me. He tilts his head, and he studies me long and hard before he lights up with a bright smile. "Baby girl? Hot damn, you got fat." His tone is playful and teasing.

"What?! I'm not fat! I'm pregnant!" I brush my hands over the dress, worried it is the source of making me appear fat, not the almost fully baked child inside.

"Who is the lucky son-of-a-bitch? Is this your first one?"

"My husband. And no. This is number four."

T-Bone wolf whistles. "Damn, Baby Girl. You don't look like you've had three other children. Your fine ass is gorgeous. Please accept my apologies for my previous statement." He brings his hand to his chest and bows lightly. This man is nothing like the thug that was on my doorstep.

I huff at him, smoothing my dress again, still worried it

makes me fat.

Harold comes barreling out the door, putting himself between T-Bone and me. "Can I help you?" His voice takes that low tone Harold gets when he plays Italian mobster.

"Oh, hell no!" I smack Harold on the arm. "You don't get to play Italian mob hero with me today. I called him!"

"What? How did you even have his number?" Harold faces me with his angry father look.

T-Bone crosses his arms and has a shit-eating grin on his face.

"I randomly picked him out of the phone book. It was the first non-Italian looking construction company, alright?" I mutter as I turn bright red.

T-Bone erupts into laughter. "You finally got tired of that Italian Sausage, Baby Girl?"

"Don't you start," I point at him. "If you can't handle this job, then I'll find someone else. You have eight weeks and the budget's non-negotiable."

"I still don't even know what the job is." T-Bone holds his hands up innocently, a mischievous smile lingering on his handsome face.

"Wait. You're seriously hiring him?" Harold grouses.

"I am. You and Scapelli can... go... do... whatever it is you do with him!" I snort, fumbling over my own words with how angry I am that Harold was in on it.

"Wait. You think I'm working with Scapelli?" He frowns and his posture droops. "I'm not one of them," he protests.

"Good. Then you absolutely have no reason to stop me from hiring someone else." I chirp as I turn to head into the Oyster. "If you would like to see the plans, follow me."

I make it to church on time.

Father Kelly had his concerns about us attending the late session three weeks in a row.

I can't be bothered with his antics. He's lucky we make it to service at all after Magellan discovered what he said to me. I spend the day enjoying the kids and Magellan's company, trying not to dwell on the meeting I have planned.

Harold and I discussed my nefarious meeting. He repeatedly made clear he won't be in attendance for any reason at all. He quickly relented by telling me if I get in trouble, he will get my golden goose eggs out of the fire.

Knowing Harold has my back, makes what I'm planning to do easier. Tonight will forever change my life. I'll earn the recognition that Le Salon is my domain, or, more likely, end up dead. I'm banking on neither man wanting to kill an unborn child.

El Diablo's behavior in my office suggests he values innocent life, even if he is a monster in a suit.

Antonio Scapelli, from what Harold has told me, does not hurt women and children to get what he wants.

I kiss each of the kids good night before I meet Magellan in our foyer. "Listen. If you haven't heard from me by midnight, take the kids and run." I lean into him as he wraps his arms around me.

"Come home," he murmurs against my forehead.

"I can't do this without you." His grip tightens on my hips and he kisses me with such tenderness it brings tears to my eyes.

The cab ride to the club is the longest ride of my life.

You can do this.

You're not alone.

Everything will be alright.

I'm elated when I see Mac's car in the parking lot. "Well, I won't die alone. Or he's with Scapelli and knows how to hide the body." I mutter to myself.

"Ma'am?" The cabby raises a brow at me in the mirror.

"Nothing, rattling off the grocery list." I pay him and get out of the cab. The cocktail of emotions washing over me makes me want to vomit. I'm afraid I've poked too many tigers.

What if they attack Mick and the kids while I'm here?

What if they just shoot me?

Oh God, is that why Harold didn't want to come?

I wish I would have sent Mick and the kids to Missouri after church. As much as he wanted to attend, I pointed out that our children need at least one of us. As I'm the one they're threatening, it needs to be me who stands up for the club. We agreed if I didn't call him by midnight he is to take the kids and flee to either Missouri, or Spain. Anger bubbles to boil away the fear the closer I get to the club.

How dare these men make me feel this way. They have no right to make decisions for me. They aren't the ones who earned this club. They don't get to enjoy its spoils. I'll burn this place to the fucking ground again before I give it to them.

As soon as Harold left this morning, T-Bone, and I to talk construction business, I recruited T-Bone to my cause. I paid him privately to install cameras, a mic, and a way to record everything in Le Salon's lobby. My requirements were he couldn't tell Harold, and the setup can't be visible.

When he called me at home, he gave me the rundown on how it worked.

I gave him instructions that if I did not greet his crew in the morning, he was to give the recordings to the police.

He was smart enough to not push me for the details of why I wanted this.

I walk through the Oyster, my heart pounding, and my stomach threatening to cramp. I force myself to take slow, deep breaths as I walk. "It'll be okay. Mommy's here." I whisper as I rub my stomach. The show smile plastered on my face causes my cheeks to hurt, and I greet people as if I don't have a care in the world. When I reach the edge of the green room that leads to Le Salon, I hesitate.

"They're already inside, Ma'am." Mac says from the other side of the tarp as he pulls it back, like a show curtain. "I got your back, HM. Knock 'em dead."

I wish I believed Mac is on my side. He has always been good to me, but he was a Scapelli with Harold. While I believe Harold is out, I don't believe Mac is. Channeling Giselle, my shoulders square and I flash him a wink when I strut by to enter Le Salon's lobby. My stilettos echo with the measured stride, showing no signs of the quivering mess my emotions are. "Gentlemen," I say to draw them out of their staring contest. "Thank you both for meeting me here. We have much to discuss, and hopefully, to resolve." I cock my hip as I rest my hand on it, not feeling powerful as I am currently a beach ball in a skirt.

Mac doesn't come stand with me, which makes me feel better. He could have easily followed me in and trapped me.

I pause, realizing I forgot to set up the table for this meeting. I won't be able to stand for more than a few minutes and don't want to give them that advantage. "Mac, would you be so kind as to set up a table and chairs for us." I don't take my eyes off of the other two men.

"Yes, ma'am," his voice rumbles from somewhere behind me.

I'm glad it is dim in here as I'm flushed with embarrassment that I was not fully prepared.

The rolling of a table across the concrete foundation echoes loudly, soon followed by chairs scraping into place.

"Anything else, ma'am?"

Afraid it will seem like I'm stalling, I don't ask for water, no matter how bad I want it. "I'm good. Would you gentlemen care for anything?" I motion to the table, unwilling to allow them to get behind me.

Parler

El Diablo and Antonio Scapelli Sr. exchange mirth-filled looks as they casually take seats opposite each other.

My heart races and the muscles in my back are tighter than a laced corset. Stress is horrible for the baby. I've been lucky this pregnancy, only suffering tiny bouts pain in the last few weeks. I don't care how weak it makes me look, rubbing my belly soothes the baby, and me.

Mac brings my rolled-up map of the area I've colored all-over like an arts and crafts project and unfurls it on the table for me. He sets a small briefcase next to me after.

I make a show of putting the bag on the table and letting both men see inside before I reach for the office supplies to allow us to continue the arts and crafts during negotiations. Getting shot because they thought I went for a weapon would be my luck.

The moment the map settles on the table, all mirth is gone from their expressions.

Antonio focuses his attention on the map and the accessories I set on the table.

El Diablo shifts his gaze from me to Antonio and keeps himself aloof, like a predator silently watching his wounded prey flounder.

Relief washes over me when no violence ensues. They're at

least willing to hear me out. I want to chew against my lower lip as stage fright creeps in. I bite against the inside of my mouth instead. To show weakness now, I will lose any chance of controlling these men later. My stomach continues to threaten showing its displeasure and returning my dinner to the world.

I shouldn't have had rock soup.

Thankfully, both men are staring at the map and not looking at me who could vomit said soup all over them.

With a light shake, I send my nerves to the abyss of my mind and channel Giselle's confidence. This is no worse than the first night I walked out on stage at the Oyster.

Fake it 'til you make it, Hope-Marie.

"As you can see, I've drawn the territory lines for all of us to co-exist."

Both men sit back and assume a casual, open pose. Their arms are relaxed and hands rest on their thighs after they unbutton their jackets in unison.

I'm beginning to think mobsters own a playbook on how to intimidate people.

Chin up. Tits out.

Stella's voice flits through my mind, and I obey. She hasn't led me astray yet. I must nail this performance to save everything I care for.

"This circle," I thump it hard for emphasis and put a scowl on my face to show I mean business. "This one right here. Is *mine.*"

El Diablo and Antonio Scapelli Sr. have spent a lifetime keeping their expressions neutral, but I catch the brief reactions to my bold claim.

I get paid to read men and react to their base desires.

A minor widening of the eyes, a twitch of their lips, and I immediately know that Scapelli's interested.

El Diablo, on the other hand, glowers at the map.

"Outside of this circle, you do whatever you want. You want to shoot each other up? Go ahead. Want to sell dope? Be my guest. Pimp girls? As long as it doesn't come back to me, we're good. Inside this circle," I tap the area Harold and I purchased with Devon. "This is neutral territory. No drugs, no guns, no fighting, no nothing. You come to see the beautiful women. Or you come to get your kink on. Or you come to watch the cabaret and enjoy a good meal. It's *mine*. Not *ours*. Not *yours*. Not *anyone else* other than *me* and *my business partners*." I hold my breath as I take in the two men again.

Antonio stares at the map intently as he leans in closer to see the exact location of my fiefdom.

El Diablo's expression is pure rage. His cheeks are red. His jaw twitches and the faint growling sound of his teeth grinding is unnerving. He rubs his hand over his face and shifts in his seat, watching Antonio as if he's ready to fight at any second.

The Blue Oyster, Le Salon, and the rest of the block is highlighted to indicated the area I'm claiming as my territory. Devon worked his magic with the city to help us obtain the loans and permits to purchase all the dilapidated buildings.

After Le Salon is renovated, we will create a parking garage for guests, as well as moving the cabaret to its own building, complete with restaurant. Le Salon will host twelve salons, along with larger public playrooms, and nicer dressing areas on the second floor.

These men are all that stand in my way.

Antonio looks up and leans back. "That is... an interesting proposal. How does giving you this neutrality benefit the Scapellis?" He motions to the map before clasping his hands together.

I hadn't planned on that question. I naively thought they would agree and go away. I chew on my lower lip in thought. I know better than to ask him what he wants. That would leave the door open for him to demand whatever he sees fit. This is my negotiation, and I won't succumb to his trickery.

I shift my gaze to El Diablo, who is mimicking Antonio and staring at me intently. He raises a brow before crossing his arms, "Yeah, Gringa. What do Los Diablos get out of this?"

The answer to their questions will determine the rest of the negotiation.

My heart sinks and I frown as I come to understand why Harold isn't here. To get what I want, I will play their game and become a mobster. I reach up and run my thumb over the tiny gold cross I'm wearing.

There's no money to offer, no guarantee of success.

I need something.

They're burning the world down around us, and I can't let that continue.

Too many people count on me.

"You get sanctuary."

Antonio's eyes widen, and his mouth opens slightly in surprise. He regains his composure and asks, "What would sanctuary entail?"

El Diablo's brows knit together as he looks from Scapelli to me. He remains quiet, which makes me nervous he won't buy into this scheme.

"In my territory, no one can act on the other. If someone is in trouble, and they come to me, seeking help, we will shelter them until you can collect them. Except for active police pursuits. If your people get themselves in trouble with the police, no place is safe for them, and I won't jeopardize all the people who depend on me here." My confidence grows the longer this meeting takes.

They're actually considering this! I might walk away unscathed.

Antonio bursts my bubble. "How do you intend to enforce this neutrality?"

"By making it lucrative to play nice." I say, as if it is the obvious answer.

El Diablo leans forward and his scowl forms into a curious brow raise. "What do you mean by lucrative?"

"I mean. You two play nice together, you both make money. Having a neutral place to handle business allows better communication. Everyone knows when you communicate, you get things done. How many times have you tried to move product, only to for some Italian schmuck come bust your balls?" I don't give him time to answer. "And you? How many guys end up in the hospital when they try to fend off vultures at the docks?"

I'm guessing at their woes. Based on what Mac and Harold said, it has been World War III for the past several months. "You two are too busy dick waggling, you're losing money. You'd make way more money if you had a safe and neutral place to negotiate. That's where I come in."

Antonio's expression is like stone when he addresses me

again. "You are giving us permission to conduct business in your territory?"

"Civil business. As long as it doesn't interfere with any of my ventures and doesn't bring trouble to my door. Then I don't give a shit what you two do."

El Diablo snorts and shakes his head. "What stops me from killing you two and taking everything?"

I freeze like a gazelle who smelled the lion and my eyes go wide.

"Are you familiar with the concept of mad, young man?" Antonio smirks at El Diablo, and his condescending tone makes it hard for me to not giggle.

"Yeah. What about it, Ese?"

"It means if your people fuck up my shit, my people fuck up *your* shit, and vice versa," Antonio explains as if El Diablo hadn't just said he understood.

I didn't know the term. After Antonio's explanation, it's exactly what I figured would bring them together.

"You're saying *Los Diablos* are required to enforce this peace?" El Diablo's shoulders square and his hands rest on the table like he's going to grab hold and flip it.

"The Scapellis would also enforce peace, keeping you little devils in line." Antonio smirks at El Diablo, still leaning back, cool as a cucumber.

I get the impression he's trying to get a rise out of the man on purpose. "Gentlemen," I cut into the dick-wagging conversation. "We all enforce the peace. We create a symbiotic relationship between the three of us. I provide a blind eye. You provide whatever it is you need to do without interference from the other. When we lift each other up, we all get stronger. Awoo."

Both men turn to look at me with my little awoo.

I couldn't help myself and it felt like I needed a little rallying cry to send the message home.

El Diablo turns his gaze back down to the map and stands as he looks over it. He spends a few minutes trailing his fingers over the area. He then looks at Antonio, "In the name of this neutrality, if I were to ask for assistance in say... imports, what would the answer be?"

Antonio takes a few heartbeats to study El Diablo. He tilts his head in thought and responds, "It would depend on how much you pay."

This meeting goes from staking my claim to true negotiations.

My concessions are that I'll provide blind spots in our new parking structures that the security won't attend. I'll provide sanctuary to any soul in either organization from outsiders. Finally, I'll host continued negotiations for all parties concerned. The exceptions are if law enforcement gets involved I will not stop them, and I won't offer them help either. I'm also able to exact payment from those seeking my protection however I see fit.

I glance at my watch and it's five minutes to twelve. I gasp and stand, "Excuse me a moment, gentlemen."

Antonio smirks and waves a dismissive hand. "Yes. Yes. Go tell your husband you are fine."

"What happens if Gringa doesn't call home?" El Diablo raises a brow as he stares at me.

"Based on how scared she is, I imagine he would call the police to come looking for her," Antonio's smiling as he talks.

I turn pink and offer a sheepish smile, neither confirming nor denying his assumption.

"Fine, go," El Diablo waves me off.

I scurry past Mac who is beaming at me like a proud father, and rush to the bar. "Sam I need --"

Sam sets the phone in front of me.

I tap my fingers against the receiver as I hold it to my ear after dialing.

"Lacienda residence," Magellan answers.

"We did it!" I chirp in excitement.

He exhales audibly. "Thank God!"

"Don't wait up. We're in negotiations. It's gonna be awhile. I'll bring bear claws for breakfast. Awoo!."

"I love you, too. Awoo," Magellan chuckles on the other end.

I hang up and hurry back to the meeting.

White Picket Fences

June 1988

The quiet hours in the morning are my favorite. I get to feed Miguel and the nurses are at the station, letting all of us new mothers sleep. After my induction to the "Round Table", I had to call the doctor because of the pain I was in. He promptly admitted me and I've been in the hospital since. Miguel arrived two weeks later. The doctor has kept us for observation. While I showed no signs of the troubles I had with Angelo, he wasn't taking any chances.

Miguel struggled to feed for the first few days and his heart kept giving abnormal readings, which normalized after a few days.

Castian and Helena don't like this arrangement. They have complained that Daddy's been sad the whole time.

Baby Angelo has been a trooper. He's the quietest baby I have ever seen.

Thankfully, the actual labor was mild.

The doctor re-read me the riot act for getting pregnant, and again brought up tying my tubes.

After a long discussion with Magellan, I agree to remain on the birth control, and we will add condoms to the list, Catholic church be damned.

"Knock. Knock." Caleb Lamb appears in my doorway with a teddy bear, chocolate, and a grin on his face. "How's my favorite resident?"

"You mean the only resident?" I tease.

"Well, ex-resident?"

"What?" Panic fills my voice and I squeeze Miguel who squawks.

"Okay. Put the panic attack away. You already exceeded your hours again. I'm just here to drop off the paperwork and see the baby." He reveals the sealed envelope in his other hand. "He's a cute little bugger. You grow up and take care of your momma. You hear me?"

I stare at Caleb like he has grown a second head. He never shows this much emotion in anything. "You want to hold him?" I offer the swaddled baby up.

"Oh, he seems perfectly content, right where he is." He puts his hand up, rejecting my bundle of joy.

"Suit yourself." I pull Miguel back down into my arms.

"Are you doing well?" He picks up my chart from the foot of the bed.

"I'm dying to go home and eat some ice cream. Other than that, I feel great."

"Good," he looks over the chart anyway before returning it to the bed. "Once you're feeling better, call me. I've some thoughts on your plans for the future." He smiles and pats my leg before he leaves.

I chuckle as I coo down to Miguel. "I think he likes us."

"Who likes you? Should I be jealous?" Magellan says as he enters the room, a goofy grin on his face.

He's immediately followed by Helena who squeals, "MOMMY!"

Castian comes stomping in with his arms crossed and huffs at the foot of the bed.

"What's the matter, my little lion?" I pout at him as Helena climbs up to snuggle me.

"Babies are stupid," he grumbles and crosses his arms tighter.

I bite my lip, smiling at Magellan, who also has a bemused smile on his face. I understand Castian's feelings. Poor guy has to share all the attention with three siblings. "You want to help mommy hold him?"

"Yes," he sulks through his teeth.

Magellan lifts him and puts him on the bed next to me.

He and Helena nestle in on either side while Magellan retrieves the sleeping Angelo from the stroller. My heart swells at having all my family here.

The nurse walks in and turns our tender moment into a three-ring circus by announcing we're getting discharged. It takes a couple of hours to coordinate doctors, notes, prescriptions, and children. Once it's all settled we pile into the van, which sports three car seats.

Magellan doesn't stop grinning the whole time we're driving.

"Can we talk about it yet?" Castian calls from the back.

"Nope." Magellan quickly replies.

"Mommy present!" Helena chirps helpfully.

"Surprise. That means secret." He brings his finger to his lips. "Shhh."

I raise a brow at Magellan and turn to face the kids.

"No. Forward," he commands as he motions for me to face forward.

I pout. I face forward obediently. "Hey, wasn't that our turn?" I point out the window.

"Huh. I guess it was." he nonchalantly shrugs and keeps driving toward the bridge.

"Uhm... Did you kidnap me?"

"What? No. Is it kidnapping if you got in the van willingly?" He flashes a devilish grin.

"SURPRISE!" Helena shrieks from the back.

Magellan and I laugh.

"A little early, baby girl," he teases. "We'll be there soon."

"No! NOW!"

"Helena," Magellan's tone deepens. "We will get there when we get there."

"Mhm." She grunts.

"It's okay. We're going to our new house," Castian whispers, trying to comfort his sister.

I pretend to not hear him and keep facing forward.

The drive from the hospital has me worried as we cross the

bridge and enter New Jersey. I'm beginning to think he's really kidnapping us.

Miguel starts to fuss in his carrier.

He's soon followed by Angelo.

"Are we there yet?" Castian whines.

"Almost," Magellan chortles.

He pulls up to a security booth with a drop gate. A stone wall extends as far as I can see in either direction. He puts the van in park and fishes out his wallet, followed by his driver's license.

"Ah! Mr. Lacienda! Welcome back!" the security guard beams. He then leans down. "Mrs. Lacienda! Pleasure to finally meet you. Your pictures don't do you justice."

I blush and smile. My body is pudgy and soft, with things squishing where they shouldn't, but he thinks I'm beautiful. I give him a finger wave before he steps back. "Hopefully, you showed him the good pictures," I whisper.

"Yup. You were completely disheveled with a newborn baby. Works like a charm every time." he grins.

"Magellan, you didn't?" My cheeks flame red at how awful I must have looked in those photos.

The gate opens and Magellan drives along the winding street past mansion after mansion without answering me.

How did he pull this off in only a month?

We stop at a house set back from the others, another stone fence wrapping to an iron gate.

Magellan reaches up and pushes a button attached to his visor.

Seconds later, the massive gate grumbles to life, the chain clanking as it creates an opening for our vehicle. The driveway curves up a gentle slope and turns back on itself, as well as curling around the side of the house.

"Surprise," he smiles as he puts the car in park in front of the house.

"SURPRISE!" Helena shrieks again.

I laugh as he locks the door before I can open it.

"You stay." He points at me.

I hold my hands up in surrender.

"Good girl." He hurries out of the van. I don't think I've ever seen him get all the kids moving that fast.

The entire tribe bolts for the house as Magellan carries the two babies in.

When he returns sans children, I grow concerned he left two toddlers, an infant, and a newborn alone in the house.

"Mrs. Lacienda," he coos when he opens the door. As soon as my feet touch the ground, he scoops me up into a bridal carry.

I giggle and lean into him. At first, I'm worried that I'm too heavy and it's too far for Magellan. I'm a fat cow in my mind.

He doesn't even break a sweat, carrying me to the door. "Welcome home," he murmurs against me as he crosses the threshold.

"Surprise!" everyone shouts, causing me to jump.

When Magellan sets me down, standing in my massive new foyer are Maman, Papa, Magellan's parents, Tristan Wolfe, and Tristan Lacienda.

Maman and Magellan's mother are each holding an infant.

Helena and Castian bounce back and forth happily in front of the crowd.

Drooping along the upstairs handrail is a massive hand-painted 'Welcome Home' banner.

Tears well in my eyes, and I kiss Magellan for all he's worth.

"Awoo!" Papa shouts.

"AWOO!" we all call back.

Biography

J. R. Froemling was born in Indiana, the second eldest of three. She met her first husband in an online writing community. She met her second husband at a board game convention in 2015. She has a Bachelor's of Science in Information Technology from Western Governors University of Indiana. She got her start in an online writing community for Star Wars fan fiction. She has transformed that love of fan fiction into works of her own. You can find all the latest information at her website.

jrfwriting.com

Other Books By J. R. Froemling

Savannah Nights Series

The Triple Six

The Night Rangers

Poltergeist Girl

The Wolfe Legacy

Mistress Giselle - Book One of Hope-Marie

The Naughty List - Book One of Elijah Joseph

Chronicles of Nodd

Fall of Avalon - Verse One

Immortal Love Saga

My Viking Alpha

My Celtic Luna

www.ingramcontent.com/pod-product-compliance
Lightning Source LLC
Chambersburg PA
CBHW072027220726
48293CB00016B/517